HOW NOT TO SUMMON DEMONS

VAMPIRE INNOCENT
BOOK SIX

MATTHEW S. COX

DIVISION ZERO PRESS

How *Not* to Summon Demons
Vampire Innocent Book 6
© 2019 Matthew S. Cox
All Rights Reserved

Cover art by Alexandria Thompson

ISBN (ebook): 978-1-949174-98-4

ISBN (paperback): 978-1-949174-99-1

CONTENTS

UNLIFE'S LITTLE INCONVENIENCES

S
tressing out over schoolwork isn't something I ever expected would be an issue for me—I mean, seriously… who winds up in college after they've been murdered?

It's not as though I haven't prepared for the biology test presently sitting on the desk in front of me. Time is something I have loads of now, thanks to my mostly nocturnal schedule and lack of a job. Not that I'm lazy on purpose. It's hard to find work as an eighteen-year-old when the sun can kill me.

Being offset from my friends' schedules gives me too much time to myself once everyone's asleep. So, I studied plenty for this test. Lack of knowledge isn't what's causing me to struggle at filling in a scantron sheet full of little circles. I've been sitting there with my face in my hands for a while trying—and failing to tune out a crapload of distractions.

Frustrated, I glare between my fingers at the guy three seats in front of me and one row right who's been robo-clicking his pen like a woodpecker on high-octane meth for the past ten minutes. He's merely the most recent layer of torture. The girl behind me? Her stomach is auditioning for the lead tenor in *Phantom*. A guy two rows left and one seat back has farted every thirty seconds almost like clockwork. It's like his colon is cheering him on every time he answers a question. I suppose it *could* be worse—at least I'm not sitting behind him.

The girl right in front of me has been tapping her fingernails on the desk for the past half hour in a desperate attempt to transmit top secret orders to a World War II submarine crew with Morse code. For the first ten or so minutes of the period, the guy directly behind me kept swishing saliva around in his mouth. Mercifully, that stopped. Oh, and the guy to my right? He keeps scratching his leg. Fingernails on jeans is as loud as a power drill inside my eardrums. Seriously, the dude's either got fleas or skin cancer. A late-thirties woman trying to 'better her career' in the front left corner has a major case of restless leg syndrome and a squeaky shoe.

Everyone is breathing too loud.

Professor Connolly's chair springs haven't been oiled since 1913. Every time he breathes, it sounds like an old Wild West steam train screeching into the station with bad brakes. And this freakin' annoying-as-hell cellphone at the back-middle of the room has been buzzing near-constantly since the test started. Despite being on vibrate, it feels like my entire skull rattles whenever it goes off. That guy's either got the worst kind of possessive-clingy girlfriend or there's a medical emergency in his family. Seriously, who calls someone every minute and a half for an hour? This dude is about to make history as the first person ever to have a cell phone go from a full charge to dead exclusively from ringing.

I can't get away from all the damn noise.

Sometimes, being a vampire is a real pain in the ass.

With a resigned sigh, I lower my hands from my face and have a quick daydream of mild violence... Like taking that perma-buzzing cell phone and using it as a cork for Fart Man. Throwing the teacher's chair out the window. Breaking Tapper Girl's fingers. Swiping Robo-Clicker's pen and stabbing it straight into his forehead. You know, mild suggestions to stop *all the goddamned noise.*

Sigh.

No way would I ever do anything like that, but it's so damn

frustrating. I need quiet for a test. Silence is torture to someone with amped-up hearing. And I'm not even going to mention what Fart Man is doing to my supernatural sense of smell. Argh! I've been so damn distracted by a million little noises or odors, I'm only done with eighteen of the twenty-five multiple choice questions, haven't even started on the essay ones… and there's only about fifteen minutes left.

Sarah Wright is no super nerd, but I also have never failed a test in my life.

Time for extreme measures.

I wad up a tiny ball of paper, set it at the corner of my desk, and flick it at Pen Clicker. My improvised missile flies true, nailing him in the ear likely with enough force to sting. The instant he glares back over his shoulder, I make eye contact and dive into his brain.

Stop clicking the damn pen.

His expression goes glazed for a few seconds, then he returns to his test. The clicking, however, ceases.

About ten people near us emit noises of relief.

I twist to my left and stare at the fart machine.

Hold it or go to the damn bathroom.

The guy fidgets in his seat. And yeah, I know it's not like anyone can really fart on command, but he can try to hold it.

A poke to the shoulder makes Miss Morse Code look back at me.

Stop. Tapping. Your. Nails.

She does a perfect derp face in response to the mental command washing over her brain. A moment later, she turns away, resuming her test without any tapping.

Can't do much about the girl with the gurgling stomach. Other than not eating before the test, it isn't in her control. I sigh and look at the question booklet again, trying to tune the remainder of the noises out and focus. Despite what everyone at my old high school thought, I've never been in the 'nerd squad'. Some people consider anyone who gets mostly straight-As with an occasional B a nerd. My definition of nerd is a little different—Brian Grant. As a sophomore, he used to fill entire classroom whiteboards with math that would make PhD physicists rub their chins. He skipped junior and senior year and went straight to college. *That's* a nerd. I probably could've handled AP classes, but never felt any urge to push myself.

All I ever wanted was to be normal.

Yeah, that worked out for me, right?

Still, I'm not used to the concept of failing a test, especially for something as stupid and totally in my control as not *finishing* the darn thing. The mere thought that I would ever struggle to finish a test never crossed my mind. Of course, I also never imagined I'd be able to hear the breath whistling in and out of a teacher's nose from forty feet. The truly frustrating thing is I haven't figured out how to turn it off yet. Like, with my night-vision eyes, I can dial them back so headlights don't blind me when driving. My ears? Not so much. And don't even get me started on my sense of touch. I've had to cut every tag off every article of clothing I own. If you can't imagine how annoying that is, picture someone who stands behind you for twelve hours a day tickling the back of your neck with a feather and you *just can't stop them.*

And no, I don't feel guilty about breaking the clock in my philosophy/sociology classroom. That old mechanical thing ticked like giant stone blocks being dropped off the roof of a building. Ten minutes of that in an otherwise quiet room could legit trigger homicidal rage. Chinese water torture has nothing on 1950s clockwork.

Anyway... gotta focus.

The last few questions are fairly easy. Honestly, I should've breezed through this test and been finished twenty minutes ago. Once I finish filling in the dots, I swap the pencil for a pen and attack the essay questions while people continue getting up to leave, making me feel more and more like a failure. The girl who forgot to eat dinner hurries out, as does Fart Man.

And then there were five.

Only way I'm going to finish this test on time is to cheat, and I don't mean academically. I hunker down over my desk, read the first essay question, and write the answer as fast as I can make my hand move, which to anyone else in the room has to look like something out of *The Matrix*. My perception accelerates with my reflexes, so to me, it doesn't feel too weird—the rest of the world is in slow motion.

How many students ever have to worry what the thermal ignition temperature of ball point pen ink is? One good thing about being a vampire: I don't get hand cramps. Or any kind of cramps anymore. Even *those*.

Best thing ever.

Actually, best thing ever is being able to fly. But no more monthly cramping is easily second. I mean, seriously. It's *totally* unfair that guys don't have to deal with that. Okay, wow, here I am complaining about distractions while distracting myself with random tangential thoughts.

It is kind of ironic for me to be sitting in this classroom learning about biology when I've gone outside the system. Something tells me that most 'natural processes' no longer apply to me. My mitochondria may or may not even be doing all this fancy chemical tangoing. Yeah, I still have cells and stuff, but who knows what's going on at a microscopic level in Sarah 2.0. It's a bit gruesome to think about, but I always have been kinda squeamish about medical stuff. My youngest sister, Sophia, screams at even cheap horror movie gore. Like, even when you can obviously see the actor squeezing the blood bag, she still shrieks. I can handle *good* special effect gore, no problem. But something like a medical drama where they don't even really show the surgery? Ick, no. It still makes me squirm, even at the mere thought of it.

Fortunately, this is general intro biology and *not* med school. A hint of smoke teases at my nostrils, the paper nearly igniting as I fill eight pages with the answers to the essay questions over the last six minutes of the period. I finish the last sentence of the last question with fifteen seconds to spare before the bell.

Hate cutting it this close. Really… what is wrong with me? I'm *never* one of the last few people in the room during a test. Grr.

Pen Clicker—who hasn't made a sound since I brain zapped him— is still here as is nail-tapping girl. It's obvious why they spent more time making annoying noises than taking their test... bet they forgot to study. I should've been out of here a half hour ago.

"Okay, that's it for the class period," says Professor Connolly, while giving me a strange look.

The last time I saw that expression on someone's face before, they'd caught me flying. I poke into his brain and sure enough, he noticed me moving blurry fast, but suspects it a product of a brain tumor or lack of sleep. After gently removing that memory so he doesn't lose sleep over worrying if he's got a grapefruit growing inside his head, I drop my test materials on his desk, smile, and head out the door.

Few times in my life have I ever been this happy to get out of a classroom.

No, it's not the work or the teacher. That total silence thing made it hell. You'd think after two months at Seattle Central College, I'd have gotten used to hearing all those little annoying sounds every damn time there's a test. But no. For some inane reason, I keep thinking 'you'll get used to it' and forgetting about it until the next time I want to rip my hair out.

Next time there's a test, I am bringing earbuds and MP3s. There will be background noise to drown everyone out, even if the teacher needs to be forced not to care about me listening to music.

Once outside, I take a nice deep breath of crisp October air. The whole school is full of Halloween decorations. Every window, doorway, bench, pole, or fence is plastered with cheesy ghosts, spiders, and bats. Is this college or pre-K? Good grief.

I lazied out on a costume for the school's Halloween event last Friday. Wanna hear something ironic? To dress up as a vampire, I used makeup to make my face paler and sprouted my real fangs. Someone had the nerve to call them 'fake looking.' Guess they're too small for her. Not sure why the administration scheduled the event last Friday instead of tomorrow—actual Halloween. Maybe someone thought asking people to show up to class in costume worked better on a Friday before a weekend than on a Wednesday?

And really, who scheduled Halloween on a Wednesday anyway? I need to file a formal complaint with the calendar guy. Then again, Halloween kind of wants to be a real holiday when it grows up. No one gets off work for it and schools don't even close. Then you have people like Paige Westcott, a former classmate of mine from high school. She's *all* about Halloween. We never really spent any time with each other outside of school, but I bet she'd totally lose her shit (in a good way) if I revealed myself to her.

So yeah, tonight is Halloween Eve for some people. I've never been *that* into it, at least not since I outgrew trick-or-treating. Ashley's a giant child. She adores dressing up in costumes and going around begging for candy even as an eighteen-year-old. It's kinda funny that I could get away with it more than her this year. Since becoming a vampire, most people who don't know me take me for sixteen. Though, there are plenty of prigs who would give anyone over like twelve attitude for showing up at their door in costume. Saw a thing on Facebook a while back about a town somewhere that even wanted to make it illegal for teenagers to go out in costume.

How miserable and wretched does an old person have to be that they want to suck even that little bit of childish joy out of a kid?

Once I turned fourteen, I mostly lost interest in it… but every year, I wound up going anyway—either with Ashley or the littles. As of three years ago, the parents trusted me enough to chaperone the littles without them. Last year, I skipped the costume entirely, dressing up as 'responsible older sister.'

Anyway, time to go home.

After slipping into a shadowy spot between buildings, I start to zip into the air but make it only a few feet off the ground before remembering the Sentra is here. Dammit. It's so much easier to fly, but it hadn't quite gotten dark enough before class. Grumbling, I land and trudge down the street to the parking deck, then make my way up to the second level.

A baseball on the floor at the top of the stairs strikes me as odd, but insignificant… at least until I reach the row where I parked and notice a few more pieces of sports equipment on the ground behind an older blue pickup truck that's wedged into the parking space right next to Dad's Sentra.

It looks awful close, and I'm fairly certain the pickup crashed into the wall.

Worried, I rush over and stop short at the sight of the Sentra's driver side door mirror smashed and on the ground. The son of a bitch shaved it straight off my—I mean Dad's—car.

"Ooh!"

Overcome with a sudden flash of anger, I lash out and kick a poor, defenseless soccer ball sitting too close to me. The ball blurs across the garage, hitting a concrete column one lane over and exploding on impact with a loud *boom*.

Despite me causing the noise, the loudness is so unexpected, it startles me and I let out a clipped yelp of surprise—as do about five or six other people. One guy manages to turn 'what the F was that' into a single word.

Grr. I glare at the pickup, fuming. I just sat through ninety minutes of torturous silence only to walk out here and find some idiot smashed the mirror off the Sentra. The truck looks older than I am, covered in dents, scrapes, and even a rust hole or two. And yeah, whoever drove it *did* crash into the wall at the end of the space, but not hard enough to cause serious damage. Maybe drunk, maybe in an extreme hurry... who knows?

I sprout claws and consider shredding all four of its tires.

After a moment of rage-breathing, calm returns. Nah. That's not who I am. Just the frustration talking.

Suppose I could sit here and wait for the owner, or take the plate number down and try getting them to pay for the repairs. That's the civilized thing to do as opposed to shredding rubber. I fold my arms, tapping my foot and scowling at the piece of shit.

And, this truck really is a POS. I mean, sure, the Sentra's old, too. It's no 'sweet machine' either, but at least the body is—was—intact. Who would drive such a hunk of junk? *Hunter...* I bite my lip. Of course, it's not his truck, but its owner has to be in a similar financial situation as him, working two or three jobs to pay their way through school or rent or whatever. The person driving that apocalypse wagon couldn't afford the $200 or so it'll cost to replace the door mirror on an '08 Sentra.

Damn. Ashley's right. I really am too nice.

I take a few photos of the scene just in case Dad freaks out. There's nowhere near enough room for me to squeeze between the truck and car on the driver's side. Even a field mouse couldn't fit. I write 'learn to park!' in the dirt covering the driver's door window, then trudge along the right side of the Sentra to the front end, walk around, and pick up the mirror. Little glass bits are everywhere and the plastic housing is smashed beyond usefulness, but abandoning it here doesn't seem like the right thing to do.

My head's a conflicting mess of anger and pity with a touch of shame for just rolling over and taking a broken mirror without fighting back. It shouldn't bother me as much as it does. Of all the things that have happened to me over the past five months, a smashed mirror is totally trivial. With a sigh, I return to the passenger side of the Sentra, toss the mirror onto the floor in the back, and climb over the seats to get behind the wheel.

Like a complete idiot, I try to check the door mirror—that's gone —to see if I have enough clearance to get out. At seeing a hole where I expect a mirror to be, I sigh again, and twist around to look.

Naturally, the truck's rear bumper is in the way since he's parked it skewed at an angle. At least, I assume it's a guy. Somewhere between it being a pickup and the moronic parking job makes me think boy. But it's not like the guys have a monopoly on aggressive driving, or owning trucks.

Still, I don't feel comfortable trying to get out of the space with such little clearance. I'll be jockeying back and forth two inches at a time for an hour. Grr! Dammit. I want to get out of here. I have stuff to do tonight!

There's always leaving the car here and flying for now... but, then I'll hear it from Dad.

I really am a sad excuse for a vampire, still worried about getting in trouble with the 'rents.

Once again infuriated, I scramble out of the car and run around to the back. Out of sheer cavewoman fury, I grab the tail end of the truck, growl, and push it away from my car, straightening it out in the space so the Sentra's not blocked in.

"There..."

I start to turn to my left, dusting my hands off, and freeze—staring into the eyes of a cop who's looking at me like he's watching space aliens for real. The only thing that would make his expression more perfect is if he had a cigarette hanging off his lower lip. Vape rigs are a little too heavy for that.

"Oh, heh," I say in a cheesy voice. "Guy parked a little close."

He blinks at me.

"... and you don't need to remember seeing that."

The cop's eyes flutter. He blinks away the momentary confusion, then fixes me with the usual 'cop stare' when they aren't sure if they're looking at a suspect, victim, or innocent bystander. "Someone discharged a firearm here a few minutes ago. Did you see anything unusual?"

"Firearm? No... someone ran over a soccer ball and it exploded. You're talking about that loud bang?" I point at the column. "There's still fragments of the ball on the ground over there somewhere. No one fired a gun."

And wow, I don't even need to use powers of mind control.

"So you don't know anything about a gunshot?" He walks up and gives me the once-over.

It's obvious he's picked up on something not being quite right, but the guy doesn't know exactly what. He suspects I may be lying and have a gun on me, but he also doesn't think I 'look like the type' to be carrying a weapon—or using one. Since I'm already agitated between the test and the mirror—as well as impatient—I hit him with a little mental prod and send him off to examine the exploded soccer ball.

Ugh. Gunshot indeed.

I hop in the Sentra. *Swear... if this thing doesn't start, I'm going to leave it here.*

It starts without a problem. Dad's owned the car for ten years. He doesn't drive it much and he brings it to the shop regularly, so aside from merely being old, it's in good shape. Not even a lot of miles on it. 52,084 isn't much for like a ten-year-old car, right? *Finally, something goes right for me tonight.*

Relieved, I exhale an unnecessary breath, back out of the space, and begin the drive home.

2

GATE NIGHT

Ashley and Michelle are waiting in front of my house when I get home.

Amid me apologizing for being late, I tell them about the idiot parking job with the truck on the way inside. This, of course, metamorphoses into me explaining the smashed mirror to Dad, showing everyone the photos on my iPhone, and re-explaining everything again. Sophia smiles that I'm not gonna harass a poor person to replace the mirror. Sierra gives me this 'really?' look. And no, she's not *that* mercenary, she's just thinking it will encourage the guy to continue being a dick to other people.

Anyway, Ash and 'Chelle head down to my room with me. Sophia gives us a look I can only describe as mildly jealous as we walk out. She knows she's welcome to hang out with us if she wants. My days of chasing her away died when I did. But, she stays in the living room reading. Her choice. Once in my room, we all turn back into tweens— at least in terms of personality. We put a movie on but don't really watch it, instead talking about our respective lives, loves, and random weird crap we saw on Facebook.

The girls laugh their asses off at my frustrating explanation of taking the test. Michelle's freaking out because she's starting to really think Corey might be 'the one' even though he's only her like fourth boyfriend ever. Ashley's a little sad as she doesn't presently have a romantic partner. She's given up on specifically trying to find a girl 'this time,' and is just waiting for the universe to send her someone she's compatible with.

We lose track of time, due to it having been a while since we just hung out with no major worries. Michelle repeats her invitation to a Halloween party someone from her school is throwing, and we both 'yeah, yeah' her and assure her we'll be there. Eventually Michelle realizes it's late, and my friends zoom out the door. Typical Ashley, she doesn't even bother putting her shoes on to run home since she's only four houses down the street that passes our cul-de-sac. I stand by the door watching Michelle drive off, her tail lights glaringly bright to my eyes. History replays in my mind, tiny Ashley, barely six, running off home after we had to stop playing for the day. Then Ashley at twelve, riding her bike home. Michelle joining in at around fourteen, both of them riding their bikes home. Now Michelle driving.

I sigh. Why the hell do I feel old at eighteen? I'm not supposed to have nostalgia yet. That's like an old person problem. Smirking, I back up, shut the door, and turn around, staring into my living room. The hairs on my arms and the back of my neck stand on end.

Yeah, I know I'm dead, but somehow that shit still works.

My home doesn't feel right after Ashley and Michelle leave.

A strange sense of wrongness hangs over everything now that I find myself alone, and it worries me big time. For one thing, I haven't been afraid of the dark since like age eight, but mostly, I freak out because the eerie feeling comes too close to a sense like I am somewhere I don't belong. Like this house isn't even mine anymore and I'm invading it, a monster on the outside looking in at a happy family I'm no longer part of.

As attached as I am to my family and my home, it scares the shit out of me to get this uneasy notion that I'm breaking the rules by staying with them. I'd feel *less* out of place sneaking into the records room at school to steal my test scores than walking into my own house.

Has something about my vampire nature finally cracked and the universe doesn't want me to stay here anymore? I try to ignore the feeling, but as soon as I'm in the basement, it's like the cops are going to come out of nowhere at any second and drag me away. Overcome by grief at the idea of no longer being able to stay with my family, paradoxical panic drives me out of the house. With no better ideas on what to do or how to handle my emotions, I fly off into the night seeking advice.

Which is how I end up reclining on the roof of an apartment building, hanging out with Glim and talking. He doesn't think anything paranormal occurred to chase me away from my home. It's not like he's known many people who stayed with their family after the Transference. I'm the first. But, he sounds confident that whatever I picked up on wasn't any inner notion of needing to leave home forever. Vampires don't have any natural urges to be with or away from people. The whole convention of disappearing after death and severing all ties with mortal friends and relatives is purely one of laziness. Few vampires want to put up with the supervigilance of trying to keep their secrets and scrub the minds of everyone who figures shit out. Of course, being an Innocent who can tolerate some sunlight, faking it is a lot easier for me.

And besides, it's pretty ridiculous for me to be afraid of the dark. I'm really not. Seriously, a vampire who's afraid of the dark would be the butt of every joke imaginable. Also, there really *isn't* any true sense of dark to me unless I close my eyes. Can't be afraid of what doesn't exist.

That means I picked up on something else. Whatever inexplicable source of information Glim has whispering in his ear all the time has yet to say anything about my house or family, so we're both hoping whatever I felt is a minor thing. Since my type of vampire isn't known for developing much in the way of strange powers, he doesn't think I had a premonition. His suggestion—that I merely sensed the presence of a malign ghost walking by—didn't exactly settle my nerves.

Coralie never made me feel like I wanted to run out of my own home. Of course, she's not a 'malign' spirit.

"There is more on your mind, isn't there?" Glim takes a sip from a can of Busch beer I brought him. "Perhaps the anxiety simply came from your not wanting to be alone after everyone went to bed?"

"Maybe." I gaze up at the stars, fingers laced behind my head, mind wandering about what life would be like now had I remained normal. Probably exactly like Ashley and Michelle's: school plus work. We still wouldn't have the kind of hangout time we used to. No sense blaming vampirism for us no longer spending ten hours a day together. That's just how adulting works. "Hey, do you know how to turn down hearing?"

"Turn down hearing?" He glances sideways at me.

"Yeah…" I explain trying to take a test with all the noises. That brings the frustration right back to the surface and my rant continues straight on to the idiot who broke the side mirror. By the time I catch myself shouting and stop, I'm sitting up cross-legged with two fistfuls of my hair. Fortunately, I've had the self-control not to growl or snarl in class. Ever since the change, me growling or snarling sounds more like a cougar or mountain lion than a girl.

He grins—I think. "That sounds maddening. I'd suggest going with your plan of headphones. The quieter it is, the more acute our hearing becomes. In a noisy environment, we notice it less. As far as I know, the process is outside conscious control."

"So if I go somewhere loud, my ears become less sensitive on their own, but I can't turn down the volume on purpose?"

"If that is possible, I am unaware of how to do it. Though, it may be a simple matter of trying. The trick is how to make your brain flex a mental muscle that you're not used to having."

"Right." I sweep my hair back over my shoulders and take a deep breath of night air. Never in my wildest dreams did I ever think I'd be sitting on a rooftop at two in the morning, stargazing. It's quite peaceful, really. "So, do you think I'm too much of a pushover for not doing anything about my mirror?"

Glim tilts back his second can, draining it in a series of gulps. Loaning him my ability to tolerate food and drink is hardly the most awe-inspiring use of vampiric power imaginable, but seeing the joy in his yellow eyes makes it totally worth it. He savors the last mouthful, reacting to the budget beer like he's tasting fine wine.

"Nah."

"You don't?" I raise an eyebrow.

"Nope. If that had been a Beemer, you would've made the driver pay for the repairs. You're not a pushover; you're a decent person. Someone driving a beater like that would have struggled with the financial burden."

I fidget at my shoelaces. "Thanks, but I'm not sure I'd have thought that way without meeting Hunter."

"How so?"

"Used to be, I never really thought about money and stuff. Like, I'm really lucky. My parents both have really good jobs. We never wanted for any of the important stuff and had plenty for unimportant things. It never really hit me before that other kids didn't have it so good. When I started dating Hunter, the reality of his life kinda hit me over the head and made me guilty for simply existing."

Glim opens can number three with a *pssh.* "Well, no one chooses the parents they're born to. Don't take blame for things you have no control over. And you're certainly not the type of person who feels superior to others because you're rich."

I can't help but laugh. "We're nowhere near rich. But… I guess to someone who isn't sure *if* they'll have food to eat, we are."

"I was mostly teasing by calling you rich." He winks. "Rich people have far more than they need. Being comfortable isn't rich. I'll start making fun of you when you have trouble deciding which yacht to take out for the weekend."

"Hah. Having *one* yacht counts as rich."

He chuckles. "So, any plans for Halloween tomorrow?"

"Umm. Probably escorting the sibs around for a bit. Michelle's invited Ashley and me to a party some people from her school are going to."

He nods. "Are you planning to dress up? I've seen a few vampires parade around in public claiming to have high-end costumes with theater-quality fangs. It's almost tempting, but I wouldn't want to give anyone a heart attack."

"Aww…" I lean against him. "You're not *that* scary. And nah. I'm not really interested in dressing up. If I do have my arm twisted into it, I'll probably do something goofy again. Me dressing up as a vampire would be too meta."

Glim wags his eyebrows at me. "You could go as a Girl Scout."

My unexpectedly strong laugh blurts out of me with a noise like a kicked chicken. "Yeah, right. Buying a costume hasn't even crossed my mind with everything else going on. They had this thing at my school, but I totally phoned it in. Right up until five minutes before I left the house, I wasn't going to dress up at all, but I changed my mind at the last possible second. Just some makeup to look pale and had my fangs out. And you know this woman thought the teeth looked fake?" I scoff. "The nerve."

He snickers, shaking his head. "Yeah, makes sense. Think I stopped bothering with trick-or-treating around sixteen myself. No younger siblings to go out with and my friends all thought it was 'for little kids.' Hmm. Perhaps losing the urge to dress up on Halloween is like the canary in a coal mine, warning us of the impending death of childhood. First, we lose the joy in trick-or-treating, then one by one, everything else goes from being wondrous to routine."

That comment would've made me sad, but I'm not going to grow up. Or… grow up any more. Unless something serious goes wrong, I'm going to be the girl who's eighteen but looks sixteen forever, which is really cool. If I'm feeling goofy, I can act immature and be taken for a kid. If not, I can act like an adult—and still get taken for a kid.

Sigh.

"Are you okay?" I hug him.

"Quite. Just feeling nostalgic." He takes a long sip of beer. "I don't want to be a child again. Couldn't drink this stuff when I was young enough to go door to door on Halloween."

"Heh."

Maybe Ashley has the right idea. She's not goth or morbid by any stretch of the imagination. However, she adores Halloween, typically dressing up 'cute.' As in, Disney princesses, cats, rabbits, or something like that. She's the reason I probably *am* going to wind up putting on some kind of costume for the party tomorrow. Considering I haven't bought anything yet and tomorrow is Halloween, I'm either going to make a panicky, rushed shopping trip and get stuck with one of the costumes no one else in the world wants, or recycle last year's outfit and go as Hermione again, assuming I can find it. When I was too little to have any control, Dad used to dress me up as retro Eighties characters. At four, he turned me into a tiny Daphne from *Scooby Doo*.

"Planning any fun for Mischief Night?" asks Glim.

"What the heck is that?"

He chuckles. "I grew up back east. We called the night before Halloween 'Mischief Night.' Did all sorts of random annoying crap. Egging houses, smashing pumpkins, TP in trees, that sort of thing."

"Uhh." I shake my head. "No, never heard of it."

"What about Gate Night? Some people around here call it that."

"Nope. New to me… and what the heck does Billy Corrigan have to do with mischief?"

"What?" He stares at me in total confusion for a second, then rolls his eyes. "No, not music. Smashing *actual* pumpkins. People would leave Jack-o-Lanterns out on their porch steps, and sometimes, we'd splatter the ones belonging to neighbors we didn't like."

"Oh. That's kinda mean."

He shrugs one shoulder. "Stupid kids doing stupid things. What can I say?"

"Yeah, well, I've never done anything like that. Never even knew the night before Halloween was a thing other than simply being the night before Halloween."

Glim finishes his third can and lets it dangle from his fingertips, arm draped over his knee. For a while, he stares into space as if lost in thought. I don't mind the silence. He does that sometimes. At least here, no one's constantly clicking a damn pen. Though, I really could do without the dude spanking it in the apartment across the parking lot from us. At least, I assume he's taken matters into his own hand as he's the only one moaning. Here and there, refrigerators kick on and whirr or a horn beeps in the distance.

There's real peace in silence sometimes… at least as silent as it gets to me. Maybe I'll fly off into the woods somewhere and sit to experience real silence away from the noise of civilization. I wonder if I'll hear the trees breathing.

"They say tonight is a powerful supernatural event. The realm of spirits and the mortal reality we know are at their closest, hence 'gate' night."

"Okay, random. Where'd that come from?"

Glim peers at me, doing a perfect impression of a creepy fortune-teller. "The darkness whispers of strange energy gathering around your home. Perhaps that is what you sensed."

I blink. "Uhh… yeah, I hear there's a legit vampire living there."

He keeps looking at me with 'serious face.'

"Are you messing with me or trying to freak me out?"

"No." Glim shakes his head. "Be careful."

"Umm." I sit up straighter, my mind racing around in circles of worry. "What kind of energy? Is this St. Ives coming after me? Dammit. I'm only eighteen and I haven't even been a vampire for a full year yet. I'm too young to have an archenemy."

He gazes up at the sky. "This does not feel like anything that woman is doing. However, I cannot rule out the possibility that it might be. The warning is not particularly dire, so you should be fine as long as you stay alert."

"Great." I wrap my arms around my legs, hugging my knees to my chest. "Telling me to stay alert is going to have me jumping at shadows for days."

"Boo," says Glim.

I smirk at him. "I mean jumping at shadows, not at Shadows."

He flashes a daggery smile and pats me on the back. "I'm sure you'll be fine."

"Thanks."

Glim springs to his feet. "Now, if you'll excuse me… the beer wants out."

"Yeah, I suppose I should get back anyway. I've got reading to do for school tomorrow."

He quirks an eyebrow at me, clearly trying not to laugh at the idea of my still going to college despite being a vampire. "Then, good night. May the forces of evil become disoriented on their way to your abode. Thank you again for the beer."

I float into the air, hovering cross-legged in midair like the old master from some kind of bad kung fu movie before landing on my feet and hugging him. "You're welcome."

There's no need for me to say I know how much it means to him, and I'm happy to do it as often as he wants. I'm sure he understands. After I release the hug, he disappears amid a shadowy pillar of smoke. It looks cool, even if it really is nothing more than an illusion he's tricking my brain into seeing.

Anyway, time to go home. And no, I don't think I'm going to get much reading done... unless that weird feeling is gone.

Something is in my house that shouldn't be there, and I don't like it.

3

MISCHIEF

To make a long, boring night short, I couldn't find a damn thing.

When I got home, I checked on the 'rents and the littles, all of whom slept peacefully in their beds. The odd feeling remained, but it had weakened quite considerably since I'd hauled ass out of the house. On top of Glim talking about 'gate night,' realizing the weird energy had been stronger at the stroke of midnight made me feel like a little kid afraid of the dark again.

Ugh. So annoying. I guess 'focus issues' are another one of my vampiric superpowers.

If I had to assign a hierarchy to them, flight is tops, followed by no periods, then the ability to eat whatever I want with zero guilt. Well, *almost* zero guilt. I'll never gain weight, but I still feel a little bad wasting food. Not so much for things like ice cream or chocolates. Those aren't exactly 'nutrition' I'm taking away from someone who actually needs it.

Mom thinks the best part is I'm forever eighteen and I'll never wind up a 'struggling-to-stay-thin' forty-something who longs for the days I can fit into my high school wardrobe. Don't tell her, but I think she's projecting a little. And it's not like she's overweight, or even slightly thick. If she was skinnier than she is now in high school, she would've looked like Sophia, taller. I swear that girl could hide behind a broom handle.

Anyway, speaking of ice cream…

I require a therapy session with Dr. Ben and Dr. Jerry to get me through my fear of the dark while dealing with some calculus homework and reading a few chapters in the comp sci book. Sunrise sneaks up on me, and even though my bedroom is completely dark with no windows whatsoever, my body reacts to the time and out I go.

Dad calls it having a 'qwerty sandwich.' As in faceplant the keyboard.

The next thing I know, I'm slumped over my desk trying to absorb information via osmosis. I didn't actually kiss my keyboard, more like drooled all over my textbook. It's a few minutes after two in the afternoon. Another tick in the 'plus' column for vampire me: no muscle soreness from sleeping in such an awkward position. I could curl up on hard concrete and not suffer for it. My bed is awesome, but comfort only matters while I'm awake.

My phone's weather app says it's heavy overcast but not raining, so I peer out into the basement. Looks nice and dim, normal. Though, there's a new red-and-gold throw rug near the far left wall that Mom must've bought yesterday, since it hadn't been there before. Guessing it's in the basement until she figures out where it's going to end up living permanently upstairs.

Satisfied the sun's friendly—and by that, I mean hiding behind clouds—I grab a change of clothes and creep to the top of the stairs and test-open the door a half inch. It's toasty in the kitchen but well within tolerable ranges. Time for a shower. For that, I can use the basement bathroom. No point dealing with burning 'calories' resisting sunlight unless I'm going to luxuriate in a bath. Once I'm finished cleaning up, I head to the first floor and check Dad's computer room—and find a note stuck to his screen explaining that he had to go to the office today. Sometimes, I forget he's not a freelance programmer and has an actual job since he works from home so often. Evidently, the manager wanted everyone to be there for some Halloween event.

Knowing my father, he either dressed up as Egon from *Ghostbusters* or Dr. Grant from *Jurassic Park*. And yeah, the dino film wasn't from the Eighties, but it's one of his favorite movies. I'm guessing he was one of those little boys who had millions of plastic dinosaur toys. My brother Sam likes dinosaurs, too, but Dad is obsessive with them. Then again, he's got two settings for any given activity/movie/fandom: 'it's okay' or acting like he's the one who created it. Like his thing with Eighties movies. You'd think he directed them all.

With the house to myself, I go back to my room and resume reading for my computer science class. I don't realize until almost an hour into reading that the weird feeling I picked up on last night is gone. Or at least *really* weak. It didn't appear to be noticeable at all upstairs. Whatever's causing it must be hanging out in the basement. I can sympathize, being a fellow 'creature of darkness,' but this particular basement is already claimed.

A brief exploration of the entire basement—including the creepy unfinished room with the furnace and hot water heater—fails to reveal anything unusual. Ghosts, of course, *can* still hide from me if they want to, but I have a much easier time seeing them than a normal person. The way Coralie explained it, a spirit has to force themselves to appear to humans and force themselves to disappear from me. A ghost who merely exists, neither trying to hide nor manifest, I'll usually be able to see at least a partial hint of.

As I've spotted nothing at all, I'm hopeful there's no ghost here. Maybe that doll, Rebecca, came back to visit. But, she'd have shown herself… and I don't know that Glim would have read her as 'dark energy.' At least, I hope not. Souls trapped in dolls are freaky enough when they're *not* evil.

I'm quite thoroughly done with having focus issues, so I grab the comp sci book and head up to the living room. Tolerating warm rainy-daylight is less distracting than wondering who or what is standing behind me, watching.

A few minutes into reading, I nearly jump off the couch at a sudden, heavy pounding at the front door. It takes me a second to recover from having the crap scared out of me. Whoever it is wallops the door again.

Geez. Hasn't this idiot ever heard of doorbells?

I mark my spot, set the book down, and stomp over to the door. The instant my bare foot hits the chilly square of linoleum—Mom's demilitarized shoe-permitted zone—it hits me that I'm offline. At the moment, I'm no more of a badass than I was in high school. Meaning, if there's some raging creep out there, he legit *could* kill me.

Annoyance becomes worry. I sneak up to the door and peer out the peephole at a late-sixties guy with a formerly-athletic build, squarish head, wispy white hair and a powder blue polo shirt. He looks mad enough to choke someone, but I'm not *too* worried since I recognize him: Mr. Neidermayer from two houses left around our cul-de-sac.

All the kids in this area know him.

He's our 'get off my lawn' guy. I think every town has one. Only this guy legit says 'get off my lawn.' Probably has an entire steamer trunk in his house filled with stolen Frisbees, baseballs, soccer balls, and such... everything that landed on his property he got to before the kid who lost it could run after it. Now that I think about it, he's exactly the kind of prick who'd try to outlaw teenagers trick-or-treating.

Why he's hammering on our door, I have no idea.

Grr. Right when I'm getting used to being a vampire and happy in my newfound powers, I am stuck once again feeling like a defenseless young woman home alone. Granted, this guy is merely a self-righteous asshole. He wouldn't attack me or do anything serious... I think. And he's old. If he *did* try anything, even mortal me could at least get away from him.

I open the door. "Hi, Mr. Neidermayer. Is something wrong?"

For an old dude, he's in pretty good shape. Taller than me by a decent amount and broad-shouldered, even if his arms are so weathered they look like beef jerky. My dad said something once about him being retired military but I can't remember what branch.

"You're damn right something's wrong," he shouts. "Those undisciplined kids of yours caused holy havoc on my property last night. They've gone too far this time. Your parents are going to need to pay for every bit of damage or I'll be getting the police involved."

You know that scene in *Back to the Future* where McFly is standing in front of that enormous loudspeaker that throws him off his feet? Yeah, that's kind of how I feel bearing the brunt of this guy's shouting. Too bad I'm offline at the moment and can't literally fly away from him to make a visual sarcastic joke. Honestly, if I didn't have a face full of dreary sunlight, I'd wallop him in the brain with a command to go the hell home and leave me alone.

Alas.

"Umm, I have no idea what you're talking about. My sisters and brother didn't go outside last night. Besides, they're not the type of kids who would cause real damage. Sophia would never even play a prank at all, much less a destructive one."

He points at me, then wags his finger at the sky. "Don't lie to me, young lady. I have cameras. Motion activated."

"You have cameras?" I fold my arms. "Then you clearly haven't looked at the video yet, because my siblings were not running around last night on their own."

Mr. Neidermayer half turns toward his house, gesticulating wildly at it. "Four windows broken. Fence smashed. Plants torn up, flowerbeds trampled. Fountain knocked over, goddamned balls everywhere. I can't take a step without balls. Everywhere. Balls. Balls. Balls."

It takes all my strength not to laugh.

He again thrusts his finger into my face. "The police can get fingerprints off baseballs ya know."

"Who's fingerprints? Whoever threw them around your yard last night, or the kids who played with them before you stole them?"

"You really want me to get the police involved here, missy?"

Ooh… he's so damn lucky I'm offline right now. Missy? Seriously?

Who does this guy think he is? "Look, if you have cameras, go look at the video. You obviously haven't or you wouldn't be here right now. Go ahead and get the police involved. I'm absolutely confident my siblings had nothing to do with whatever happened at your house."

"Bull—" He catches himself, going red in the face. Evidently, screaming curse words at a girl my age bothers him. "There are footprints going from my backyard straight to yours."

I gesture at him. "You're in our front yard, but you don't live here. It's possible whoever vandalized your property cut through backyards to avoid being seen out on the street. Have you looked at the video at all? Just because the trail goes to our yard doesn't prove it was someone who lives here."

He gives me this weird stare, like still trying to be furious but also unnerved. "Of course I watched it."

"And…?" Dammit! I *really* want to read this guy's mind. Stupid sunlight. "It didn't show my siblings because they weren't the ones responsible for whatever happened."

Mr. Neidermayer dials back the anger. Honestly, it's the first I've seen him where he didn't look like the stereotypical old bitter neighbor who hates children. He almost looks worried. Maybe if he hadn't shouted at five-year-old me for riding a tricycle too close to his grass, I'd feel bad enough to offer some kind of help. But, considering how much of a shit he's been to me and any other kid who's grown up within about a quarter mile, I can't find the desire.

After a long, silent stare, he gives a slight shake of the head and walks back across the cul-de-sac to his house, muttering something about 'damn kids' and 'makes no damn sense.' Figures, my amped up hearing drove me nuts yesterday and right now when I'm super curious and *want* to hear a flea fart at a hundred feet, I can't.

Irony can go straight to hell.

I shut the door and return to the couch. Half a chapter later, a muffled man yelling breaks the silence. It's mostly indecipherable, but the cadence makes me think he's yelling 'what the F' or some variation thereof. Ugh. What now? It sounded like Mr. Perry next door on the right, but they're usually quiet. I don't pay it much mind and keep reading... until a knock comes from the patio doors in the kitchen.

Stretching up to lean past the end of the couch lets me look down the short hall at Mr. Perry standing on our deck. Like Neidermayer, he looks ready to hit someone. Unlike the old guy, he's neither tall nor muscular. He's also not *old*, being around Dad's age. Every time I've ever spoken with him, he's been like this sweet guy, so seeing him furious is both unusual and kinda funny. Almost like watching Ned Flanders from *The Simpsons* have a meltdown. If Mr. Perry had a mustache and glasses, I'd have burst out laughing.

Curious, I climb over the back of the sofa and pad up to the door, flick the lock, and pull it aside. "Mr. Perry?"

He flails, then jabs his hand like a knife toward his house over and over again while yelling, "Your dogs shredded my kitchen... ripped open the fridge, tore up the cabinets, tossed stuff everywhere, ate half of it."

"Umm. Mr. Perry, you know we don't have *a* dog, much less multiple dogs."

"Huh..." He calms a bit, sets his hands on his hips, and sighs. "Oh, well... it ran to your yard."

"It what?" I blink.

Mr. Perry points at the fence separating our backyards. "I saw some weird dog run across the yard and jump the fence here. Ran after it, but the darn thing disappeared. I figured it came inside."

"Wow, that's messed up." I shrug. "Sorry... but we don't have a dog, or a cat, or even any pets. Well, my brother's got a pair of frogs and, umm, strange as they are, I doubt they have the ability to make a mess in your kitchen."

"Frogs..."

The front door opens, admitting Sierra, Sophia, and Sam, in the midst of a discussion about why Mr. Neidermayer had been glaring at them while they walked down the cul-de-sac from the street. They all appear equally confused as they shed their backpacks full of schoolbooks and kick off their shoes.

"He just hates kids," says Sophia. "Thinks we're gonna do bad stuff just because we're not grown up."

"Yeah." Sam frowns. "He's a butthead."

They notice Mr. Perry at the back door and walk into the kitchen. The girls chorus, "Hi, Mr. Perry" almost simultaneously while Sam merely waves.

"Hello... umm, did any of you see a weird little dog running around?"

They shake their heads.

"Nope. We just got off the bus," says Sam.

Mr. Perry grumbles, then looks at me. "I'm guessing you have no idea who might have a dog around here?"

"The people who live in the brown house to the left out on 167th Ave have a black lab." I scratch at the back of my head. "But, I don't really know them."

"Don't think it was a lab, but..." Mr. Perry sighs. "Hard to tell, the damn thing ran off so fast. Probably a stray."

Sam fishes around the cookie jar while standing on a chair by the counter. "How'd it get into your house?"

"Not sure to be honest. Took off work early to set up for Halloween. There's all sorts of noise coming from the kitchen. Back door was open, but no idea how it got that way." He sighs. "Sorry for yelling at you before. I assumed it was your dog."

Sophia clings to Sierra, shrinking in on herself. Given how timid the girl is, she might make that frightened face at the presence of an angry neighbor, but it's more guilt than fear. Ugh. She's been wanting a pet for a while. *Do* we have a dog that I simply don't know about? Is she hiding a stray she hasn't told our parents about?

"Before I make a complete idiot out of myself, is there an animal in the house that I'm unaware of?" I ask.

"No," chime the kids.

Sierra and Sam are casual about it, but Sophia answers without looking up from the floor.

"Soph? Are you hiding a dog in your room?"

"No." She shakes her head fast. "I swear."

"Why do you look worried?"

She fidgets. "I dunno."

"She read some spooky book last night and had a nightmare," says Sierra. "She's thinking it wasn't really a dog, but something *else*." The girl waves her arms making cheesy woo-woo spooky noises.

"Stop!" Sophia swats at her.

Mr. Perry laughs. "Darn. Well, I've got a big mess to clean up and a candy bowl to get ready. Sorry again."

"No problem." I wave at him and slide the patio door shut.

"Time to go trick-or-treating!" cheers Sierra. She grabs Sophia by the hand and drags her down the hall to the living room, then upstairs.

"Ashley left something for you," says Sam around a mouthful of cookie. "On the dining room table."

"Huh? She what? When?"

"This morning real early." He walks out, following his sisters upstairs.

In the dining room, I discover a plain white box. She got me a costume, I bet.

Well, that's one less thing I have to worry about.

"Where is it?" yells Sophia. "It's gone!"

Ugh. She better not be talking about a dog.

Soft thuds indicate Sierra marching across the hall to her sister's room. "It's right in the closet where you left it."

I peer up at the ceiling. Something is bothering Sophia. Then again, she acts this guilty over trivial stuff like staying awake a half hour past her bedtime to finish reading a chapter in a book. Meh. It's probably nothing. She's worse at lying than I am, crying within seconds of fibbing. Telling lies doesn't make me cry, but I evidently can't keep the worry off my face. Anyone who knows me can tell I'm lying right away.

The costume can wait for the party. I am *not* going to class in costume tonight. Nor am I going to wear it to escort the kids around. No, this afternoon, I am going dressed as 'older sister.' That decision made, I pick the box up and carry it downstairs to my room. It's gloomy enough today that I'll fly to school. That will let me get home after class in time to change for Michelle and Ashley to pick me up for the party.

Once in my room, the temptation to peek becomes irresistible. I lift the lid to see what Ashley did to me this year. If she thinks I'm going to go out in public as Raggedy Ann, she's sorely mistaken.

… and it's a Tinkerbell dress. With fairy wings and cute green slippers.

Groan. That skirt is so damn short I'm going to wear a bikini bottom with it instead of panties. At least I have one a matching shade of green.

Great. Tinkerbell.

Very funny. I just know Ash is going to ask me to fly around.

4

TRICK OR TREAT

My siblings are excited to go out for 'loot and plunder' as Sierra puts it.

Not long after Mr. Perry leaves, the trio comes downstairs having changed into their Halloween costumes. Sierra's dressed up as Wonder Woman, which is a little odd to see as she doesn't usually go out of her way to call attention to the fact she's a girl. I mean, she's no tomboy, but it's *weird* seeing her in a skirt. Predictably, Sophia is wearing something pink, frilly, and quite extra, along with white face paint. I almost think she's trying to dress up as a porcelain doll like the ones Aurélie collects, but when she opens her mouth to show off plastic vampire teeth, I give up trying to guess who she's supposed to be. Maybe Claudia from *Interview*? Of course, since I'm a vampire, it was a foregone conclusion Sophia—who idolizes me —would want to dress up as one. Sam, aside from having hair a little too long for the outfit, rocks a 'Young Sheldon' costume scarily well.

He glances at Sierra, then looks up at me. "Sare, someone stole Sierra and replaced her with a girl."

Sophia giggles.

"Nice bowtie, nerd," says Sierra.

"Thanks." He raises his chin and adjusts the tie.

She scoffs. "Why are you wearing that? It doesn't even look like a costume."

"I calculated that seventy-four percent of trick-or-treaters this year will be wearing one of two costumes: Batman or Wonder Woman. I decided to be unique."

Sierra's face reddens… but hey, at least she doesn't make a fist.

"You got me, Soph," I say. "Not sure who that is."

My youngest sister shrugs. "Not supposed to be anyone specific. I'm a vampire doll." And with that, she play bites Sam on the neck, causing him to scream and flail his arms.

"Where's your costume?" asks Sierra.

"Not gonna put it on now. I need to run to school like right after we get back, and there's no way in hell I'm going to wear a costume to class."

All three of them *aww* at me.

"But, Sare, it's Halloween!" whines Sophia. "You *gotta* dress up."

"Seriously." Sierra gives me a rare, pleading look.

"Yeah, c'mon." Sam rubs his neck. "Even Sierra dressed up as a girl."

She slugs him on the shoulder—and proceeds to launch into a rant about how the new *Wonder Woman* movie inspired her and it's about damn time (her words) Hollywood started having more female-led movies. Sam stares at her with this look on his face like a mouse stuck in quicksand watching the eagle diving at him.

"Oh fine," I mutter, not loud enough to overpower Sierra's tirade.

I race down to my bedroom, fling off my clothes, and grab my green bikini bottoms. After pulling them on, I open the box. The Tinkerbell dress is on the skimpy side but not quite so much that the costume feels pervy… at least no more so than the actual cartoon. It includes a wand as well as a set of thin plastic faerie wings that Velcro-attach to the back of the dress. I'm not dying my hair blonde or bothering to put it up in a bun, so I'm going to be 'the faerie with the same dress as Tinkerbell' tonight.

Sigh.

The littles cheer when I return to the living room in costume. Sierra gets the case of the giggles, attempting to comment about how I can actually fly. Sophia catches on that Ashley must've done that on purpose and she, too, starts laughing. Sam remarks that a character with wings is merely the most logical choice for a costume. Sophia helps me out by zipping the back of the dress. I may have amazing dexterity and agility as a vampire, but the Transference didn't give me extra bendable joints. That done, the girls argue over the position of my wings, taking a good ten minutes to decide they're on 'straight enough.'

"Come on, come on. We're running out of time." I usher them out the front door. "Got your bags and stuff?"

They show off their treat bags (mom's reusable cloth grocery bags) and head out the door.

We make our way around the cul-de-sac first, skipping Mr. Neidermayer's house as usual. In all the years I've ever gone trick-or-treating, that house has always been off the list. The guy's so nasty to kids, he'd surely just yell at anyone who dared ringing his bell. If any kid actually dared to ring his bell, they'd probably get chocolate-covered Brussels sprouts. Here and there, groups of other children wander around in costume—and they all avoid his place, too.

At each house, Sam says things like he doubts the existence of spirits, but the candy is tempting or he calculated the odds of this house giving out good treats as favorable. The girls go with the traditional 'trick or treat' chime. Mrs. Perry *awws* at Sophia until she smiles, baring her plastic fangs, then pretends to be scared. She head-pats Sam and grins at Sierra.

We make our way out to the street and go house-to-house. A few people give me odd looks, but once they realize I'm not out begging for candy—merely chaperoning the littles—they lose the attitude. Not that I *want* to go trick-or-treating as a teen, but seriously, who cares? Wearing a silly outfit is hardly the worst thing a kid my age could be doing at night.

The fifth house down the road, a middle-aged guy in a blue tank top regards us with a mostly unimpressed look. I get the feeling he finds constantly answering the door irritating, but he's not mean enough to ignore the kids entirely.

"Heh, cute," he says to Sophia while dropping a few candies into her bag.

"Thank you," chirps Sophia.

The guy nods at Sam, drops candy in his sack, then raises an eyebrow at Sierra. "Kinda scrawny for Wonder Woman, aren't you?"

Sierra glares at him, but by some miracle, holds her tongue.

He laughs, drops candy in her bag, and shuts the door.

"What are these?" asks Sam. "Like some kinda hard candy."

"Asshole," mutters Sierra.

Sophia gasps at her.

"You *are* skinny," says Sam. "We all are. But you're also eleven. You're supposed to be skinny."

Sierra shifts her glare to him. "You're not helping. He's stingy and a butthead."

"The man gave us candy. He didn't have to. He could've ignored the doorbell." Sophia tugs at her. "C'mon."

Mini Wonder Woman shoots a final glare at the house, then turns to follow us back to the sidewalk. We barely take a step before a loud explosion goes off in the yard behind the place, a mixture of deep, *booms* with sharper rapid-fire snaps like a small machine gun firing.

The sky above the house lights up with fireworks. Car alarms go off everywhere. Roman candle orbs come skittering down the driveway, hissing and whirling about. An orange one misses my head by about three feet.

"Run!" yells Sophia.

Something goes into the air with a deep *whoosh*, followed by a painfully loud *bang* and a rushing crackle. A spherical bloom of sparks erupts maybe fifty feet up. The littles sprint down the sidewalk, Sophia hiking up her voluminous dress so she can run. Not wanting to eat a firework, I hurry after them. The angry screaming of the homeowner drowns under the continuous barrage of shrill whistles, loud explosions, and crackling.

A large group of kids and parents collect at a safe distance to watch the fireworks show.

Once we get far enough away that nothing seems likely to hit us,

Sierra erupts in laughter. Sophia stares at me with a face like I'd caught her murdering someone.

Sam cheers at the fireworks. "Awesome!"

I can't tell if the smoke smell is coming just from the fireworks or if the guy's house caught fire. Considering the detonation went off in the backyard, I'm guessing he had a tool shed that's now burning. Unfortunately, I left my iPhone at home since this silly little pixie dress has no pockets.

Meh. The guy's aware of the fire… he can call 911 himself.

It does bother me that Sophia looks so damn guilty. It's almost like she thinks Sierra somehow set off those fireworks with an angry glare. Before I can ask her about that, a weird sense that we're being followed comes out of nowhere. A quick look back doesn't reveal anyone trying to sneak up on us, so I stop walking and face to the rear, scanning the trees and hiding places between houses. There's plenty of costumed kids and parents around, but none are watching us. A dad is checking out my butt though. Ugh. Still, I can't shake the sense that someone with worse intentions than that guy is stalking us.

The area we live in is nice, and I've never had—or even heard of—a problem around here involving a creep stalking kids. Still, that doesn't prove it could never happen. It's not quite gloomy enough for me to come 'online,' yet, so the shadowy spots in the trees and bushes remain too dark for me to see into. Though, if someone *is* really watching us, they'd have to be a little kid since there's nowhere in line of sight big enough to allow an adult to completely avoid detection.

Maybe I'm just on edge after the other night. That strange energy saturating the basement still hasn't quite faded out of my thoughts. When we reach the next house, I stay on the sidewalk watching back the way we came from while the littles run up the walkpath to the door and ring the bell.

A heavyset older woman in a witch costume answers, all smiles, and spends a few minutes talking to the kids in character as the 'not-so-wicked witch.' She playfully tries to negotiate a fair price in candy in exchange for Sam, who she wants to bake into a pie. Neither of my sisters is willing to sell, which makes him smile. The woman pretends to be annoyed, then hands out a generous amount of candy before telling them how cute they are, waving to me, and going back inside.

A little later, we bump into Nicole, the girls' friend, who's dressed up as original Harley Quinn in the black and red unitard. She's out with only her mother, so they decide to join our 'pack.' I wind up chatting with Mrs. Pierce about random mundane things as we walk along, waiting on the sidewalk while the kids run up to each house. Nicole's recently decided she wants to learn how to play the clarinet. Her mother's simultaneously excited about this new musical interest but the off-key disaster of the girl's practicing is making her want to jump off a high-rise building. I try to encourage her to give it time, assuring her Nicole will either improve or give it up soon.

That makes her laugh.

The kids storm back over to us from the twenty-somethingth house, all with sour faces.

"What's wrong?" asks Mrs. Pierce.

Sierra reaches into her sack and holds up a Ziploc bag with a mini-toothpaste, brush, and floss kit. "This! She gave out freakin' toothpaste for Halloween. Who does that?"

"Seriously," mutters Nicole.

Even Sophia looks disappointed.

"Lame," says Sam. "Halloween is supposed to cause cavities, not prevent them."

A loud *boom* comes from the direction of the house.

The kids all jump. Mrs. Pierce yells in shock. I go statue still, blinking. The reaction strikes me as odd. In the past, startling me triggered a very Sophia type reaction—a scream. Lately, I've noticed that I react to jump scares by tensing up and holding still. Is that because I'm a vampire or because of stuff I've experienced after becoming a vampire?

My brain restarts once the shock wears off. The house doesn't look damaged, no fire... but all the interior lights are out. The woman inside shrieks like someone jumped out at her with a knife. The five of us stand there, staring at the darkened home while the occupant screams and bangs on things. A couple minutes later, the front door flies open apparently all by itself. Four seconds after that, the woman runs out onto the porch holding a broom like a warrior with a two-handed sword. She glares around at her front yard with a wild-eyed expression half terror, half rage.

Sierra and Sophia exchange a look.

"What did you guys do?" I ask.

"Nothing," says Sierra. "That's just weird."

"The door opened like automatic." Nicole points. "The woman wasn't even there."

"It's mechanical." Mrs. Pierce shoos the kids down the sidewalk. "Halloween stuff to scare you."

"Oh." Sam nods. "Neat effect."

Since Mrs. Pierce is with us and can keep an eye on the kids, I keep standing there, watching the woman with the broom search around her yard. If she's acting, she's damn good. She makes eye contact with me, her expression asking 'did I see that?' Clueless, I offer a weak shrug and mouth 'no idea.' She looks around one last time, then goes back inside.

This is seriously getting weird.

I jog to catch up to everyone else. Rustling in the trees to my right makes me stop again and spin. The sudden motion startles a yelp out of Sophia and Nicole.

"Quit it!" yells Nicole. "Not cool."

Nothing's moving in the shadows. Grr. Sometimes, it's a real pain in the ass being offline. How did I ever survive life as a normal human? I miss my powers!

We resume trick-or-treating. That feeling of being watched and/or followed persists the whole time we make our rounds going down every side street within like three blocks from home. This pudgy guy on 158th Street calls Sierra's Wonder Woman 'rad,' but gives Nicole crap for wearing the 'old' Harley Quinn outfit instead of the *Suicide Squad* version.

Sierra gets into an argument with the guy about how the whole Harley Quinn character is taken the wrong way by fans. She insists the woman is trapped in an abusive relationship that she can't escape from and no one seems to realize that when saying they love her and Joker together. The man appears unprepared for a serious comic book character debate with an eleven-year-old. He stumbles for a moment, then apparently decides to talk to her like she's an adult and the two of them go in circles about the toxic relationship between a pair of fictional characters.

Sam and Sophia walk back to stand with me and Mrs. Pierce.

"This is almost like going to a convention without having to buy plane tickets," whispers Sam. "Dad says this is all people do there—argue about cannons."

Sophia rolls her eyes. "He said argue about canon. Not cannons."

"More cannons are better than one cannon." Sam grins.

"No, dork. Canon. One n."

Sam blinks, then biffs himself in the forehead. "Duh. Maybe I should've dressed up as Sponge Bob. Now I feel dumb."

Seven minutes later, Sierra and the guy appear to reach an accord and shake hands. With a pleased look on her face, my older-younger sister marches back to us.

"Amazing," says Sam, shaking his head. "I'm supposed to be the nerd here."

"It's not nerdy to talk about comics. It's geeky." Sierra peers down into her treat bag, shaking it, seeming happy with the contents.

"Can we not have another hour-long debate about the difference between nerd and geek?" I ask. "I've got to go to class soon."

"All right." Sierra starts off down the sidewalk.

Sam and Sophia follow. Mrs. Pierce yells and starts to fall over, but I grab her arm, holding her steady. She looks down at her sneakers, the laces tied together. She glances at Sophia and Sam somewhat accusingly, but her expression goes bewildered after only a few seconds.

"What on Earth? Did one of you do this?" She sits on the sidewalk and picks at her laces.

The kids all say 'no' more or less at the same time. Again, Sophia gets this guilty presence about her. Could be she's hurt at being accused when she didn't do anything. She really *is* that sensitive… but this seems deeper than that.

"What's wrong, Soph? You seem a bit worried tonight." I pat her on the head since her dress has super-puffy shoulders.

"I'm sad someone pranked Mrs. Pierce. They shouldn't do that. Whoever did mean stuff to her should leave her alone from now on."

I raise an eyebrow. Why does it sound like she's telling someone to stop?

"Are you talking to anyone in particular?" I ask.

"The spirits of Halloween," says Sierra in a creepy voice. "What else would be causing mischief today?"

"I can think of several names," mutters Mrs. Pierce.

It takes her a few minutes to untangle her shoelaces and retie them. "I have no idea how anyone could've done that to me while we were just standing there watching Sierra debate that guy."

"Ghosts," says Sierra before making wee-ooo noises.

Sophia rolls her eyes.

Finally, Mrs. Pierce gets back to her feet and we resume going door-to-door.

Still being followed by someone…

Or something.

5

ON THE OUTSIDE

The littles made out like bandits.

By the time we called it a night for trick-or-treating and went home, both of our parents had returned, already in the process of preparing dinner. Smelling garlic and onions in the air momentarily made me want to skip class tonight so I could eat with the family, but not *having* to eat food let me force myself to be a good little student.

I did, however, change back into my T-shirt and jeans. *Not* wearing that Tinkerbell costume to school.

Due to the gloomy day, my down-to-the-wire departure didn't cause me to arrive late at school. Flying is *so* much faster. No traffic, no speed limit, straight line. Pretty sure if I flew at full speed, those flimsy plastic costume faerie wings would break. I just *know* Ashley's going to demand to see me flit around while wearing the costume. Yeah, it's a little embarrassing, but I can't say no to her.

Computer science and intro to calculus go by pretty fast. Except for one guy in math who came in with a movie-quality Deadpool outfit, no one else is wearing a costume. Glad I left Tinkerbell at home. Besides, that skirt shows off way too much leg for an academic setting.

As soon as calc lets out at 9:28—ugh, Dr. Mercer *always* goes over time—I hurry outside and pull my phone out. It had been more or less constantly vibrating ever since 8:58. Michelle and Ashley are both trying to call me and text me at the same time. Ashley happens to be the one ringing at the moment I get the thing out of my pocket.

"Hey, Ash. Sorry. Just got out of class. Mercer's a slow talker. On my way home now."

"Oh, cool. I was worried."

"I didn't forget."

"Umm. That's not what I was worrying about. You know, thought something *weird* might have happened."

"Ahh. Yeah, well, I suppose that is a valid concern these days. See ya soon."

"Cool."

I hang up, slip into a dark spot, and take off.

Michelle calls six seconds later.

"Hey. Sorry. Class ran long. On my way home now."

"Sweet," says Michelle. "We'll pick you up."

"Okay."

A few minutes later, I land in the yard behind home and go inside. The kitchen still smells like garlic-onion, but also something else that's probably a cream sauce. Mom had to have made chicken pasta. Unable to resist, I pop the fridge open and help myself to a few forkfuls of leftovers out of the Tupperware. Even lukewarm, it's still awesome. I always tease her that she cooks well enough to open her own restaurant if she wanted to. But of course, turning something she loves to do into *work* would make her stop loving it… so she hasn't gone pro chef.

Like the thief I am, I sneak the Tupperware back into the fridge, toss the fork in the sink, and hurry to the stairs. It's mildly strange *not* to see Sierra in the living room on the PlayStation. Yeah, we all have our own computers in our rooms, but she prefers gaming on the massive screen down here. Maybe she got a new PC game? Could be working on a school project. Meh. I can hear them upstairs, so I don't worry at all, and hurry to my basement room. In the midst of changing into the Tinkerbell outfit—meaning as soon as I'm topless in my bikini bottoms and reaching for the little green dress—Mom walks in.

Being murdered has done a lot for my ability to tolerate my parents being annoying. Old me would have jumped onto the bed, rolled up in the blanket, and screamed at her to get out, then proceeded to rant about her habit of barging in. I'm calmer now. Almost losing my family left a wee bit of a mental scar.

I turn to face her, hands on my hips. "Didn't we reach an agreement on the barging in thing?"

Mom blinks, blushes a little, but doesn't break eye contact. "Oh... sorry. What are you doing standing around topless?"

"I wasn't *standing around*. You walked in on me in the middle of changing."

Something weird happens next... we go from mother and daughter to a dynamic more like two girls in a locker room. She loses the blush and plucks the dress off the bed, holding it up.

"This? Where's the rest of it?"

"It's Tinkerbell's outfit."

"You should really put a bra on."

I snag the dress from her. "If I had a strapless one, sure."

"Don't let your father see that outfit. He won't let you out the door."

"It covers more than my bathing suit." I pull the dress on and turn my back to her. "Zip me?"

She sighs, and does. "Well, it does look like Tinkerbell. Have you noticed Sophia being weird?"

"Yeah... for the past few years."

Mom pokes me in the side. "I mean more so today."

"A little. Seems like she's guilty about something but whatever it is can't be too bad 'cause she hasn't said anything. The way she keeps looking at me, it's like she's afraid I'm going to ask the wrong direct question."

"Wrong direct question?" asks Mom.

I hand her the wings. "Velcro me? And yeah. You know she's even worse at lying than I am. If you ask her a question she'd be tempted to lie to, she'll just start crying instead of answering. It's like she got all of Sierra's remorse. Soph's got too much and Sierra, not enough."

Mom chuckles and affixes my wings to my back. "You know, the outfit really is cute."

I hold up the green slippers with the pompoms on the toes. "Check these out."

"Adorable. You surprised me. Never thought you'd pick a faerie costume."

"Ashley chose it." I float up off my feet. "For reasons."

Mom cracks up. "Oh, that's too funny."

"Yeah, except I can't exactly go flying around in public. People will freak out, I'll go viral, the People-in-Black will show up and spank me for being naughty... bad idea."

"I wasn't suggesting you do that." She pats me on the cheek. "But you are *so* adorable in that outfit. Remember the last time you had a faerie costume? What were you, six? Seven?"

"Umm... I think I was about—"

Mom grabs me and bursts into tears.

"Uhh... sorry I forgot the laundry. I'll get it later."

She regains her composure after a moment. "Sorry..."

"It's okay, Mom." I hug her back. "Was that 'I can't believe my baby is eighteen' crying, or the other thing?"

She steps back, wiping her face. "Little of both. Where did the time go? Wow, it feels like just yesterday you were so tiny."

"You're always so busy with work, driving Sam or Sophia around to stuff... no wonder time's blurring. Want me to bite everyone and freeze our family in time?"

Mom taps her finger on her chin in a fake 'thinking it over' gesture. "Tempting, but... nah. I can't ask my kids to stay kids forever if they don't want to."

"Good. I couldn't do it to them." I smile, but the mere thought of basically killing my siblings is enough to make me want to cry. Biting them at all feels beyond wrong, no way could I drain them so much they died. And shit, there goes my voice. Damn lump.

Mom rubs my back. "We should stop making ourselves sad now."

"Good idea," I rasp.

"So what do you think is bothering Soph?"

"Dunno. Want me to look into her head?"

My mother ponders this for a few seconds, then shakes her head. "Not yet. I know you promised not to invade our thoughts, but if she keeps acting weird and won't tell anyone what's going on… I want you to look."

Great. Some parents install nanny apps on their kids' smartphones to snoop on them. There's a fine line between snooping and protecting, and it depends on whether you're the kid or the parent. My parents have a nanny app to snoop on their kids' brains: me. Mom's worrying that someone might have like done something icky to Sophia and she's too ashamed to say anything. She also can't imagine when that might've happened… Not like Sophia goes off on her own for any length of time anywhere. And I'm sure Sophia would be *way* more upset if anything like that happened to her. She got the same talk at ten that the parents gave me around twelve. So, no, I don't think anyone like touched her. That look on her face wasn't shame or fear. I know her guilty look. Pretty sure she did something that she thinks is bad, but probably isn't. Once she makes up her mind about whether the 'it' is bad or not, she'll either confess or stop being guilty.

A car pulls into our driveway—at least I'm guessing based on the whirr of an engine outside.

"Sure. If she keeps acting weird, I'll check. But, I gotta go now. Michelle and Ash are here."

"How do—"

The doorbell rings.

"Heard the engine." I hug her quick, then dart past her. "Love you."

"Be careful!" shouts Mom.

"I will!"

MICHELLE DRIVES US TO THE PARTY AT THIS EVENT HALL, BASICALLY A giant space that people can rent for whatever kind of soiree they want to have.

She met someone in a study group at Seattle University who knew someone who invited her to the party. At the moment, she's planning to apply to their law school once she's done with her bachelors… unless she can land a scholarship to a school with more prestige.

On the ride there, she explained how they were originally going to have the party at a house east of the school that four guys rent, basically as a dorm. But, they had a lot more people interested in going than the house could handle, so they decided to float the idea of using this place and seeing if people would chip in. And… here we are. Michelle seems to think the people organizing the event are trustworthy—not 'frat boys' so to speak—and isn't at all worried about the sort of scene we're going into.

It helps that Hunter and Corey are with us, though someone got the genius idea of all going in Michelle's little Kia Soul. I had to remove my wings and cram into the back seat with Ashley and Hunter.

After a brief ride and by the grace of Garmin, we find the location without too much difficulty. It's a large warehouse-sized building nowhere near the school, closer to downtown Seattle. When she first invited me to the party, I'd been expecting like a frat house with cars on the lawn, people hanging out windows to vomit, other people sneaking off upstairs to make out—or more. Guess that means I've watched too many of Dad's Eighties college comedy movies.

With any luck, a giant laser beam won't fry me tonight.

After we park, Hunter helps me put my wings back on. He threw together a low budget cowboy costume… which in certain parts of the country wouldn't look like an obvious Halloween getup. Like, if we went to Texas, he'd just look like everyone else… though the plastic Lone Ranger revolvers do kinda stand out.

I grin and float up off my feet a few inches. "Hey, Ash."

Ashley's doing Princess Merida—again. Her hair is nowhere near that curly, but it is red... so close enough. Guess I'm not the only one too busy to put a lot of effort into costume shopping. She wore the same dress last year. But it's a nice one, theater quality.

"Yeah?" She turns to look at me, realizes I'm hovering, and squeals. "Can I take a pic?"

"Sure, but if anyone asks, I jumped to make it look like I flew."

She sticks her tongue out at me. "Like I'd go sharing it. It's for me."

"Something you two aren't telling us?" asks Michelle, putting on and adjusting her Maleficent headpiece, which had been too tall for her to wear while driving.

"Oh, go to hell." Ashley giggles, snaps a pic with her phone, and stuffs it back in her purse—which she leaves in the car.

Michelle hands out tickets.

"Wow, you paid for our tickets?" I ask.

"Don't worry about it." She winks. "I got ya covered."

Corey's going as the Phantom. No, not the obscure superhero movie, the opera one.

We cross the parking lot to the entrance. A handful of zombies and a sad attempt at Freddy Krueger are hanging out to the left of the double doors, vaping. Michelle takes point, leading us past them and inside. After a brief stop at a counter to get our tickets punched, we head through a black curtain and down a hallway to a big set of double doors. As loud as the music seemed outside, I'm surprised my head doesn't implode. Okay, Glim was right. My ears auto-adjust to obscene levels of volume.

Except that everyone is wearing costumes, the layout reminds me of a wedding reception or a corporate Christmas party. Dance floor on one side, small stage (but no live band), and a bunch of round tables and chairs set up everywhere else. Long tables at the far wall hold an assortment of treats like cupcakes, macarons, hors d'oeuvres, cookies, cake, pie, mini-eclairs, and soda/tea/water. They *do* have a bar, but it's staffed and big signs announce they check ID.

Not that I care. Alcohol doesn't do much for me. Though, I start debating if I should cave in when Michelle inevitably asks me to compel the bartender to skip her ID check. We drift into the room, Michelle and Corey heading toward the dance area while Ashley goes for the sweets. I kinda feel bad for her being dateless, so I follow. Hunter trails after me.

Ash grabs a chocolate sphere about the size of a golf ball and hands it to me, then takes one for herself. "Chocolate mousse balls!"

I burst out laughing too hard to take a bite. And of course, I tell her the story of Mr. Neidermayer screaming about balls.

"Can't say I ever wanted to eat moose balls." Snickering, Hunter grabs one and bites it in half. He makes a 'holy crap that's sweet' face.

Ashley daintily takes a small nibble, looks appraisingly into nowhere while chewing, then tosses the rest of it into her mouth all at once like a true barbarian princess. I eat mine in three bites. It's good, but I'm nowhere near the mousse fiend Ashley is. If I don't pull her away from the table, she'll keep on eating them until she throws up.

The three of us peruse the sweet stuff for a little while, then Ashley shoos us off to the dance area. Hunter isn't terribly thrilled with the idea since he's still super shy. Dancing in a bedroom, no problem. Out in public? That kinda bugs him. Still, he puts up with it. Considering there are over a hundred people here and roughly half of them have masks on, I guess it's surreal enough to calm his nerves.

We don't pull a John Travolta/Uma Thurman routine and wind up having everyone stare at us, but we do get into it more than most for a while. At least until *Monster Mash* comes on. That's far too silly for him and I don't insist that we make asses of ourselves trying to do that.

I've never been much of a party person, and the awkwardness of being at one is already slipping its hands around my neck from behind. Being out and surrounded by loud isn't my idea of a fun night. I'd much rather be at home cozied up with a book or video game. Or a few close friends and a movie. I'm not antisocial, just anti-macro-social. Big groups of people I don't know are well out of my comfort zone. At least *some* familiarity helps. Like, at my old high school, I had no problem with big events since I kinda-sorta knew everyone. However, my comfort zone has grown fangs. Things that used to terrify me—like walking from school to the parking garage after dark alone—don't anymore.

Hunter doesn't object to me heading off to one of the tables and sitting down. I'm stuck holding this silly magic wand since the dress lacks pockets. Really, I should've added a cute belt with a holster for it.

We sit, holding hands and failing to have much of a conversation over the music while some thirty people on the dance floor lope about like drunken Frankenstein's monsters. Speaking of which, there's at least one guy wearing that costume out there.

I lean against Hunter watching people make fools of themselves. There's a few Elsas, a bunch of Wonder Women, a small army of Batmen, several other cowboys, one Chewbacca—poor guy. He looks miserably hot. This other dude has a bedazzled homemade giant mouse head on. I'm not sure if it's supposed to be a *fabulous* Mickey or Deadmau5.

"Be right back," half-yells Hunter by my ear. "Bathroom."

I nod, and continue people-watching as he hurries off among the crowd. Most of the attendees are students at Seattle University, which makes me feel like an outsider already. Sure, I'm technically a college student, but not at this school. I'm also not studying law or anything really prestigious. The vibe in here is kinda hoity-toity. My family's doing okay, but even I feel out of my league. No wonder Hunter's uncomfortable. I bet he really wants to leave. That makes two of us. But… Ashley would be hurt if I bailed on her. And Michelle would be hurt if the three of us bailed on her and Corey.

Not to mention, Ash still hasn't completely unpacked her emotions over what happened to me. Dalton gave her a false memory of watching a bear attack me, but in reality, she witnessed Scott stab me to death. Once I told her that yes, he did kill me, the memory implant peeled away. Ashley didn't want me to make her forget since she said almost losing me strengthened our friendship. Probably the same reason I didn't bite my mother's head off for barging in on me earlier.

Humans would be a whole lot nicer to each other if it didn't require something as drastic as death to make us reevaluate what's important. No one ever seems to have a reality check of that magnitude without losing someone or coming damn close to losing someone.

But, am I really even human anymore? All these people dancing, hanging out, scarfing down sugary treats... they're all going to have ordinary lives. Some will start families, some won't. They'll all grow older. At some point when someone in this room has a great-grandchild, I will still look exactly like I do now.

That sense of not belonging here for not fitting in among the elite set worsens. More than for social class reasons, I don't belong here because I'm not even human. Sitting here at the table by the edge of the room is a metaphor for my vampiric existence—watching society from outside it.

Or, maybe I'm just not a party girl.

I look down at my feet, raising and lowering my toes in the thin slippers to make the pompoms wobble. Yeah, it's the party thing. I'm more maudlin over the end of my childhood than I am at not being mortal anymore. But that doesn't make sense either. Dad thought it weird for me to even think of it. He didn't start wishing to go back to being a little kid until after he'd passed forty. And no, I'm not wishing to be six again. My father has stress issues, misses the days of being a kid where he had no responsibilities more pressing than what game to play or what movie to watch. It worries me a bit that I'm having feelings like that at only eighteen. I shouldn't even be thinking about time or age or anything like that. Michelle and Ash certainly don't. They're all about 'I can't wait until I'm twenty-one' or 'I can't wait until I have my own place' and so on. You know, like normal people our age.

Sometimes, I think Sam might be on the spectrum. That makes me wonder if I am, too. At least a little... or if my more recent habit of feeling detached from everything, looking in at myself like I'm analyzing someone else's life came from the vampire stuff.

Bleh.

I think I've had enough party for one night. But… Ashley.

She's mingled in among a small group too far away with too much ambient music for me to hear what they're talking about. A tall, thin guy with belt-long black hair appears to have gotten her attention. He's wearing a strange, oversized top hat with a bunch of metal discs around the bottom, and a suit like from the 1800s with long coattails. I have no idea what character he's supposed to be, but he's throwing off a steampunk anime vibe.

Out of nowhere, I get this weird feeling of jealousy. Like, why did Ashley drag me to this party and then not even hang out with me? Of course, she's probably trying to give Hunter and me space. Michelle and Corey are still dancing. Guess they're having a good time since we've been here almost two hours and she hasn't yet asked me to help her get alcohol.

My stomach growls.

Darn. Oh well. Might as well get *something* out of this party. I stand, scanning the edges of the room, and target a post-apocalyptic punk in a tank top. Nice open neck. He's also alone, which helps. He looks over at me when I approach, and his first thought is wondering if I've come over to suggest we go off somewhere alone. While that *is* technically what I had in mind, he's expecting an entirely different sort of activity. Sorry, buddy. Just need a quick bite.

It's easy to overwhelm his thoughts, and we walk off together toward a small corridor that looks empty. Hunter, making his way back across the room to where we'd been sitting, stops and stares at us, the beginnings of worry and hurt in his eyes.

Needed a quick snack. Played chicken with the sun earlier.

He slouches, feeling like an idiot for assuming the worst. Yeah, it's cheating to look into his thoughts, but I can't go having him thinking he's not good enough for me and I'm going to ditch him as soon as a better option comes along. That's not happening. At least, as of right now, I'm like really in love with him and thinking he's the one I'm going to spend the rest of my life with—only, that's a long damn time. The only way I could spend the rest of my life with anyone is if someone destroys me before they die, or they wind up becoming a vampire, too.

So, no… I don't want to spend the rest of my life with Hunter. I want to spend the rest of *his* life with him.

I lead Mr. Post-apocalyptic into the corridor and down to a second set of doors that opens to an unused space full of folding tables and chairs. It's a smaller event area than the one we're using, but that doesn't matter. All I need from this room is a few minutes of alone time. A closet would've worked.

The guy stands there like a mannequin while I attach myself to his neck. Hmm. His blood tastes like charred meat. By the third gulp, I'm getting a mildly-burnt Chinese spare rib flavor. Wow, this is so weird. I only had them like once, but I guess it fits his costume.

Once I'm full, I seal the bite wound and erase myself from his memory, slipping back into the hallway before he recovers from the mental fog. He's going to be confused as to why he's in that room, but as long as he doesn't remember me, no big deal.

I head back to the party and bee-line for Hunter, who's again sitting at the table. He's having cake at least, and he grabbed a piece for me. He smiles at my approach, and smiles wider when I sit in his lap.

"Sorry for scaring you like that."

"It's okay. Sometimes, I forget you're so amazing. And by that I mean, you know…"

"Yeah." I kiss him. "Thanks for dealing with this party tonight."

"It's okay." He pats my butt. "Even if we're stuck here, I'm still spending time with you. That why Ash disappeared?"

I glance around until I spot her again, still talking to Top Hat Guy. "Probably wants to give us space."

Momentary guilty about her being alone while 'Chelle and I brought boyfriends, I peek a little into her thoughts. She's not bummed out at all, much to my surprise. As far as she's concerned, this party didn't count as a 'girl's night' thing. So all that angst about

Hunter coming between me and my oldest friend is purely my brain looking for reasons to get all emo over nothing.

Hunter eats a bite of cake. "I don't mind hanging out with her, too. You guys were friends like forever. She doesn't need to be alone."

"Ash is fine." I rotate to face the table and start on my cake. "Just me being weird. I swear, death is like a total drag on hormones."

He coughs.

Our conversation drifts into our childhoods. I tell him about hanging with Ash, back when we were small. Roller-blading, watching cartoons, dolls, video games, and so on. Hunter confesses to having been a 'bit of a nerd' as a kid, playing with Transformers and GI-Joe stuff, except when his father was around. He didn't approve of any toys or games that didn't practically leak testosterone when squeezed. His dad terrified Hunter's friends so much they wouldn't go anywhere near his house except during the guy's long absences. He would disappear for months at a time due to a combination of working on a fishing boat, deciding not to be around for a while, or prison. Hunter's not entirely sure if his old man actually went to jail or not, just suspects it happened due to something he overheard his mother say on the phone once when he'd been around eleven. As the story goes, dad started a fight in a bar with a man he accused of checking him out.

Considering the violence I witnessed personally, it wouldn't surprise me if it happened.

I try to steer the conversation toward less depressing topics at least until someone nearby says, "just got up and walked right out of a morgue around here somewhere."

Crap! I stop short in mid-sentence and glance sideways toward three girls and two guys at the table to our left. They're probably students at U-Seattle, and are all wearing *Ghostbusters* jumpsuits. I eavesdrop on them discussing a supposed paranormal event of a dead girl waking up in the morgue 'somewhere around here' and walking away. One of the guys says he saw it on YouTube and pulls out a smartphone to find the clip. The redhead among them says she heard it was a little girl who got hit by a car and mistaken for dead. Both other women swear it was a high school kid, while the guy not looking at his phone thinks the story is made up.

"Sarah? Are you okay?" asks Hunter in a low voice. "You're blushing."

"I, umm…"

Remarkably, I'm not embarrassed at the memory of streaking across town after leaving that body cooler. The blush is coming from fear. Hearing them talk about *my* waking up in the morgue is as scary as hearing people talk about seeing someone who kinda looks like me pull a major prank at school when I thought I got away with it clean. Not that I ever had the proverbial balls to do anything like that. No, I was Follows Rules Girl.

"Weird," says the guy with the phone. "Can't find it."

I slouch with relief. Wow, wonder if my government friends managed to kill that video. Or maybe it simply drowned in the labyrinthine mess that is YouTube's search results. At Hunter giving me a confused look, I stare into his eyes.

They're talking about me and they don't know it. Waking up in the morgue?

"Ahh." He nods.

"Bummer," says the girl beside him.

"Give me a sec…" I whisper to Hunter, then get up and walk over to their table. "Excuse me… couldn't help but overhear you talking about paranormal stuff. You said something about a zombie in *this* area? Like for real?"

"So Bryce says." The brunette elbows smartphone guy.

"Cute costume!" chirps the redhead.

Both guys sit taller in their seats to check me out. The blonde (who I think is way prettier than me) gives me this look like she thinks I'm trying to steal her man. There she is stuck in a jumpsuit and I'm rocking a barely-there Tinkerbell dress. Dad's genes are all that's keeping me from being considered a weapon of mass distraction. Though I've filled out a bit since being a tween, I'm still pretty noodly. If Michelle put this thing on, she'd probably get arrested.

I stand there talking to them for a few minutes about what they heard, where they heard it, and so on. Fortunately, there's no need to mess with any of their memories as it feels like they've mostly heard rumors mutated from already-mutated rumors. Apparently, I killed six people on my way out of the morgue by making them drop dead from sheer terror.

"If you guys are looking for a good paranormal tour, check out the Old Ellensburg Jail. Went there a couple months ago and I'm pretty sure they have several legit ghosts. A chair fell over in the cafeteria and no one was near it."

The guys, Bryce and Dan, begin debating if the place rigged a wire to it, while the redhead, Parker, gasps in fright and starts insisting that they go there as soon as possible. The oddity of her seeming frightened yet eager to go there catches me off guard.

Out of the corner of my eye, I catch a glimpse of a small figure zooming across the back end of the room and vanishing under the long tables holding the snacks. As far as I know, nobody brought a five-year-old to this party. But, maybe they did. I haven't exactly been checking IDs at the door.

Another rapid motion happens near the empty stage. I spin toward it, but only spot a flutter in the curtain. A dude dressed up like the scarecrow from *Wizard of Oz* is standing right next to the spot and didn't react at all. So, I'm either seeing ghosts he can't, or there are actual children here playing hide and seek and the guy is ignoring them.

Hmm.

"So what's it like there?" asks Parker, staring up at me wide-eyed.

I give them a brief explanation of my experience with the paranormal jail tour, though I leave out the jackass Ashley had been dating at the time. Laurie, the blonde, has a mild panic attack when I tell them about the solitary confinement cells and refuses to do that, swearing to 'like legit unfriend you for real' if anyone shoves her inside.

Confident they know nothing about my truth, and having planted the seeds of a different conversation in their heads (the old fashioned way), I head back to my chair.

"You know them?" asks Hunter.

I shake my head. "Nah. Just heard them talking about being into ghost stuff."

He nods.

We sit near each other holding hands and continuing to talk about fun things we did as kids while watching everyone else dance, eat, drink, or hang out. Michelle and Corey are standing in a group with others, likely new friends of hers from school. Ash is *still* talking to Top Hat Guy. Uh oh. Wonder if that's gonna be a thing. I resist the urge to peek into their heads and keep checking out the various costumes. Some of them are pretty amazing... others, not so much. And, whoa. I thought my dress was on the revealing side, but there's a 'vampire' near the bar in an outfit that's basically goth lingerie in dark crimson and black with a corset. Good grief, her boobs are squeezed so much they look like bubble wrap a second before it pops.

Merely looking at her makes mine ache.

How can you breathe in that thing?

She spins to peer behind her. "What?"

Eep! I glance away before she notices me staring at her. Still, I watch her surreptitiously. She spins back and forth in search of whoever spoke to her. Whew. At least telepathy isn't obvious. No like weird echoing effects or anything. Unless someone knows my voice and is looking right at me to see my lips not moving, it's pretty darn hard to recognize as *not* normal speaking.

Seconds before I stop looking at her, a guy standing near her dumps something into her drink when her back's turned searching for who spoke to her. He acts casual, though hovers close, watching her.

Ooh, bastard.

I leap out of my chair and fast-walk over to the bar, right next to the guy. As soon as he glances at me, I gesture at the glass and mutter, "Drink," while forcing the command into his head.

He gapes at me for a second or two, then grabs the glass, chugging the contents.

"Hey!" yells the 'vampire' girl. "That's mine!"

The bartender looks at her, at him, back to her... and doesn't seem like he's going to do anything.

I poke the guy in the arm. "You should buy her a new one."

"Bacardi Limonade," says the girl. "And what the heck are you doing just grabbing random drinks?"

Mr. Roofie pulls out his wallet, hands the bartender a $20 bill, then seems to realize he just drank a cocktail full of sleepytime. Panic washes over him. He takes off for the door, bumping several people out of his way. Ugh, I really hope he's not going to attempt driving home before the drug hits him.

"Wow, what an asshole," mutters the girl. "Did you see that?"

"Yeah," I mutter. "Some guys..."

The instant the dude reaches the curtains at the exit hallway, all the lights go out. I notice this mostly due to the room going from 'kinda bright' to 'comfortably lit.' That, and everyone around me starts screaming simultaneously.

"The lights are out!" shouts a guy in a Captain America costume.

More like Captain Obvious.

People flail and grab others nearby. Hunter stands from his chair and looks around blind. The girl in the vampire underwear grabs me and holds on as if the mere absence of light is an earthquake that could knock her over.

"Everyone please stay calm," yells the bartender. "Probably only a circuit breaker. Just stay where you are and remain calm." He crouches, opens a cabinet door, and feels around the shelves. "Hmm. Damn, where'd the flashlight go?"

I grasp the girl's hands gently and redirect her to holding onto the bar for support. Before I can walk around to help the guy with the flashlight, painfully bright strobe flashes start up along with the deafening *bwooooop-bwooooop* of a fire alarm.

Absolute chaos erupts in the dance hall.

A guy in a chicken suit makes a run for the exit, only he charges into the wall and nearly knocks himself out. People scream and go in random directions. Half a dozen bodies crash into the curtains by the exit and tear them down, falling in a heap, buried under yards of black fabric. I fly up near the ceiling, looking around for my friends. A tiny woman dressed up as a Smurf gets knocked over in the panic and people just start running her over.

I dive into the crowd, knocking four or five people aside and scoop Smurfette up before they can trample her.

She screams, kicking and punching blind.

"Easy!" I shout. "I got you."

Tables and chairs clatter from partygoers racing full speed in the wrong directions. Something small and dark zooms by on the left. I spin after it, but lose it in the chaos. Seconds later, the lingerie vampire's loud scream draws my attention to her. A figure that resembles a tiny child in a ninja suit clings to her chest after having ripped her corset and top off. She punches the little bastard in the head, knocking him away into the crowd. Unfortunately, he appears to have stolen half her costume.

What the hell was that?

I carry Smurfette to the nearest spot of open floor and set her on her feet. Since there's no smell of smoke in the air, I'm confident this is some jackass' idea of a joke and give the girl a 'stay calm' command.

Michelle and Corey are standing their ground near the back corner, largely avoiding the panic by *not* running. They huddle together, clearly unable to see much. I can't find Ashley anywhere, but there's so many people swarming back and forth, screaming, grabbing, and pushing at each other that Lady Gaga could show up in a dress made of Christmas lights and no one would notice.

A loud *clank* precedes a hiss from above—and a deluge from the fire sprinklers.

Once again, everyone screams. Only, this time, I shriek right along with them. The water is effing cold!

People stack up in the corridor leading to the exit. A few near the front scream that the doors are stuck. Some wail for help while others shout "stop pushing" or "you're crushing me!"

Uh oh.

There's too many effing people in the way for me to even think about shoving my way past them. So, I do the only thing I can: fly like

Supergirl horizontally over everyone's heads. Random flailing hands smack me here and there, but no one notices what they hit. Upon reaching the front of the crowd, I hang in midair for a few seconds, looking at the panicking mass of bodies attempting to fight the double steel doors with brute force. The instant I spot an opening, I plunge in and shove a guy out of my way, but everyone's packed so close they *can't* fall over.

People smush into me from behind the instant I'm on my feet at the head of the crowd, squeezing me against the doors. There are too many people in too high a state of frenzy for me to even attempt mind-zapping anyone. Instead, I hammer the push bar, shoving at the door. The little metal bit opens, but the door is still stuck closed like some prankster idiot super glued it shut.

Grr.

This shouldn't be harder to open than a stupid mausoleum door… but I can't get a running start when sixty people are crushing me into the steel.

I brace myself and push back at the crowd to make a little room, then swing my leg up and stomp-kick the door with as much vampire strength as I can channel into my foot. The guy crushing into my back groans. Oops. Think I broke his rib.

With a *boom* that sounds like a cannon, the left door flies open, a noticeable dent where my foot hit it. A bizarre flash of yellowish light bursts from the doorframe, but it's so quick I'm not entirely sure I didn't imagine it.

The crowd shoves me forward, out into the parking lot. I have little choice but move or be moved, so I sprint a bit to break away from them before turning around to look. The second door opened as well, allowing a stream of freaked out people in drenched Halloween costumes and ruined makeup out of the building. A few with body paint have melted into unrecognizable messes.

No one has coats and we're all soaked to the skin. Fortunately, cold doesn't bother me anymore. Soon after emerging into the late October night air, mass hysteria gives way to quiet shivering and people asking what happened. A couple guys drag trample victims out and arrange them on the sidewalk next to the entrance. Two women and a guy appear to have suffered injuries serious enough that they don't try to stand up.

There's still no trace of fire anywhere I can see or smell. That means someone definitely set off the alarm as a shitty prank. Okay, so I *did* want the party to be over with already, but I can't be happy about the circumstances that brought it to an abrupt halt.

The girl in the skimpy vampire vixen costume (or at least it's lower half) runs outside with her hands over her boobs. She's shaking pretty hard, and turns in place looking around at everything for a few seconds before starting to have a meltdown. Her thoughts are a scramble between who ripped her top off, ack I'm outside half naked, wanting her coat, wanting her purse (and car keys), and being too wound up by the fire alarm to have the mental capacity to do anything much past stand there feeling overwhelmed.

Ashley finally exits the building, helping a guy in a Daredevil costume who appears to be legit blind. The poor girl looks like a drowned rat, all her hair matted down and soaked. She somehow managed to lose her shoes as well. I hurry over to them.

"Ash! You okay?"

"Yeah… fine. Just helping Randy not get crushed. He said there wasn't really a fire, so we took our time."

"Hi." Randy waves at me. "Don't smell any smoke."

I sigh with relief. "Where's Hunter, Michelle, or Corey? And what happened to your shoes?"

She wiggles her toes. "I left my slippers under the table, and I have no idea where the guys went."

"Right here." Hunter walks out of the building and hands me the wand I left on the table.

"You seriously went back inside for this?" I ask, holding it up.

Ashley pouts. "That's your wand! And why not? There's no fire."

"Someone did this on purpose," I say, narrowing my eyes.

Randy opens his mouth as if to say something, but hesitates.

"What?" I ask.

"Nothing. I thought I heard something strange in there before the shit hit the fan, but it's probably just a Halloween ambiance track." He pulls off the Daredevil mask and wrings it out.

The guy's pretty cute, though he's gotta be like twenty-three or so, probably a grad student. "Seriously, what did you hear? I thought I saw something weird, too."

"Don't think I'm crazy."

"I won't."

Michelle and Corey wander over from the far end of the parking lot, approaching us.

"It kinda sounded like tiny voices giggling and hissing. I couldn't understand what they said since it was *not* English, and I only heard them for a few seconds. Made me think of little critters from a horror movie."

Whoa. "Umm, yeah. You're right, that's probably just something they had on the sound system."

Ashley raises an eyebrow at me.

Not sure what's going on yet, but I don't need to start ghost stories.

She nods.

"Be right back."

I zip inside and—because I can see just fine—collect vampire girl's purse from the bar along with Ashley's shoes and everyone's coats, which also got a fair drenching from a sprinkler in the coat room. Ugh, so much for warmth. They'll make us colder. I drop Ashley's shoes on the ground beside her, hand out coats, then head over to Vampire Girl, whose white face-paint has almost entirely run down onto her chest. The fake blood she had on her lip is gone, too.

"Here." I hand over the purse and coat.

She still seems to be too upset to speak or even process what the object is I'm trying to hand her. A few seconds of staring later, she blinks as if snapping out of a daze and rushes into the coat, zippering it. "Holy shit, thank you!"

"No problem." I smile.

"Hey, this is mine. Like, my actual coat. How'd you know?"

"Oh, umm. Just got lucky…"

"So weird. Thank you!" She hugs me. "Did you see the creep who ripped my costume off?"

"It was totally dark in there." That's technically true, so hopefully my face doesn't make my lie obvious. Like Sophia, I'm really bad at it. Stupid conscience and guilt. Besides, telling her a 'four-year-old in a ninja suit' did it wouldn't go over well. She'd either think me insane or messing with her.

"Oh. Right. Grr. Damn assholes."

While she pulls out her phone, I hurry back over to stand with my friends and Hunter. Randy-slash-Daredevil is still with us, so 'real' talk will need to wait for later.

"Does anyone know what happened in there?" asks Corey.

Hunter shakes his head.

"The sprinklers went off." Ashley makes a silly face, despite her teeth chattering.

Sirens grow louder in the distance.

"What are they bothering with? Nothing's on fire." Michelle eyes her Kia. "Are we supposed to stay here or can we leave?"

"Fire alarm's probably tied right into the system, so it called them." Hunter puts an arm around me. "Some people got hurt, so I think we should stay. The police are going to want to interview everyone."

"Ugh. Hope it won't take too long." Ashley swipes her hair off her face, then stares at me with an intense, questioning glint in her eye.

You're going to think I'm crazy, but I think I saw like... gremlins or something.

She covers her mouth and stifles a giggle.

Yes, I'm serious.

Ashley blinks, picturing the cute creatures from that movie.

No. Not like that. Kinda looked like a tiny ninja. All black, generally person-shaped. About the size of a four-year-old.

Her eyes go wide. "Wow, that's messed up."

"Huh?" asks Hunter.

Michelle and Corey look at her.

"What is?" asks Randy.

"Just what happened. Setting off the alarm and people getting hurt." Ashley twists to look over at the three injured people.

One of the women looks better, sitting up and taking deep breaths. The guy's face is a bloody mess and the other woman broke her wrist, probably when she fell and got trampled. Whoever—or whatever—did this isn't playing cute pranks.

They're freakin' evil.

6

THE NEW NORMAL

Surprisingly, the police didn't keep us long.

They took a quick statement from everyone, which mostly all turned out to be similar variations of just standing around having a good time when the lights went out, then the alarm, then water. Chaos. I gave a statement like everyone else, claiming I couldn't see anything, people were grabbing and pushing... then somehow I wound up outside.

Another surprise, there actually *was* a fire—in the alarm console. A few of the firemen going by were kind enough to share their thoughts with me unknowingly. In a massive twist of irony, the fire alarm system shorted out and ignited a small electrical fire in the room containing all the circuit breakers, phone hardware, and other electronics. The space is almost entirely made of cinder blocks, so it probably wouldn't have spread into an actual fire.

I can't help but picture one of those mini-ninjas stabbing the alarm panel with a little sword until it exploded.

Ugh. What's wrong with me?

Anyway... once the cops let us go, we wind up arriving home at roughly the same time we would have without the chaos ending the party early. Well, I say 'home' but I mean Ashley's house. The three of us plus Hunter and Corey plan to hang out there for a while, watching a movie. Since I live just down the street—and can fly—I zip home to change into dry clothes, a T-shirt and sweat pants, fuzzy socks, and Uggs. Being at Ash's does not require wearing 'real' clothes. I can be comfortable.

When I get back, Michelle's changed into a borrowed dress and the boys are both shirtless and wearing these hideous khaki shorts. Ash fills me in that the shorts belonged to her father and he left them here years ago when he divorced her mom. The boys are borrowing them while their actual clothes are in the laundry machines.

Corey is still out of the 'vampire loop,' so I don't bother trying to explain anything about what I think I saw. Ashley is, of course, a wiseass, and offers to put on the movie *Gremlins*. I shrug, having no opinion. Michelle, Corey, and Hunter consider it a kids' movie, to which Ashley replies "So what?"

Ultimately, the group settles on *Cabin in the Woods*.

Oh great, I get to have nightmares apparently.

Ashley and I mostly scream at the same places. Hunter's reaction to the scary parts is wider eyes. Corey looks ready to shriek, but manages not to. Michelle's face is frozen in a sort of 'oh hell no' expression for the last two-thirds of the movie. Note to self: Sophia is not allowed to watch this one. She'd chew her way into the sofa cushions like a nesting hamster and never come back out.

Hunter makes an unfortunate rapid exit when the movie's over and his clothes are dry. Since it's Wednesday night, he's got class tomorrow early and is already up later than he'd like to be. We have a brief romantic goodnight on Ashley's porch before he hops in the car with Michelle and Corey for a ride back to her place—and his car.

Ashley and I talk for a while, and I finally give her all the details of what I saw.

"Ooh, sounds like that dance hall is seriously haunted by something." She rubs her chin. "Shadow people maybe? You know that ghost show I always watch? They have this device with Xbox parts that draws stick figures whenever it detects a ghost and a lot of times they're super small. Like only two feet tall. Could be one of those?"

"I have no idea. When I woke up in that fridge, I didn't have a copy of 'Vampires for Dummies' next to me. There's no instruction manual that explains all the weird stuff."

She laughs. "This is ghosts. Maybe you should ask Coralie."

"That's a thought." I tap my foot. "If she shows up. She's not living with us anymore, but she does pop in sometimes to visit Sophia or me."

Ashley grins. "That's really cool how your sister can see ghosts."

"Not sure 'cool' is the word I'd use for that. What if she sees one so freaky that it scares her right into a mental institution?"

"Aww. They only do that because people don't believe in ghosts. She has you right there to talk to."

I shrug. "Maybe."

We kill a little more than an hour talking about school and Ashley's job at the veterinary clinic. She's super into animals and even though she's a glorified janitor at the moment, she adores being there.

Eventually, she's yawning almost too much to keep on talking, so she finally admits she needs to go to sleep. We hug, and I make my way home… for some strange reason, on foot. I guess it reminds me of normal times before my life 'went to plaid' as Dad would say. A faint *snap* in the trees to my left breaks the silence. I look toward it, but spot only a squirrel hauling ass across a lawn. Gah, I'm getting jumpy already.

Eleanor St. Ives still hasn't retaliated for my helping Coralie get to Arthur Wolent's place instead of hers. Almost enough time has passed that I'm beginning to consider the possibility she won't come after me. Hang on, she's a vampire, not a high school kid. A few weeks of calm doesn't mean she forgot about it. She could do something ten years from now. That's *so* damn annoying that she considers not helping her to be the same as attacking her. Is that an Academic trait or is she just a bitch?

Snap.

I stop short at where the cul-de-sac meets the road. A pattering of bare feet like a highly-coordinated toddler sprinting over pavement goes behind me. When I whirl to look, I catch a fleeting smear of black vanishing into the trees on the opposite side of the street.

"Who or what are you?" I ask. "Why are you following me?"

A tiny, surprised gasp comes from the trees.

"Hello?"

Only birds answer. I face that direction and scan the area, looking for anything that shouldn't be there. It's not dark to me, so if this critter is relying on shadows to hide, he's out of luck. Minuscule scratches on a trunk stand out as new, but there's no sign of what made them.

"There you are," I mutter.

I fling myself into the air, flying low, and charge at the scratch, grabbing at it as if attempting to catch an invisible small creature. Alas, I mash my hand down on tree bark. However, a wisp of sap in the air convinces me the three small scratches really are fresh. Based on the distance off the ground and a generally human shape, the little dude's head would barely be past my knee. That's too small to be a four-year-old child. In fact, it's too small to be a human capable of walking.

Looking straight up the trunk, assuming the creature climbed, doesn't help. The tree's empty. I stand there listening, for once *wanting* to hear sounds as faint as the stomach gurgles of the girl in the last row. Just birds, a distant boat engine, and a handful of jet planes.

Screw it.

I trudge across the cul-de-sac to my house, trying to think of reasons a creature that's clearly not human would want to hide from me. It's probably a good sign if it's afraid. Maybe whatever it is can tell I'm a vampire and a serious threat? He certainly didn't seem to have any problem with jumping on that one girl's chest—but the lights had been out then. No one would've been able to see him, at least as far as it assumed. Why did it attack her? My dress was skimpy, too—though nowhere near as revealing as hers. A few other women had almost nothing on, like a *Mystique* costume involving a blue bikini, red wig, and a crapload of body paint.

I go in the front door, kick off my Uggs, and secure the deadbolt behind me.

Ugh. I don't really want to burn off brain cells trying to figure out something this weird. It's Halloween night, so maybe it's just sheer random paranormal mischief. Oh, son of a bitch. I stop halfway down the stairs to the basement. That little guy is probably what Mr. Perry saw running out of his kitchen. Could it have been responsible for ripping up Mr. Neidermayer's yard? Why this year? Why not past Halloweens?

Because I wasn't a vampire last Halloween, says my brain.

How is this my fault? My mere existence is attracting crap?

…

Right, my brain can only answer questions I already know the answers to. I proceed down to the basement and again stop, staring around at the common room. Zero moonlight makes it past the tint film Dad put on the small windows near the ceiling. That shadow I thought I saw move in the corner couldn't have been something outside. Also, the room feels like it's staring at me.

"Who are you?" I ask.

Nothing replies.

"Coralie? Rebecca?"

Come to think of it, the figure is about the same size as Aurélie's dolls. However, none of them have ever gone walking around much less jumping on people. They may or may not have turned their heads. My jury is still out on whether or not I imagined that part. Thinking about that creepy doll store makes me shiver. Multiple shelves of eerie dolls always seemed to be looking at me no matter where I stood in the room.

I search the basement, peeking in the washer and dryer, checking the little bathroom, poking my head into my bedroom, all without noticing anything unusual beyond a constant feeling that something is here with me.

"If you're a ghost, please show yourself. Maybe I can help you."

After a few minutes of having no luck at finding anything, worry pushes me upstairs. One by one, I peek in on the littles. They're all in their beds, sound asleep. Sam's smiling like he got away with something, but the smell of chocolate in the air tells me he probably snuck candy after brushing his teeth. Sierra's in her usual 'crime victim sprawl,' sleeping with her mouth open. I creep in and move her arm back under the blankets, then pat her on the head. She doesn't react.

In Sophia's room, I find her curled up on her side with the blankets pulled up to her nose. That pose usually means she went to sleep scared. Could be, Dad hit them with a movie. Or, maybe Sophia's seen the little creeper running around and she's afraid to mention it because she doesn't want us questioning if she's gone nuts. When those mystics from the Aurora Aurea magically possessed her, stealing her body to use as a living recon drone, they did something to her unintentionally. Exposure to that spell unlocked a talent she had but couldn't access—or so they told me. So far, she appears to have gained the ability to see ghosts. Aww. She's probably afraid we'll be scared of her. Or she could be afraid we'll blame her for weird stuff.

I need to talk to her soon, tell her I saw the little thing, too.

"It's okay, Soph." I kiss her on the head. "It's not your fault."

She squirms a little in her sleep.

The sound of something small going by in the hallway outside nearly startles me into screaming. I jump away from Sophia's bed and run, hanging on the doorjamb into the hall while looking left and right. Assuming I'm not hearing things, the little guy is damn fast. It sounded like it went from my right to my left while I had my back to the door, so that puts it going toward my parents' room or the upstairs bathroom. As quiet as can be, I peek in on Mom and Dad. They're asleep, nothing looks out of place, and the room doesn't give me any strange feelings.

Bathroom's clear, too.

Again, I check on Sam. He's still asleep with that strange little smile of victory. No eerie energy in there, either. Sierra's room, however, has gone full creepy. The instant I go in, anxiety wells up inside me. This is exactly how I would feel walking from night school to the parking garage alone if I remained a mortal girl. Wait, not exactly. This is how I'd feel at night alone with a big man following me, taking the same turns I took trying to lose him.

"What the hell do you want?" I whisper. "What are you?"

A tiny noise comes out from under the bed. I swear it sounded like a gasp of awe. Like, this little goblin-whatever is startled I know it's here. Within seconds, the sense of oddity in the air goes away. It's well after midnight, so maybe it just ran out of time and went back to wherever it came from until next Halloween.

And seriously, what the hell am I afraid of? I *am* a creature of the night! I'm the one that's supposed to be scaring other people. Ashley's right. This is so messed up. I have claws, fangs, night vision, can fly... I am not afraid of a little twenty-inch-tall goober. Annoyed, I tromp—quietly—out into the hallway and shut Sierra's door.

I'm about to go to my room when I notice Sam talking about *Fortnite* like he's explaining what the game is to a farm kid who's never seen a PlayStation before. Curiosity pulls me to his door and I peek in.

My nine-year-old brother is sitting up in bed, one eye open, one shut like Dad on an early morning before coffee. He kinda looks like he's sleep-talking, just rambling on and on about his favorite game.

"Sam?" I whisper.

He stops talking and looks over at me. "Yeah?"

"You're awake?"

"Yeah."

"Who are you talking to?"

"The closet monster," says Sam in the most blasé tone imaginable.

I walk in and stand beside his bed. "Sam, there's no such thing as closet monsters."

He shrugs. "Tell that to him."

I glance to my right at the closet—at two glowing red eyes floating within impenetrable darkness. A faint, but deep growl follows, like a 200-pound dog.

"Gah!" I jump onto the bed and grab my little brother from behind like he's a big teddy bear that will protect me from the evil thing.

"Don't be scared." Sam grips my arms, both presently encircling his chest. "He's not a bad closet monster."

Wait. What the hell am I doing? *I'm* the monster. I relax my grip, slide off the bed to my feet, and point at the door. "You, out of the closet."

The glowing eyes fade away.

Another thing that bugs me once I think about it… how the heck does the closet appear *dark*? I saw two glowing eyes floating in blackness. Stuff is *not* supposed to be dark to me, dammit! A nudge from my foot moves the door all the way open. The unusual blackness dissipates, revealing a quite normal—albeit messy—assortment of toys, games, and clothes. Hmm. Glim can make me see black smoke. This could be a similar mind trick. A faint hint of rotten egg smell lingers in the air. Crap… something really had been here. Unless that came from Sam.

"Aww, you scared him away." Sam sighs, then flops flat on his back, pulling his blankets up. "Why'd you yell at him? He was nice."

"He growled at me."

"Just playing. He growled at me, too."

"Did you fart?"

"No."

I stand there for a moment, blinking at Sam, not quite sure how to interpret his non-reaction to glowing eyes and growling in his closet. Is he really that brave? He's always been fairly reserved emotionally. Could he simply lack a fear response? Or, he knows his big sister is a vampire and a tiny growling thing in his closet isn't scary by comparison. I believe him that he didn't fart, since he's quite proud of them when they happen.

Edgar and Alan, Sam's frogs, watch me from their terrarium, their beady eyes gleaming in the moonlight.

"What are you two looking at?"

Neither frog reacts.

So creepy the way they stare like that.

"Night, Sam."

"Night, Sare."

I leave his room, shut the door, and head downstairs to mine. The basement still feels weird. Now I'm blaming *Cabin in the Woods*. It's not even three in the morning and I already want to crawl in bed and hide under the blankets from how creepy it feels in the house.

Tonight has caused too darn many questions.

Hopefully, whatever that creature is, it'll go back where it came from once Halloween is over.

That would be nice... but nothing is ever that easy, is it?

7

SPOOKY STUFF

U nfortunately, one thing I can't do is fall asleep at night.

Bed is comfortable, but boring. Staring at the ceiling was frustrating enough when I *could* fall asleep during the night hours. Eventually, I get over my unnatural fear of the dark enough to crawl out from under my blankets and sit at my desk, killing time playing *Skyrim*. I'm mostly caught up with schoolwork. Still have some reading for English Lit, but it's Wednesday night (technically Thursday morning) and I don't have that class again until Monday, so I have time.

And my brain is mush at the moment. Any studying I do now, I'd have to repeat. Need something mindless.

Eventually, the first traces of sleepiness begin poking at my consciousness. Usually, I sense the approach of dawn by feeling tired. Panic pretty much stomps that into oblivion if I'm doing something stupid and flying around outside too close to sunrise, trying to race home before incinerating myself. In those situations, I go from total panic adrenaline city straight to unconscious when I'm no longer in danger. Since I'm already sitting in my safe room, my body reacts to the approaching sun simply by gradually becoming more and more tired.

Okay, time for sleep.

I save my game, shut down the PC, and crawl into the awesome softness of my bed. At least I can enjoy it for the half a minute it takes me to pass out.

CONSCIOUSNESS RETURNS WITH THE POINTLESS MUSING ON comfortable beds.

Normal people aren't consciously aware of how nice their bed is while they sleep. Like me, they only notice it while unable to sleep, on the way to sleep, or just spending a lazy/sick day in bed wide awake. So maybe I'm not being wasteful having a real bed. I get the same amount of benefit out of it. The real difference is muscle stiffness afterward. I could sleep folded in half in a metal can and be totally fine when the sun went down. Not that I have any interest whatsoever in using a fifty-gallon drum as an emergency shelter like a certain English vampire who shall remain nameless has done numerous times.

Speaking of soft beds, I enjoy mine for a while… in no hurry to go anywhere.

Mostly, because I feel groggy and stiff. No, it's not from sleeping wrong, it's a sign that the sun is in a pissy mood. Vampires aren't supposed to be awake during the day at all. The rest of the bloodlines *can't* wake up until sunset, unless presented with an immediate threat to their unlives. I'm still not quite sure how that works, but Dalton said that if someone ever snuck into my room while I slept with intent to destroy me, I'd snap awake—and it wouldn't be pretty. Apparently, we're not fully ourselves in that state. More of a wild beast. Though, if someone is trying to like legit destroy me, I can't say I'd feel sorry for them if I ripped their face off.

I stretch out and grab my phone from the nightstand to check the weather app. Sure enough, sunny and nice out, if a bit cold. Talk about unnerving. Cold doesn't bug me anymore, and I was the girl who *always* felt cold. Two sweaters and a blanket burrito in the winter and

I'd still be constantly asking my parents to turn the heat up. Pretty sure I could go make snow angels butt naked when it's below freezing now and be more worried about someone seeing me than getting frostbite.

And yet, wearing warm, fuzzy coats and snuggling in blankets still feels as wonderful as it should. Sometimes, I just don't understand myself.

That's not metaphysical. I literally don't understand the inner workings of vampiredom yet.

Like, how am I able to ignore cold but warm still feels good? Whatever. Vampires are magic. Magic makes no sense. I have fangs. If Chewbacca lives on Endor, everything is invalid.

My phone rings. Caller ID says 'Chelle,' so I answer.

"Hey."

Sniffling comes over the line. "Hey… Sarah?"

I sit up fast. Shit. If Michelle's crying? That's rare. Something bad happened to her parents. If Corey left her, she'd be angry. "What's wrong?"

"My life is shot to hell."

"You bought a Bieber album and liked it?"

She sob-laughs. "No, dammit. I'm serious. My career is over before it started. I just got fired."

"Whoa. What happened?"

"I don't know!" she almost yells. "I went down to the records room to grab some files for Mr. Wallace. It's in the basement. This big-ass room full of old file drawers and stuff, because they have to keep legal records in hardcopy for seven years—longer if the case is still going. So, I find the stuff I need to grab, and all of a sudden, *everything* goes crazy." She breaks down in sniffles, breathing hard. "And… and… all the cabinets opened, papers are everywhere. Like someone set off a bomb in here. They think I did it. I got fired. They're going to sue me and press charges if I don't put everything back where it belongs. It's gonna take me days. He's going to complain to the school and they're going to kick me out. Nevermind what I'm going to hear from my dad. The only reason I even got that job is my father went to high school with Mr. Kirkland. Do you know how hard it is to get a job, even fetching coffee, at a law firm at eighteen?"

I shrug. "Umm, no."

"Impossible!" shouts Michelle. "I'll never be able to get into law school if my record shows that I tried to destroy records. I didn't!"

"I believe you." I narrow my eyes at my closet door.

"Sare, can you *please* fix this? I know I've been kinda funny about what you can do with people, but this is my whole life about to go up in smoke." She lowers her voice to a whisper. "Can you fiddle around with Mr. Kirkland's head and make him forget this?"

"Yeah, sure. No problem. Umm… can it wait a couple hours? The sun's a bit too brutal for me to go anywhere right at the moment. I'll zip over there as soon as I can, probably on my way to class."

"Umm… he's probably going to be gone for the day by then, but okay. Don't hurt yourself. Maybe he won't call the school right away."

I cringe, feeling guilty—but not *too* much. "You're also forgetting that I can't do anything when the sun's on me. Unless I can convince him to go with me into a windowless basement, it would have to wait until after dark anyway."

"Oh. Yeah, duh. Umm. I'll be here all damn night… so whenever you can."

"You got it. Try to hold it together? I'll fix whoever I have to fix. Even if he calls the school, I can deal with them, too."

Michelle's sniffling quiets. "Yeah. Cool. I didn't even think about that. Wow. I'm so upset right now my brain's not working."

"Relax. Everything's under control. I got you."

"Thank you *so* damn much…"

"I haven't done anything yet, but I will fix it." It's possible that whatever happened to her is the direct result of something I may have potentially caused. Undoing it really is the least I can do for her.

We talk a bit over the rustle of papers in the background. There's thousands of files from a ton of six-drawer file cabinets bigger than refrigerators, and every single one of them is on the floor. Putting it all back would be impossible if not for every document being stamped with a case number. Not only does she have to pick up papers and stuff them back in manila envelopes, she has to make sure all the papers for each particular case are together, and put back in the correct drawer in the correct chronological order.

What an effing nightmare.

Eventually, she calms down enough to release the lifeline of having me to talk to, figuring she'll work faster with both hands. After we hang up, I grab the textbook for my sociology class and start reading what I had to read for tonight's class.

Within minutes, the littles walk in upstairs, home from school. I'm tempted to go check on them, but the sun's kind of keeping me locked in for the time being. Besides, Dad's probably up there. If, for whatever reason, he had to go out somewhere, he'd have left a note sending the three of them down here so I can watch them. However, I can hear them despite being downstairs.

"… it's not right," says Sophia. "We gotta do something."

"Rachel Cartwright has been picking on you for two years. Who cares if she trips into a trash can?"

"Sierra!" whisper-shouts Sophia. "You know she didn't *trip.* You know exactly what's going on."

"This girl always teases you for being too squishy and nice… and here you are feeling bad because she's clumsy. Maybe she's right. You are *too* nice."

A raspberry flutters over the sounds of the girls going up to their rooms. I strain to keep following their conversation, but eavesdropping from the basement on a pair of whispering tweens on the second floor is asking a bit much from even my ears. Too much house in the way.

I do, however, hear *far* more than I ever wanted of my brother exploding in the bathroom.

Eww.

He's too small to make noises like that. Gah. Damn, I really need to figure out how to control these ears. They always seem to ramp up to eleven when I *don't* need them to. Soft, rapid footsteps come down the stairs again. Ooh, the girls must be hunting for a snack. Perfect. With a 'target' to focus on, I can concentrate on their conversation and tune out unrelated distractions of the methane variety.

They're still chattering about that Cartwright kid going headfirst into a trashcan right in the middle of the cafeteria and everyone laughing at her. Evidently, this kid is the pretty blonde 'popular girl.' I feel kinda sorry for her really. A kid who peaks in fifth grade is going to have a messy life. Sophia sounds super guilty, though. Almost like she'd telekinetically thrown the girl into the can. Nothing the girls say remotely approaches suggesting that's what actually happened, but Sophia is acting as guilty as if she pushed her in.

"Ms. Stein's chair kept flying out from under her when she tried to sit, too," says Sophia. "Something happened. We gotta make it stop."

"Nothing happened. You're getting freaked out for no reason." Sierra sighs. "Umm, you want iced tea or... what's this purple stuff?"

"No idea. Umm, tea."

Good call, kiddo. Never drink unidentified purple substances.

The fridge closes with a *whump*.

"Here," says Sierra. "And Ms. Stein is like the worst teacher in the whole school. I had her last year. She's so mean. Falling on her butt is getting off light."

Sophia whines.

"It's just spooky stuff. Stop being a baby."

Grr. Something happened. I close the book, set it on the bed, and head out into the basement. The tinted windows make even bad days tolerable. However, when I pull open the door to the kitchen at the top of the stairs a half-inch to peek, it feels like I'm at the entrance to a volcano. Damn, it must be clear and cloudless today.

"Hey you two," I say. "Come down here a sec."

I shut the door and hurry downstairs.

The girls, Sierra in a T-shirt and jeans, Sophia in a cute pink dress, come down, each holding a cup of iced tea. Sophia's expression is a mask of total guilt. Sierra doesn't have a shred of it, or hesitation. I don't think she's gone full psychopath, so there's something strange going on here.

I set my hands on my hips and look back and forth between them. "What happened?"

"We did magic the night before Halloween," whispers Sophia. "And it really worked."

"No it didn't." Sierra rolls her eyes. "We pretended to cast a spell and you got all sorts of scared because it's Halloween Eve and ghosts can cross over more easily."

Sophia faces her. "We really did something! I hear it whispering."

"You need to stop watching any movies scarier than like *Sesame Street*," mutters Sierra.

"Hold on, guys." I raise both hands. "One, there really is something running around. I've seen it, too. And it's messing with people. What did you do?"

Sierra blinks. "Holy crap, really? Are you serious?"

I nod, and explain the two neighbors complaining as well as the blackout/alarm at the party plus the mess at Michelle's job.

"And the fireworks!" Sierra laughs. "That had to be it because you —well, *we*—got mad at that guy."

Sophia looks down. "I'm sorry! I swear I won't do it again. But I don't know how to turn it off."

"What did you do exactly?"

Sierra shrugs. "Just drew a circle and put funny marks on it like the thing showed. We chanted some made up words and nothing happened."

"Nothing *looked* like it happened!" Sophia shivers, hands balled into fists at her sides. "We really did open a gate. Guess something actually did come over."

"I *told* you something was wrong when the marker didn't wash out!" half-yells Sophia.

Uh oh. Glim called it 'gate night.' I wonder if that's just a coincidence.

There's no need to freak them out too much, so I don't bother telling them I saw some little goblin type thing running around. "Something probably did show up, yeah. Maybe it'll go back on its own, but just in case it won't, I'll ask some people I know if they can help."

"The people who cursed me?" Sophia folds her arms.

"And sent you to the bottom of the ocean?" adds Sierra with a raised eyebrow before turning back to Sophia. "Besides, you're not cursed. You got magic powers out of the deal. What are you complaining about?"

"They weren't trying to help me!" Sophia stomps one foot, nearly spilling some tea. "They used me as a... a... *meat puppet!*"

I make a silly face at them. "Open for suggestions if either of you are aware of anyone else who thinks magic is real."

Sophia sighs, then clings to me. "Okay. I guess it would be stupid to ignore them out of spite. Maybe they can help."

"Obvs," says Sierra. "They totally did real magic, so they gotta know something."

"We opened a doorway." Sophia holds on tighter, speaking in a whispery half-voice. "Something came across. It's bad. We did something real bad. The little man that came through the gate isn't nice. He's not nice at all."

Sierra pauses, about to take a sip of tea. "Umm, can you like *not* say creepy, ominous stuff?"

"Sorry," whispers Sophia.

I'd make a joke here, but she's legit trembling. Whether or not these two genuinely had anything to do with what's going on, she believes it's her fault. She's always been clingy with me, though I have no idea what I ever did to deserve the almost hero-worship she's regarded me with for years. Prior to my transformation, I'd usually only tolerate it for a little while before pushing her away. Thinking about my family almost losing me forever is still fresh in my mind, right next to my dread of watching them grow old and die.

So, yeah. I fully tolerate all clinginess now. She's mostly stopped bracing for me to snap at her to 'get off,' but there's still a trace of tension in her muscles, like she's afraid I'm going to get mad at her. Said tension fades when I put an arm around her and pat her back.

"You saw one, didn't you?" I ask in a gentle tone.

"Yeah. Didn't say anything 'cause Sierra would've made fun of me and anyone else would've called me nuts. Well, except you, but I didn't want you to get mad at me."

I pat her on the back. "Don't freak out, Soph. We'll deal with it... somehow."

THE GIRLS HANG OUT IN MY ROOM FOR A WHILE, BOTH ABSORBED IN their tablets, researching whatever they think they did. Eventually, Mom pokes her head in to summon Sophia off to dance class. At that point, Sierra decides she's done enough reading about occult weirdness and goes up to the living room for video games.

I throw some time at studying, checking the weather app and clock. According to the 'net, the sun's going down at 5:52 p.m. tonight. My philosophy class runs from 7:00 p.m. to 10:00 p.m. since it's a once-a-week affair. An hour should be enough to sort out Michelle's issue before class. If not, I'll pull a classic Dracula and sneak into someone's bedroom in the middle of the night.

At a couple minutes to six, I change into a purple sweatshirt and jeans, then toss my backpack over one shoulder before heading upstairs. Dad's in his office, hammering away at the computer. He only usually types that fast when he's really into whatever project he's working on. Sure enough, the screen is full of computer code. After a few seconds of me standing there obviously watching him, he stops and looks up with a smile.

"Hey. Welcome to the surface world."

"Good morning to you, too, Dad." I hug him. "Daylight was a pain today."

"Yeah, tell me about it. I had to put on sunscreen to work indoors."

I stare at him.

"They can't all be funny."

"Dad, no 'dad joke' is funny. They just have varying degrees of eye roll."

He laughs.

"Something weird is going on and I wanted to give you a heads up."

"Weird like the Cleveland Browns making it to the Super Bowl?"

"That's not weird, that's apocalyptic," shouts Sierra from the living room.

I glance back and forth between them, confused. "Umm, whatever. No, I mean weird like…" I extend my fangs. "Thith."

"Vampire stuff?"

"Noth exthathly." I retract the teeth. "Not exactly. Paranormal weird. There's some kind of little critter running around causing mayhem."

Dad gives me a flat look. "Sarah, we've talked about this. His name is Sam."

I snicker. "No, I'm serious."

"Ooh." His eyes metaphorically light up. Gotta say 'metaphorically,' since in my new life, actual light-up eyes are apparently a thing. "Have you seen *Critters?*"

"Yes, Dad. You made me watch it when I was nine and it gave me nightmares."

"Wimp!" yells Sierra.

My father snaps his fingers in disappointment. "Aww drat."

"You can still screen it for the littles."

Dad shrugs. "Maybe. But I'd feel too guilty about traumatizing Sophia. Sierra would laugh at it, and Sam would keep staring at me with a 'this is supposed to be scary?' face."

I chuckle. "I'm being serious though."

He listens as I give him a quick explanation of what I've seen so far. "Well, that does sound difficult to explain away. Okay. I'll keep my eyes open."

"I'm not sure what, if anything, they might do here. It was talking to Sam last night and seemed well-behaved. When we went trick-or-treating, I think it followed us, and anyone that the girls got mad at, it pranked. It's probably not going to do anything here if my theory is correct and it's working for them."

He nods. "All right. You look like you're ready to head out. Little early?"

"Yeah. Michelle has an issue at work that I think this thing caused… so I'm going to try to undo it as much as I can."

"Be careful."

"Yep. Any lapses in care can be patched by abuse of mental powers."

He points at me. "Until you run into a situation where that won't work."

"Mostly kidding there." I flash a cheesy smile. "Be back after class."

"Have fun."

"Won't be as fun as calculus."

"Hey, I liked math."

I stick out my tongue. "So do I. That wasn't meant to be sarcastic."

"You think math is fun?" asks Sierra. "You have a sick mind."

"Umm…" I lean out into the living room to look at her. "Don't you want to develop video games when you're older?"

"Yeah."

"That's almost *all* math."

She pauses the game and glares at nothing in particular. "How can math be involved with video games? That's like fun colliding with anti-fun. It would explode and annihilate the known universe."

"I got this one." Dad winks. "Go help Michelle."

"Okay." I pat Sierra on the head while walking by on my way to the shoe staging area, where I claim my sneakers.

Mom pulls into the driveway as I go out the door. I delay my departure long enough to hug them both, then jog around to the side of the house where it's dark enough to conceal my takeoff.

Flying will never not be amazing.

Wind at my face, my hair whipping about, I bask in the awesomeness. Maybe after a couple decades, it might start to feel routine, but for right now, it's way too much of a thrill. Driving still feels strange to me, like I'm getting away with something I shouldn't. Even though I did get my license a couple months before death, part of me still feels like too much of a kid to be driving on my own. Mom and Dad don't feel odd about driving. I wonder at what age the 'OMG factor' of it wore off for them. Motorcycles would probably be a better metaphor for flying. I can see driving becoming routine for someone, but riding a bike? That's gotta be scary even after thirty years.

Says the girl doing 120 miles an hour 600 feet off the ground without a helmet.

But, honestly, flying is safer. No traffic up here to crash into.

I turn toward Seattle and zoom, not quite sprinting as fast as possible. When I reach Lake Washington, the air takes on the smell—and flavor—of saltwater. From this altitude, the lake looks like a hole in reality, so dark compared to the land surrounding it. There's so many lights everywhere on the ground, but the sky still looks black. It feels like I've been sucked into the computer in *Tron.*

My phone provides a GPS app that leads me straight to an office building downtown. I swoop in for a landing in a nearby alley, then walk a block or so to the main entrance. A man and a woman wearing security guard uniforms staff the front desk, both giving me weird looks as I enter.

"You waiting for your mom or dad, hon?" asks the female guard.

"No, I'm checking on a friend of mine. She works here."

The male guard shakes his head. "Sorry, kid. Need a valid badge to get inside after five. Employees only."

Sigh.

I give the woman a ride to derpville with a mental jab, then focus my attention on the guy, commanding him to make me a temporary ID badge with security guard rights so it opens everything in the building. Also, he's not going to log it or remember me.

While he programs a white plastic card, I erase myself from the woman's memory.

The man mechanically holds up the visitor badge.

"Thanks." I take it and head past the reception counter to an alcove full of elevators and doors.

Kirkland, Morris, and Patel is on the ground floor, so I skip the elevators and badge-swipe my way into the door at the back end of the lobby. That leads to a small area with hallways going in different directions to various offices. The law firm is straight ahead, so I keep going up to a pair of huge glass doors marked with 'Kirkland, Morris, & Patel Attorneys at Law' in front of a deserted reception area. A white wall behind the desk has several shiny brass strips attached to it, trying to be a sculpture of like waves or clouds or some abstract concept of storks. The badge reader at the doors also chirps and turns green, allowing me inside. Two corridors, one on either side of the wall, lead deeper into the place. There are a ton of desks, side rooms, and cubicles, but no people.

I run around looking for Michelle for a few minutes until I spot a door marked 'storage' that leads to a stairwell. As soon as I open it, the rustle of papers reaches my ears along with Michelle muttering to herself. She alternates between commenting about how screwed she is and hoping I'm going to able to help.

The hallway at the basement level has eight doors, three on the left, four on the right, one at the far end. It's fairly obvious where Michelle is since the middle door on the left is open, with a light on. The sounds are coming from there.

When I reach the door, I stop short and gasp in horrified awe. The room looks like it had a snowstorm—of paper. It's easily half a foot deep in places. Pale grey metal cabinets as tall as I am with wide drawers line all four walls, plus three aisles composed of the same cabinets arranged back to back. Every single drawer is open, and empty.

"Holy shit," I whisper.

"Sare!" Michelle springs to her feet from where she'd been kneeling. Her skirt suit makes her look like she belongs working for a high-end law firm, but her mascara's run and she's taken her shoes off. "Oh my God... I can't believe this."

I fly over the paper drifts and glide up to her, hovering. "This is... wow. How on Earth did they believe you actually did this in the few minutes you were down here? It would take hours to create a mess this bad."

She rakes her hands up through her hair, drawing a hissing breath inward. "I dunno. Mr. Wallace probably doesn't know either. And Mr. Kirkland like totally freaked out. Called me ungrateful for the opportunity, wanted to know why I would do something like this to the firm giving me a chance... when I said I didn't do it, Wallace accused me of lying and said I'm too dishonest to be a lawyer. Kirkland looked sad."

I laugh. "Wow. He really said dishonesty is bad for a lawyer with a straight face?"

"Hey." She playfully punches me in the shoulder. "I'm trying to be a lawyer here. Not *all* of them are crooks."

"I guess. Just the ones who know their clients are guilty and still try to get them off."

She grasps my shoulders. "I don't have the time or the composure to get into an ethical debate about it with you now. Can you fix this?"

Looking at the mess makes me *meep*. "If you're asking me to snap my fingers and make all these papers jump back where they belong, no. I can't do that. Changing your boss' perception of this event, that's easy. I'd even offer to stay and help you pick this crap up, but I wouldn't know what to put with what, and this badge is not going to let me stay in here for long without causing a problem." I show her the blank card.

"It's okay. If you can make it so I'm not fired and my whole life is shot to hell, I'll happily deal with putting this crap back where it belongs."

I flash a cheesy smile. "I could make Mr. Kirkland tell you to shred it all to save time."

"No... the firm could get in serious shit if they're ever subpoenaed for any of these documents and don't have them."

"Umm. Aren't there electronic copies? Couldn't they just print them?"

"In some cases, but a lot of these papers have ink signatures or notarized attachments stapled in."

I slouch. "Ugh. That blows."

She gives me side eye. "Do you know what the hell did this?"

"Yes and no."

"Just what the shit is that supposed to mean?" She leans back, arms folded.

"It means I have an idea which entity is responsible, but not a damn clue what it is or why it did this."

She raises an eyebrow. "What is it?"

"Remember the chaos at the party last night? Same thing set that off."

"What did you do?"

I hold my hands up. "Hang on. I have no idea where it came from. If it *is* my fault, it's a total accident. And I can't think of anything I might have done to cause this, other than simply being supernatural. Anyway, where's this guy live?"

She steps into her shoes. "C'mon. I gotta look his address up in the system. Oh… shit. I can't. They locked me out of the network when they fired me." Michelle looks down like a scolded child having her dreams crushed before her eyes.

"Aww." I hug her. "Don't be sad. I'll fix this. Unless they kill you, I can undo whatever they do to you."

Michelle exhales, bows her head, then nods. "Okay. I'll try to stay calm. Counting on you…"

"On it."

I fly to the corridor to avoid stepping on any papers, and run back upstairs. Mr. Kirkland's office is pretty obvious since it's the biggest one and his name's right on the door. There's no computer on the desk, just a monitor and mouse connected to a docking station for a laptop he's obviously taken home with him. I blur around the room searching for an address, checking wastebaskets, desk drawers, anything that looks like a day planner or business card. I'm about to give up when I spot some magazines on a table by a small sofa—dude has a huge office.

One of them has a mailing address for Paul Kirkland in North Beach, on Loyal Ave. I snap a photo of the label with my phone for good measure, then program the address into my GPS app. After sending Michelle a text of 'got the address, OMW,' I head out to the lobby.

Both security guards startle at my approach.

"What are you doing in here?" asks the man. "Where'd you come from?"

"Are you lost, sweetie?" The woman stands. "Does your dad work here?"

I walk over to the desk. "Nope. Just leaving. Oh, I found this badge on the floor."

The male guard swipes it from me like he's taking a hand grenade away from a small child.

A minute or three of memory tweaking once again leaves the pair standing there, staring off into nowhere. Neither will remember seeing me. I hurry out the main doors before the mind fog wears off, and jog back to the dark alley.

THE FLIGHT TO MR. KIRKLAND'S HOUSE DOESN'T TAKE TOO LONG.

It's like eight-ish miles from the office as the vampire flies. I land in a thick cluster of trees in front of the house next door, enough to hide my descent from most eyes. A flight-assisted leap carries me over a chain link fence and I walk west one house to a weird looking rectangular place that looks like an experiment in artsy architecture inspired by the wrong kind of drugs. The façade is dark grey on the left, with a narrow strip of dark grey over the main face that's pale grey and crammed with windows of different sizes, some square, some rectangular. It's like the builder had a bunch of stray windows left over and decided to use them all. The door is set into an area of wood siding that's totally at odds with the modernist design of everything else.

You'd almost think someone from Microsoft designed this place, since it's got so many windows.

I ring the bell, and clasp my hands in front of myself, waiting.

A friendly-looking older guy, probably early fifties, with fully grey hair and blue eyes answers a moment later, giving me a bewildered glance. "Can I help you, young lady? Are you sure you have the right address? Who are you looking for?"

"Paul Kirkland?"

"That's me... but I don't recognize you."

I smile. "You wouldn't. I'm just a messenger."

"Oh." He smiles. "Very well. Do I need a pen to sign or is it electronic?"

"Neither." I stare into his eyes. "The message is about an intern working at your firm, Michelle Gerard." My intrusion upon his brain stalls the words rushing to his mouth.

Surprisingly, he's shocked and dismayed at what happened, genuinely hurt that Michelle 'betrayed' him by trashing the records. He didn't want to believe she did it. Whew. That makes this much easier.

To avoid attracting unwanted attention, I nudge him inside the house and pull the door closed behind me. Yeah, that whole 'gotta invite vampires inside' thing? Total BS. Anyway, I rearrange his memory such that he thinks Michelle went down there to get something and found the room like that. Now, he remembers her being the one who reported it to him, having returned from the basement in barely five minutes. I reinforce the idea that it would have taken someone hours to empty all those drawers and throw stuff around. There's no possible way Michelle could have done that.

I also get an address for Mr. Wallace (the lawyer who walked in on Michelle while she stood there staring aghast at the chaos) from this guy's head. And, purely because I feel bad for my friend, I give Kirkland the idea that the firm is going to pay her a fair wage for the time she spends cleaning it up. Oops. Gotta undo the firing, too. A few minutes later, Mr. Kirkland believes someone hacked into their network and faked his email to HR. He's going to get that fixed first thing in the morning, reinstating her as an active intern. Fortunately, he liked her and couldn't believe she'd do something like that... so he hadn't yet called her school to complain. One less thing for me to undo then. Good.

With the guy in a fog, I let myself out and take off again.

The other lawyer lives in Wallingford, more or less east from here. His is a normal suburban type house, though in an odd coincidence, the siding under the double roof is the same shade of charcoal grey as the dark part of Kirkland's house, the rest of it red bricks.

A tween boy answers the door this time. I smile at him, but skip the conversation and give him a mental prod to go back to whatever he'd been doing before the bell rang. As the boy runs off down a hallway, I step inside and close the door.

Wow, this is kinda like super weird and wrong… just walking into someone's house. But, I'm not here to steal anything or cause harm, so I force myself to ignore the idea that I'm doing something bad. I'm here to undo whatever mystical bullcrap screwed over my friend.

Following my ears, I find Mr. Wallace in the basement, in the midst of building a remote-control model airplane. The place is full of various mini-aircraft hanging from the ceiling on bungee cords. Some are biplanes, some look more modern. Most are about four-feet long, but one looks big enough for Sam to ride like a horse. Another's even an F-16. Oof, this can't be cheap.

The guy glances over at me casually for a second, starts to go back to gluing a piece of wood in place, then whirls toward me, grabbing a screwdriver like a knife. "Who the hell are you?"

"No one. I'm not even here." I smile and dive into his head.

Mr. Wallace apparently has been metaphorically up Michelle's butt since she started there. This guy doesn't think women belong in law, and he's been microscoping everything she does, waiting for any opportunity to get rid of her. It's extremely tempting to make this guy think he's the one who tossed the storage room, but that's a little too far into 'doing harm' to sit well with my overdeveloped sense of guilt. Especially considering the guy has at least one kid to take care of. I can't go costing him his job.

So, he didn't go downstairs, didn't see the room, and he's going to largely ignore Michelle's existence for as long as my compulsion lasts… which should be long enough for her to complete her internship and move on.

About fifteen minutes later, I'm back in the air, flying to school.

It's difficult to talk on the phone while flying—wind is loud—so I shoot Michelle a text 'all handled. Will call you in a few mins.'

She responds with a string of emoji smiles, hearts, and one I think is supposed to be a hug.

I land on the topmost level of the parking garage by Seattle Central College with a little more than an hour to kill before my first class. Plenty of time to talk to Michelle and explain to her what her boss believes. And how maybe I nudged his sense of appreciation toward her for volunteering to clean up such a horrible mess without expecting anything in return. Mr. Kirkland had been so impressed with her, that he's offered to pay her for the time.

Michelle squeals. "Holy crap, Sarah. That's... amazing." She can barely talk past her tears. "I can't stop crying."

"It's weird hearing you cry. You're usually such a badass."

"Well, yeah. But this went *way* past my ability to comprehend. Like, I had zero control over my life at that moment."

I nod, even though she can't see it. "Understood. Don't flip out anymore. It's all good... and I should probably get to class or I'll keep right on talking to you until I'm late."

"Okay. I owe you big time."

"It's cool. The thing that did this is probably connected to me somehow, so I'm just undoing damage. If you owe me one, I'll feel guilty."

She laughs. "All right. Ugh... this is gonna take me freakin' weeks to put back together, but at least I'm not going to be kicked out of school. Hey, if you catch that thing that did this, slap it upside the head for me."

"Will do."

I end the call and start walking across the parking garage to the stairs.

Maybe I stepped a little across an ethical line, but undoing supernatural wonkiness with more supernatural wonkiness feels justified to me.

8

STUCK AT WORK

id I mention my philosophy teacher is a vampire?

Professor Heath is an Old Guard vamp who's been teaching at various colleges for the past 130 or so years. He changes towns and schools every so often so people don't notice him not getting older. The man has a lot of leeway though, having been turned in his late forties. Some guys just don't change that much as they age past a certain point. His salt and pepper hair and hint of beard stubble could make him look anywhere from a wise forty to a young sixty.

Curiosity gets the better of me. I linger after class and bounce the situation with Michelle off him.

"I'm afraid I don't have any experience involving 'creatures' like that. I've heard a story or two, but never personally interacted with creatures more bizarre than college students… and the odd vampire or two. However, in regard to your question concerning the ethics of altering the memories of your friend's employer, I think you're mostly in the clear. However, having them pay her pushes the balance in her favor as opposed to simply undoing a paranormal event with paranormal means."

"Does it?" I lean against his desk. "She's still stuck spending hours and hours cleaning up a mess she's not responsible for creating. That time cuts into her schoolwork and she's basically not going to have *any* time for fun until she's done with it. Having them pay her for the time she's fixing the records room balances the creature's effect on Michelle. It didn't only affect the law firm."

Professor Heath opens his mouth, hesitates, then closes it. He smiles, pointing at me. "Clever. But a good point. I think—"

"Gah!" I yelp and jump as my phone goes off, ringing on vibrate in my pocket.

"Are you unwell?"

"Sorry, professor. My phone went off and startled me." I pull it out so I can check the screen before ignoring the call, but seeing 'Ash Home' as the ID worries me. She hasn't called me from their land line since we were twelve and she got her first cell phone as a birthday present. "Sorry, this could be an emergency."

He makes a 'be my guest' gesture at the phone.

I flick to answer. "Hello?"

"Sarah?" asks Mrs. Carter. "Do you know where Ash is?"

Crap. My stomach turns into a lead weight. "No... I haven't talked to her since last night. Did you try calling her cell?"

"Of course. It's going right to voicemail."

"Ash never turns her phone off."

"That's why I'm worried. Oh, no. Do you think someone abducted her?"

I bite my lip. That's not my first thought, but as scary an idea as it is, not impossible. "Did she go somewhere?"

"Just to work. She should have been home hours ago. Do you think I should call the police yet? Or are you girls up to something?"

"Umm. Let me go check at the vet place before you get the police involved. You know how she can get with animals. If they gave her a project, she'd lose track of time."

Mrs. Carter emits a shuddering breath. "All right, but please call me right away when you are there."

"I will. Going right now."

"Okay."

Professor Heath tilts his head in concern. "Well, that certainly sounds like a matter of concern. Go check on your friend. We can resume this discussion at any time."

"Yeah. Thanks."

I smile at him, stuff my phone in my pocket, then run out of the room, down the hall, up the stairs, down another hall, and out the nearest exit to the street. It takes a lot of willpower to force myself to not leap straight into the air, instead heading for the concealment of shadows first. I jog to the courtyard where Howell Street stops being a street for the width of one block. It's empty and dark there, offering me a good opportunity to take flight.

Worry for my best friend pushes me up to the airborne equivalent of sprinting. I'm not exactly sure how fast this is, but if I had my Uggs on, I'd lose them. In fact, the occasional blast of wind gets under my collar with enough force to pull my shirt out from being tucked into my jeans. Ignoring the flapping fabric, I keep on flying toward the veterinary office in Woodinville.

My nerves calm minutes later when the parking lot comes into view and I see Ashley's little VW Jetta there. Technically, it's her mother's. Anyway, the calming effect lasts only a moment before I think bad thoughts. If someone kidnapped my friend, they wouldn't take her car, too. But, really, who would abduct someone from a veterinary clinic? Also, she should have been out of here hours ago.

I land beside the Jetta and try to call her. It goes straight to voicemail.

Clicking draws my attention to the door of the vet hospital.

A tiny dog stands behind the glass, paws up, staring at me.

Okay, that's unusual. Why is a dog loose inside the clinic?

The little furball barks at me. Answering barks come from deeper in the building. A faint cat wail leaks past the din, sounding as though it's all the way in the back. Poor kitty. Probably terrified of all the dogs.

I walk up to the door. "Hey, boy. What happened?"

The small terrier jumps and yips at me, backing away. It waits a moment, then barks again. Wow, I thought that 'Timmy's in the well' thing was made up for a television show. This dog appears to be trying to ask me to follow it.

The cat wail happens again, but this time it sounds more like a girl yelling "Help!"

It's too faint to be someone inside the building yelling, though. I can barely hear it and my ears are considerably better than a mortal's. It almost sounds like a ghost screaming from the other side. Sorry if you're a ghost, but you're already dead. I need to find Ashley first. Any problems you have can wait.

The faint voice yells again, mostly incomprehensible, but I do make out the word 'police' at the end. Okay, that's messed up. A ghost wouldn't want cops. The little dog keeps barking, backing away, returning, and barking.

Short of breaking the door off its hinges, I don't have a good way to get inside. A bigger dog, probably a German shepherd, walks by near the counter. His right foreleg is bandaged and he's limping.

Damn. Too bad I can't read doggie minds.

I am curious to look around inside, but I don't want to break the door. However, it doesn't look like options for getting in are terribly numerous. I fly up to the roof on a lark, hoping there's maybe an access hatch, but no luck. The rear door by the dumpsters is plain black steel, but it's out of view of the street. Tempting, but the knob will most assuredly break off in my hand before the door pops open.

Ooh, better idea. I start checking windows around the outside until locating one at an empty examination room that's partially open. It's a wide rectangular slab only about eight inches tall, the type that opens by cranking. Breaking this won't be *too* destructive. I grab the underside and pull upward with both hands until the mechanism snaps, allowing me to manually open the window to its full width.

Dalton is probably rolling over in his not-grave at how crappily I'm going about breaking into a place. Pretty sure he's an experienced thief. Or at least experienced at breaking into places. Kinda odd that he brought me to a pitiful burglar for my first feeding. Isn't that like a betrayal of the thieves' code? Meh.

I stuff myself headfirst in the window, cheating by flying for propulsion to slip through without much trouble. The heavy panel of double-pane glass closes with a *whump* behind me since the struts are broken. Just as well. I rotate vertical, land on my feet, and close the lock. I'd feel guilty if someone intending to steal stuff used the window I broke to get in.

The exam room has two doors, one out to the 'public' area, and one for the employees to go into a private space in back. Since I'm in already, I might as well break all the rules and check out the 'employees only' area.

Yeah, I'm a rebel.

I open the door and step into a space that isn't sure if it wants to be a room or a wide corridor. A bunch of cubicles hold desks, probably each vet who works here has a separate workspace. Signs indicate doors leading to surgery, storage, records, and so on—and there are dozens of animals roaming around.

"Ashley?" I shout. "Are you here?"

The distant ghost-voice wails, "Yes! Sarah! Help!"

Okay, that's messed up. It kinda sounds like Ash, but why is it coming from miles away? I head in the direction the feeble shout came from, dodging around dogs and cats, none of which seem overly bothered by my presence. Of course, they're not exactly running up to me for love either. The tiny dogs give me wary looks and scoot away while the big ones, as well as cats, just watch me with neutral curiosity. About a quarter of them have bandages, but most appear healthy.

Possible-Ashley's screaming leads me down a corridor that connects to the adoption center and past a blue door into a giant room full of cages, all of which are open and empty.

"Oh, this is too weird," I say.

"Sarah!" shouts Ashley, and still sounds like she's a long way off.

I pivot to my right, tracking the source of the voice to a row of larger dog cages. They, too, are all open—except one. Ashley's stuck inside the third one from the wall, hair a mess, eyes red from exhaustion and crying. She wipes her face on her blue work smock and grabs the bars of the cage door, rattling it.

"Help!"

I run over, nudging a big pail of poo out of the way. "What the hell? Who locked you in a cage? And why do you sound so damn quiet?"

"I don't know! These cages aren't supposed to be able to lock!" She points at the mechanism. "It's just a sliding latch, but it's like welded or something. I've been stuck in here for hours screaming and kicking at the door, but I can't get out and no one came to help me."

"Hang on." I pull my phone out and call her mother.

"Sarah! Please tell me you have good news!" says Mrs. Carter, on the verge of tears.

"Yeah. I found her. She's still at the clinic, got stuck in a kennel somehow. I don't have any answers yet."

Ashley sighs. "I crawled in here to clean it like I always do. The door slammed behind me and somehow got stuck. I've been screaming my head off but everyone ignored me. My phone's dead as a brick, too."

"There's something funky going on with sound. You're like right in front of me but your voice is so faint I don't think a normal person could even hear you at all."

"What?" asks Mrs. Carter.

I turn my attention back to the phone. "Ash is fine. Situation is annoying, not dangerous. It's also highly weird. Let me deal with this and I'll bring her home as soon as possible."

"All right." She exhales hard. "Oh, thank you. You're sure she's okay?"

"Yep. I'm looking right at her. She was freaking out, but she's back to normal. Wait, no this is Ash I'm talking about. Normal's a dirty word."

Ash flips me the bird, but grins.

It takes me a moment to convince Mrs. Carter to get off the phone. Finally, I stuff it in my pocket and crouch in front of the kennel. Ashley looks miserable, but relieved to see me. She sticks her fingers past the bars to grab the latch, but it doesn't move at all. The mechanism is fairly simple, a loop-shaped handle attached to a sliding metal bar. Lift the handle, slide the bar to the left, cage opens. Only, this one's fused as tight as if it had been welded.

"After I got stuck in here, all the other cages opened by themselves. Every dog and cat in the adoption center is running around. It's like the animal rebellion!" She laughs. "I'm the only human in the building and I'm the one in a cage."

"Sec."

I grab the handle in as secure a hold as I can manage on something that small, and pull, gradually increasing strength. The instant the thought 'holy shit this thing is tough' starts to form in my brain, the handle rips off the cage door, sending me sliding into the room on my back. A faint flash of yellowish light bursts away from the bars.

Ashley shoves the door open, crawls out, and stands. "Oh, wow. Holy crap. I thought I was gonna be stuck in there for like ever."

"Your mute button stopped working." I fake snap my fingers in disappointment.

She sticks her tongue out.

"Must have been something in that light…"

"What light?" She swipes her hair off her face, trying to neaten it.

I sit up. "Did you see a flash from the door when the handle broke? I saw the same flash at the party when I kicked the door open."

She shakes her head. "Nope."

A deep growl comes from my left.

I start to smirk at the dog—but it's not a dog. I'm staring at a two-foot-tall jet-black-skinned creature that's most definitely *not* a canine. He's generally human shaped, with spindly arms and legs, gargoyle-like wings with claw-like protrusions at the joint and tip, a giant nose, beady red eyes that glow like penlights, and small, curved horns sticking out of his somewhat-oversized-for-the-body head. Though he's naked, he doesn't have any visible signs of being a boy—or girl. Maybe I should call it an it?

"Whoa. What the f—"

It makes a swiping gesture and the big orange Home Depot bucket of animal poo leaps off the floor by the cage and flies at me. Never have I been so happy to have superhuman reflexes. I fling myself to the side, rolling out of the path of the shit bomb. The bucket crashes to the floor, spilling its foul contents everywhere.

Dogs erupt in a deafening chorus of barks and snarls at the creature, which they, too, can apparently see.

Ashley screams.

I look toward her, relieved to see nothing happening. "What?"

She points. "That bucket just flew at you for no reason!"

"It had a reason." I jump to my feet.

The little creature grabs and throws a small dog at me. I catch the poor critter as gently as possible and set him back on his paws.

Ashley screams again. "Why are the dogs flying?"

"You don't see the little gremlin thing?"

"Gremlins? Are you serious?"

The *thing* runs to the left, jumping onto its wings and cruising over to a counter. From there, it begins hurling whatever it can get its hands on at me. I dodge and weave past a barrage of plastic bottles, food bags, bowls, and spoons. When I get close enough, I dive at the monster, but it zooms to the side at the last second. My knuckles brush a leathery wing.

"What are you doing?" yells Ashley.

I chase the tiny terror, following it in a circle around the kennel area. "There's a weird little creature here doing this."

"Where?" Ashley looks around in a panic. "I don't see anything."

The dogs go berserk, alternately barking at the—whatever it is—or fleeing, knocking over anything that gets in their way. A chihuahua appears to dislike the damn thing as much as I do and helps me chase it, as do a pair of cats.

Ashley runs around corralling the animals back into their kennels while I pursue the goblin up and down the hall connecting the adoption center to the veterinary area. It leads me into the back rooms where they do the operations. More kennels there are all open, though the animals in them haven't gone anywhere, likely too medicated from recent surgery to bother moving.

Not wanting them to get hurt, I stop chasing the tiny gargoyle long enough to secure the cages.

A sharp, stabbing pain hits me in the left butt cheek.

"Yow!" I yell, grabbing the spot, and jerking a syringe out.

It's impossible for me to tell if it had been empty or its contents are now in my backside. Fortunately, I am reasonably confident that drugs won't do anything to me. Even if the little bastard hit me with the 'bad' stuff they use to put animals to sleep, I'm going to laugh it off. It hovers by the door, pointing at me and making this raspy, hissing laughter.

I whip the syringe at it like a throwing knife. Of course, having zero practice at throwing weapons of any kind, I miss... but the syringe shatters on impact with the wall. The creature looks startled for a moment, then gives me the finger.

"Ooh! You little..."

It laughs and races out of the room.

To avoid trampling an army of cats and tiny dogs, I fly after it. The thing looks back over its shoulder at me, screaming in panic when it realizes I'm gaining on it rather fast. It careens into the adoption center, heading for a space full of secluded benches. It's kinda like booth seating at a restaurant, only without the tables. Probably where people can spend some time with a prospective pet before deciding to adopt it.

Since I can fly, the creature's attempt to trip me up by weaving in and out of those areas back and forth over a counter in the middle of the room doesn't work. Papers and small objects go flying off the counter from the speed with which I zigzag after this damn thing. Its sense of fear speaks to some dark part of me that I didn't notice before, the vampiric predator that's still part of my new psyche, despite being Innocent.

Maybe I really am part cat since a small, annoying thing zipping around is filling me with the urge to bite and claw the hell out of it.

It careens back into the hall and swerves into the room where I found Ashley. She's in the middle of mopping up the poop-splosion. The creature flies headfirst into her back, shoving her off her feet so she crashes down screaming right on top of the mound of animal feces she gathered. Fortunately, her chest hit the horror and not her face. Her open mouth only encountered hard floor.

Grr. This goddamned thing.

I pour on more speed, trying to grab the infuriating creature out of midair. It swerves downward and darts left, making a wrong turn into another dog kennel where it flattens itself against the inside wall, flashing a terrified googly-eyed face at me.

Its fear doesn't sway me.

Claws out, I dive headlong at it.

… and the son of a bitch thing evaporates in a cloud of greasy, black smoke.

I crash into the wall in a tangle of limbs, but no bones break.

Wham.

The kennel shudders from the force with which the cage door slams, trapping me inside.

He, it, or whatever, lands by the door, pointing at me and laughing. I uncurl from the ungainly heap I crash landed in, sitting on the floor and staring between my knees at the little monster. Really? This thing expects it's going to trap me? The thing keeps laughing at me, no doubt having watched Ashley kick at the cage door for hours.

I smirk, raise my foot, and stomp the bars near the latch. The metal bends under my sneaker, emitting a brief camera-flash of yellow light. My stomp hits hard enough to rip the entire door off the kennel and send it skittering across the room. The creature goes wide-eyed, still pointing at me, but it's stopped laughing, mouth hanging agape.

It's apparently too stunned at witnessing me rip the cage open that it doesn't even move when I lunge at it. The little monster emits a faint gurgle of alarm as I grab it by the neck and lift it off the ground so it's eye level to me. Feels like I'm holding one of those furless cats. This thing's wrinkly black skin reminds me of touching a leather biker jacket that's been sitting in the sun for a while.

"Where did you come from?"

It raspberries me.

I squeeze its neck until the eyeballs start to swell out of their sockets. It claws at my wrist, slicing my skin open... but the small wounds heal within seconds. Yeah it hurts like hell, but I've experienced worse—like that twisted Sybarite artist bitch ramming a shaft of rebar into my chest.

"Where. Did. You. Come From?" I relax my grip.

"Gate," rasps the critter.

"Go back where you came from."

It shakes its head. "Can't. Called here. Must obey."

"Where is the gate?"

"You know."

I squeeze it again. "If I knew, I wouldn't be asking you."

It flails at me, kicking, clawing, and whacking at my arm with its wings. "Basement. House."

"My house?"

It nods.

"You say you can't go back, but I think you're lying. What happens if I stuff you through the gate physically?"

"Umm, Sarah?" asks Ashley. "What are you talking to?"

I glance left at her, horrified by the giant brown spot on her chest. Fortunately, it appears that her vet tech smock absorbed the worst of it. "I'm holding the—"

A torrent of painfully hot green slime sprays out of the thing's mouth, mostly hitting me in the face. It smells—and tastes—like sulphurous rotten eggs. The creature laughs at me. Overcome by disgust and anger, I jam my claws into the tiny chest.

It emits a polyphonic wail of pain, like four or five little demonic dolls screaming at once. Burning pain makes me yank my fingers out of its body and wave my hand around gasping and muttering 'ow' over and over a few times.

Ashley screams.

"Now what?" I glance at her again, and spit slime. "This is horrendously disgusting."

"I have poop all over me."

I cringe at the hot slime dribbling down my front. "I'm not sure that's worse than this."

"Umm, okay, maybe. There's a shower in back."

"Cool. I think I'm going to use it before I throw up."

She quirks an eyebrow at me. "*Can* you throw up?"

"Good question." I furrow my eyebrows at her. "Why did you scream?"

"There's a little demon monster thing in your hand. It just appeared out of thin air."

I glance at the critter still dangling from my grip, my arm straight out in front of me. "Yeah. So you can see it now?"

"Yeah. Is it dead?"

"I think so." I shake it, making the body flop around like a rubber chicken. "Feels dead."

She walks over. My eyes water from the combined stink of rotting eggs and dog poo. "Wow. Eww. What the heck is it?"

"I have no idea. But I think I know some people who might." I drop the critter on a nearby cart with an unceremonious *clank*. "Where's that shower?"

Ashley pulls her smock off over her head without unzipping it. Doesn't look like much poop made it to her clothing underneath. "Follow me."

9

MINOR DEMONS

I didn't even bother taking my clothes off for the shower... except for my shoes and socks since they didn't get any foul green goo on them.

Ashley and I spend about two hours cleaning up the vet office after I'm de-slimed. Of course, I'm running around barefoot, but I don't care that much. Better than wet sneakers. Once we have all the animals back where they belong and all the other stuff picked up, wiped down, and mopped, we leave. It's late, almost midnight by the time we get everything back to rights. Ashley's in a surprisingly good mood for having spent hours locked in a small cage, then being shoved into a huge pile of poop. She's so happy the dead creature I'm carrying out the door didn't hurt any of the animals, she doesn't think it matters what it did to her.

It matters to me, though. This little bastard messed with my two best friends. Probably why I surrendered to anger and killed it. Well, that and it's not really a person.

She hops in her Jetta to drive home while I fly to Downtown Seattle, heading for The Brass Tap, the hipster bar where the members of the Aurora Aurea hang out. My clothes have mostly dried out by the time I land, at least enough that I can put my sneakers back on without fear of water dripping out of my jeans and soaking them.

The tiny corpse I'm carrying stinks like rotten eggs even though it's only been dead for a few hours. It isn't decomposing visibly, which gets me wondering *if* it will. Call me nuts, but I have a suspicion this thing might not follow the laws of conventional biology.

I head inside, again cringing at the ridiculous amount of brass everywhere. Yeah, okay, the place has the word 'brass' in its name, but they still take it a little too far. Feels like I've gone through a reality warp into steampunk Victorian London... with avocado toast and beard cream.

Darren Anderson, the mystic from the Aurora Aurea, is sitting at the same corner table I met him at last time, along with his friends Landon and Callum. They have a bunch of fat, old books spread out in front of them and appear to be discussing something complicated over beers and buffalo bites.

I walk up and stand by their table, the creature dangling at my side. I've gotta look like some poor lost orphan with a bizarre dolly hanging from my fingers based on the looks they give me.

"We didn't do it," says Callum.

I toss the creature on the table. It lands with a *splut* like a slab of raw pot roast. "Yeah, figured that already. Can you tell me what this thing is?"

"Fascinating," half-whispers Landon while leaning forward and nudging it with a pen.

Darren cringes from the smell, but also appears intrigued.

"Do be careful, please?" Callum pulls the basket of buffalo bites away from the creature.

I grab a chair from the adjacent freestanding table and sit at the end of their booth. While they study the creature, poking and prodding at its face and wounds, I give the buffalo bites the evil eye. Never again.

Some things, I just should not eat now.

Sure, I can enjoy the taste of food still, but that whole 'passes through unchanged' deal makes spicy things a no-no. Those damn nuggets of agony made me scream so loud my dad thought I was under attack in the bathroom. Felt like I'd eaten coals from Hell's furnace.

Anyway.

A few minutes later, a waitress walks over. "Hi, hon, can I get you —oh ack! What is that thing?"

"Silicone doll," says Darren without missing a beat. "Movie prop."

"Oh wow." The waitress leans in for a closer look. "That's amazing work. Looks so real."

"Thank you." He smiles and resumes examining the creature.

She looks at me. "Can I get you something to munch on, hon?"

I'm half tempted to say 'yeah, let me see your arm' but I shake my head. "No thanks, I'm not hungry at the moment. Just helped a friend clean up something kinda gross."

"No problem." She smiles at me, ogles the little creature a bit longer, and whisks off to another table.

Landon pulls one of the giant books closer and opens it, flipping page after page containing handwritten text and illustrations of various creatures. It kinda looks like one of Dad's roleplaying game manuals full of monsters. He finds a sketch that somewhat resembles the thing and shows it to the other two. Darren rubs his chin.

Not even really looking at it, Callum says, "Page 284."

The other two stare at him. After a moment, Landon grabs a thick wad of pages, opening the book straight to the indicated number. Whoa. Neat trick. Even neater trick, the drawing on that page looks exactly like the critter when it had been pointing at me and laughing.

All three of them take the book in turn, studying the page and pushing it to the next man. Finally, Darren turns the book so I can see it—not that I can read whatever language it's written in—Latin?

"That is an imp," says Darren. "Rather impressive you managed to kill one. They're usually invisible unless they want to be seen. The little blighters aren't terribly tough or powerful. It's more an achievement that you *found* it than slew it."

"Slew? Really? People still use that word?" I blink.

Landon smiles. "Indeed."

"My friend couldn't see it until after I killed it. I chased it around for a while. No idea if it wanted me to see it or if I could see it anyway. Seemed scared of me at one point, but it might have been trying to trick me." I explain what happened at the vet clinic.

Landon takes the book again, rubbing his greying goatee while reading. "Imps are a form of minor demon. They can turn invisible at will, though I wouldn't be surprised if your unique talents let you see them. Normal people can't unless the imp wants to show itself."

"They possess a host of minor magical abilities," says Callum. "Which they usually use in the furtherance of mischief. Imps *generally* aren't trying to hurt or kill, though their pranks are often dangerous."

Darren nods. "These creatures would much rather have someone around to torment, so they aren't usually intent on murder. However, if it so happens they kill someone, they also aren't too bothered by it. They regard injury and pain as hilarious."

I groan. "It nearly killed people at this party I went to. Locked the doors, set off the fire alarm."

The guys wince.

"Their activities ramp up the longer they're around." Landon pokes the critter, making the body undulate like a giant gummy bear... or gummy demon.

"Good thing I killed it when I did then." I smile.

"Hardly." Callum offers a placating smile. "The problem here is that imps are never alone. Only the person who summoned them is safe from their mischief... unless the bargain is broken. Then, they are free to sow chaos wherever they care to—and extract their payment from whoever summoned them."

Uh oh. I sit up. "Umm, payment?"

"What else? Souls," says Landon.

"Alas, he's right." Callum pops a buffalo bite into his mouth.

Shit. If my sisters really did somehow manage to summon these imps, we have a big problem. "Assuming that I want to prevent someone's soul from being devoured, what can I do?"

"Don't worry too much." Darren smiles. "Imps are extremely weak. They really can't claim souls too easily. Any arcanist capable of summoning them should be able to defend themselves against their attack. They're the rats of the demonic world."

"Let's say in theory a kid summoned them by accident." I catch myself fidgeting with a fork and put it down, clutching my hands in my lap to keep them still. "How much risk are they in?"

"Oh, well, in that case, a child wouldn't be able to effectively fight them off." Darren leans toward me. "But an adult—or you especially— shouldn't have any problems. No need getting yourself too worked up. These things are far more annoying than they are deadly."

"Would you mind if we kept this one?" asks Landon. "I don't imagine you have much need of its remains, and even if you did, you're quite likely to have a ready supply. Where there's one imp, there are forty."

I bury my face in my hands and grumble. "Knock yourself out. I don't want it. So how exactly am I supposed to send them back or close the gate?"

"Depends," says Callum. "What tradition was used?"

"Huh?" I look up at him.

"There are at least thirteen schools of mysticism that possess the capacity to summon imps. The process for reversing the ritual would vary accordingly."

Was that even English? "Umm. I have no idea."

Landon traces his finger back and forth over the book with the imp sketch. "I suggest you try to find out. We cannot offer you any useful advice until we know the tradition involved."

"He's right." Callum looks up from what he's been reading this whole time and makes eye contact with me. "Attempting to invoke a counterspell from, say, Thelemic traditions against a ritual from Qabalah would make the situation many times worse."

Darren winces.

"Right." I stand. "Guess I'll go try to figure that out. I'm pretty sure the summoner has no idea what they did. If I send you some pictures of their notes, will that help?"

The men nod.

"Should." Darren offers the chicken basket. "Care for a bite?"

I wave him off. "No thanks. They did bad, bad, evil things to me last time. I should really go try and find more information about how 'the summoner' did this."

"All right." He sets the basket down and looks at Landon. "Do take that creature off the table. It smells ghastly."

"Thanks, guys." I wave at them, then hurry for the door.

Great. My kid sisters summoned demons.

Shaking my head, I slip outside into a dark alley and leap into the air.

ONLY MESSING AROUND

I return to a quiet home full of sleeping people unaware of the mess brewing in Cottage Lake.

Out of habit, I kick my shoes off by the front door, then search the house as quietly as possible, starting with Sam's closet. It's normal and empty; the boy's safe in bed. My sisters are both sound asleep, though Sophia appears to be having a bad dream. I hover by her bed, whispering comforting things to her until she calms down.

Their closets are also unremarkable from a paranormal standpoint, though the amount of crap Sierra's stuffed in hers could count as a violation of physics. Sophia's obtained psychic abilities or something and evidently, my other sister is a time lord. There's nothing under their beds that looks like a portal or evidence of ritual. I spend a while rummaging their dresser drawers and desks, checking notebooks or papers or any place where they might hide magical notes. No luck. Grr. Guess I wait for the morning and ask them where they got the spell from.

Vampires are apparently *really* good at being quiet and moving around without waking people up. I don't think any legendary creature of the night ever expected that particular talent would be used for snooping on tween-age siblings.

It's highly unlikely that the girls did a ritual in our parents' room, but I still check to be thorough. Once satisfied that the upstairs is demon-free, I search the ground floor. All seems normal there, so I head downstairs to the most obvious place for tweens to conduct a demon-summoning ritual.

No, not a Justin Bieber concert... the basement.

The instant I go down there, a feeling of paranormal otherness hits me in the face as obvious as a slap. It's stronger than it had been on the night before Halloween, quite clearly external in nature at the moment. When the energy had been subtle, I mistook it for an internal notion of doubt that I'd made a big mistake staying with my family. That idea depressed me more than dying did. Anyway, knowing that's not true reassures me like a warm blanket and a hot cup of tea.

Tempting... but I need to figure out what my sisters did.

The larger area of the finished basement is still mostly empty except for the laundry machines, so I check the room at the back end that holds the furnace, hot water heater, and circuit breaker panel. That space is creepy for some strange reason even though nothing— as far as I know—sinister ever happened in our house. Could just be the presence of bare cinder block walls and machinery. Furnaces are kinda scary for some reason. Guess I've seen too many movies where the killer lives in a boiler room. At least it's no longer dark to me in here. That makes it far less unnerving.

Despite the weird energy being noticeably stronger in here, I can't find any sign of a supernatural gate.

Sophia emits a brief scream.

I look up at the ceiling. That sounded like she scared herself awake from a nightmare and tried to stay quiet so the 'rents didn't wake up. Not a good sign she's hiding a bad dream from them, so I hurry upstairs to her room.

Sophia's sitting up in bed, clinging to her giant plush unicorn, her face buried in it to muffle crying. She looks up at the sound of me closing her door. If her expression is any clue, she's merely had a bad dream.

"Hey, just a dream, right?" I sit on the edge of the bed.

She nods. "Yeah. We really messed up. People are getting hurt. I'm sorry!"

"You didn't do it on purpose. Who would really believe something like that would actually work?"

"I guess." She wipes her eyes. "We just thought it was like some cool magic type stuff. Didn't expect it to do anything."

"What exactly did you do?"

She fusses at the unicorn's mane. "The spell was supposed to open a door, but nothing opened. I didn't think it did anything. But stuff's really happening. Guess I really am a dumb blonde."

I hug her. "You're not dumb. Most people don't believe magic is real."

"Yeah, but most people also don't live with vampires. Or have their bodies stolen by buttheads."

"Heh. Okay, true. But you're still not dumb. Where did you do it? I've been all over the house twice and I don't see anything strange."

"In the basement." Her expression goes super guilty again, near to tears. "I tried to get rid of it, but I couldn't."

"There's nothing in the basement."

Sophia sniffles, sets the unicorn plush aside, and scrambles out of bed. "C'mon."

She leads me down the hall to the stairs, across the downstairs to the kitchen, and down the basement steps. As soon as I realize she's heading for Mom's new throw rug that's been sitting against the wall by the washer/dryer, I almost slap myself in the head for being an idiot. Mom didn't put it there... my sisters did.

Sophia pulls the throw rug aside, revealing a circle drawn on the beige carpet in dark blue ink, surrounded by strange marks and symbols. Other than the creepy occult overtones, it doesn't look much scarier than the aftereffects of naughty children getting their hands on markers. Still, I pull out my phone and snap a picture of it.

"It's a washable marker." Sophia rakes her toes at the writing. "But it won't come out. We tried everything. I even tested a small mark before we started and that washed out. We were gonna do it on paper but we didn't have any paper big enough."

I crouch and run my fingers over the area. The back of my hand prickles like super strong static electricity when it's above the middle of the circle, a space about the size of a pizza. "Whoa…"

"Pins and needles," whispers Sophia, also putting her hand into the circle. "I feel it, too. Sierra says I'm making it up."

"You're not making it up."

The squish of small feet compressing carpet fibers approaches behind us. Since I recognize Sierra's scent, I don't bother looking back.

Sophia looks up at me, her emerald green eyes huge with a heartbreaking stare. "What's wrong with me? Am I dead?"

"No…" I pull her into a hug. "When those mystics hijacked your body, it knocked down some kinda wall in your brain. You're like sensitive or something now."

"She's always been sensitive," says Sierra.

Sophia screams into the hand I clamp over her mouth. It's kinda fun to conspire with the littles to keep something secret from the parents. Though, I did already tell Dad about the critters. No reason to wake them up now though.

"Why won't the marker wash out?" Sophia rubs her foot at one of the blue lines.

"Magic, obviously." Sierra rolls her eyes… then yawns. "Why are you guys down here now? Can't this wait for tomorrow?"

"Maybe we just have to break the circle?" asks Sophia.

"Hmm." I extend the claws on my right hand and try scratching at it, but jump back with a startled gasp when sparks fly. My fingertips feel like I stuck them into an electrical outlet and a stink similar to burned hair hangs over the markings. "Eep!"

Sophia scoots away, gawking. "Whoa."

"Maybe I shouldn't mess with it physically…"

"The monster is going after people you don't like." Sierra pokes Sophia in the head.

"No. It's just messing around."

"It is too." Sierra pokes her again.

"Stop!" Sophia grabs the offending finger.

"It got Rachel Cartwright who you can't stand, and Ms. Stein who's a total troll, but no one else at school?" Sierra grins. "I mean, seriously, how much of a bitch does a girl have to be to get *you* not to like her. You like everyone."

Sophia looks down.

"Hey, hang on a sec," I say. "If the imp went after people you guys don't like, why did it attack Ash and Michelle? Do you not like my friends?"

Sophia covers her face in her hands and sobs.

"Uhh, Soph?" I ask.

It takes her a moment to calm down enough to speak. "I'm sorry. It's not that I don't like them. I'm a little jealous sometimes when you hang out with them, but it's okay. They're your friends. I didn't *want* anything to happen to them."

"It knows what you're thinking," says Sierra. "Great, we summoned little demon Santa Claus."

I can't help but snicker. "Okay, so think nice thoughts about my friends. And if you want to hang out with me more, it's okay to ask. Promise I won't bite."

Sierra giggles. "That actually means something now."

"Not funny." Sophia glares at her with tears still rolling out of her eyes.

Aww. She's still upset over me almost dying. "Hey, I'm not gonna go away."

"Bite jokes are hilarious." Sierra drapes herself over me from behind. "Nothing to cry over. Sare got an upgrade."

"I guess." Sophia wipes her face again.

"Gawd," mutters Sierra. "Why do you cry about everything?"

"Why do you swear so much?" I ask.

My living backpack shrugs.

"It's just who you guys are."

"So can you close it?" asks Sierra.

"Dammit Jim, I'm a vampire, not a wizard."

Sophia blinks at me like I spoke Greek while Sierra giggles.

"So…" Sierra drops off my back and drags the rug over to hide the markings. "We are going to get mega grounded if Mom sees this."

Sophia gasps. "We caused people to get hurt! We're gonna get grounded for that, not marking up Mom's rug."

Sierra shakes her head. "Mom would never believe we summoned a creature that hurt people. She *will* believe blue ink on beige carpet. Besides, you've got enough guilt already to count as adequate punishment."

"You don't seem bothered by what's happening." I try to tickle her ribs, but she dodges.

"Oh, I'm totally torn up inside." She grins. "Seriously, I still don't quite believe it myself, and it's not like we did it on purpose. It's like we played Bloody Mary. No one expects that to do anything… just make kids scream and freak out."

Sophia pales, gawking at her. "We are *never* doing that!"

"Okay, you two need to go back to bed. Nothing more to do in here right now." I stand. "Oh, the mystics need to see whatever source you used. Where did you guys get the ritual from?"

Sierra shrugs. "Off the internet. Where else?"

POWER HUNGRY

Friday must be gloomy since I wake up early.

It's 2:01 p.m. when my eyes open. I'm not groggy or sluggish at all, a good indication the weather outside is crappy. Overcast, dark, probably raining pretty hard. Oddly, I have a super strong craving for Hunter. Or, more specifically, what he could be doing for/to me right now. Maybe I lose a little time to a nice, deliberate daydream. Hey, it's not just boys who have needs.

No way would I dare bring an 'appliance' into the house. The *last* thing I need would be for Mom—or worse, Dad—to find that. One of the siblings finding it would be even worse. Ashley had (maybe still has) one somewhere, and her mother found it. I still can't process that the woman had no reaction whatsoever to it. Like, 'yeah, okay, my daughter has a plastic dong. Who doesn't?' That, of course, makes me think of Mom having the same reaction finding one in my room—and her theoretical non-reaction is more embarrassing than imagining her freaking out.

Anyway…

Once I'm done thinking about Hunter and releasing my pent up frustrations, I head out to the basement bathroom for a quick shower, then return to my room and attack my homework. Oh, I already did the calculus I needed to… and aha! Comp sci has some reading, but it only takes me about an hour.

When I finish the reading assignment, I throw some time at *Skyrim*. I'm a little annoyed, actually. No, not at the game itself, it's cool… but it's kind of old now. *Fallout 4* wasn't bad either except for some weird holes in the storyline, but it's about time for something new. I check Steam, but nothing appeals enough to me that I want to ask Dad if I can spend money on it, so I just keep on playing *Skyrim*.

About a quarter to six, my computer goes dark in time with a tremendous *boom* that shakes the walls like someone fired a cannon in the basement. I jump out of my chair screaming, so startled I fly-stick to the ceiling.

Dad shouts a bunch of F-bombs upstairs. He doesn't sound *too* upset. Thankfully, he's got one of those battery backup power supplies on his computer. I think I was about seven when a power outage made him lose two hours of work. I had a full vocabulary of interesting swear words from that day going forward, though I didn't dare repeat any of them until I hit my teens.

I think Sophia's probably going to be ashamed of cursing until she's forty, while Sierra can tell someone F-you in English, Spanish, Finnish, and Russian, thanks to *Call of Duty*.

Dad stomps down the stairs and pokes his head in. "Sarah, did you —oh, you're not here."

"Look up."

He leans back, peering at me. "Umm. Why are you reclining on the ceiling?"

"Is 'because I can' a valid answer?"

"I suppose."

I float down and land on my feet. "That bang scared the crap out of me. Literally jumped out of my seat. What exploded? Oh, shit. I smell smoke."

Dad's eyes widen and he runs off.

I follow him into the utility room.

Our circuit breaker box is on fire—and so is a dead imp attached to it by its fangs.

"Shit. Another one?" I sigh. "Didn't realize they were *this* stupid. That's not what they mean by 'power hungry.'"

Groaning, Dad grabs a small fire extinguisher from nearby—specifically one for electrical fires—fiddles with it, and sprays the panel until the fire goes out. White powder billows everywhere... I'm glad I don't really *need* to breathe. "What the ever loving fudge is this thing?"

I giggle. "Dad, I'm not five. Besides, you yelled that word about fifteen times before you came downstairs."

"You heard that?" He peers at me, both eyebrows up.

"Umm... the Perry's next door heard you."

He coughs to cover his embarrassment. "Yes, well. The power outage startled me. What the hell is this thing? Did you find some strange creature, bring it home, and feed it after midnight?"

"Huh?"

"You haven't seen *Gremlins?*" asks Dad, as shocked as if a Canadian admitted they didn't like hockey.

"I have a feeling you're going to remedy that horrible tragedy."

"Damn right," says Dad.

I laugh. "Actually, I did see it. You made me watch it when I was eight. How can you not remember me waking up every night for a week, screaming?"

"Oh. That was *Gremlins?*" He scratches his head. "Thought you did that after watching *Critters.*"

"Critters?"

"Little furry ball-shaped monsters? Whole bunch of them like stick together and form a big critter boulder that rolls over a dude, leaves just a skeleton on the ground?"

"Nope, sorry. Don't remember that one."

He snaps his fingers. "Gotta fix that. Should re-watch *Gremlins,* too. Now that you're older, you'll appreciate it more. Though, it might be too much for Sophia."

"Ya think?" I poke the dead imp. "Especially with these things running around."

"So that *is* a gremlin?"

"No. It's an imp. A minor demon. Not even as powerful as the ones who work for the IRS."

He laughs. "So, are they after you?"

"I don't think so. At least, they haven't directly messed with me yet." I sigh. "Dad, I think the girls did it."

"What?" He twists toward me, still holding the fire extinguisher.

"They found something online that looked like 'cool magic to mess around with' and tried it… and apparently, did it correctly. They opened a little gateway and didn't realize it."

He blinks, making a series of faces like he can't decide between wanting to laugh, call me nuts, or be concerned. "So… imps."

"Yep. They're supposedly more annoying than dangerous."

Dad pries the crispy demon off the breaker box. It disintegrates to ashen dust before hitting the floor. "Well, annoying is right. I'm going to have to replace the main breaker and at least two others. We're going to be powerless for a couple hours at least."

"You could just call an electrician."

"I could, yes, but then I won't have the satisfaction of doing everything I can to royally mung it up before caving in to your mother telling me I don't know what I'm doing and ultimately calling the electrician anyway."

"Does it have to come from Mom, or can I save you the trouble now and say you don't know what you're doing?" I smile.

"In theory."

"I could compel you."

"You promised not to mind control your family."

"How about compulsion by guilt instead of vampiric powers?" I make Sophia's pleading face at him.

He sighs. "Fine. You know I can handle fixing this breaker box. It's just removing modules and putting new ones in."

"And when the house is on fire…"

"Yeah, yeah…"

"Or you get shocked and thrown across the room…"

"All right. I promise I'll call the electrician." He kisses me on the forehead. "Really."

I hug him. "Don't get hurt."

Since my computer is dead, I follow him upstairs. It's super gloomy out but not raining. Smells like it had been raining most of the day, though. According to Google, sunset's about five minutes off.

Dad leans over to peer at my cell phone screen, notes the time, and looks at me. "Have you seen your siblings?"

As if on cue, Sam walks in the sliding glass door to the kitchen.

"That's one," says Dad. "Sam, have you seen your sisters today?"

"Only one." He points at me.

I listen for a few seconds. "They're not upstairs."

Dad grabs his cell from the mini office and tries to call Sierra. He walks back to the kitchen shaking his head. "Straight to VM." He attempts calling Sophia, same thing. A vein rises on his forehead.

"Calm down, Dad. They're not ignoring you. Sierra might turn her phone off to avoid you and Mom, but Sophia wouldn't dare."

"Something happened." Dad eyes me with worry. "I didn't notice them come home from school. Figured they went straight to Nicole's."

"I didn't see them leave," says Sam. "Thought they cut school early after the fire alarm went off."

Dad looks at me like this is somehow my fault.

"Relax, Dad. I'm on it."

"You're awfully calm for your sisters both being kidnapped!"

"Dad!" I grab his shoulders and open my mouth, about to declare that they haven't been abducted. But… then again, Eleanor St. Ives is still out there and mad at me. There's an off chance she might disregard the threat of Aurélie's wrath and attack my family, but I'd like to think that merely not giving her Coralie wouldn't be *that* much of an affront. "I'm pretty sure no one kidnapped them. We were talking about closing the gateway last night, and that might've broken whatever contract or agreement came along with their spell. If the imps are free of the girls' control, Soph and Sierra are probably stuck somewhere like Ashley was. And, the fire alarm went off at the school? That's got imp written all over it."

"What happened to Ashley?" Dad tilts his head. "Is she all right?"

"Fine, but an imp locked her in a kennel at the vet place."

"What's an imp?" asks Sam.

"Tiny demon."

"Oh." He nods. "I think there's one at school. Mrs. Ferguson almost died today."

Dad and I blurt "What!?" simultaneously.

"She almost got electrocuted in the gym. And the fire alarm went off. They evacuated everyone outside. We had to stand in the rain. Teachers think a kid pulled the alarm, but they don't know who did it or how they did it without being caught on camera."

"She got electrocuted?" I blurt.

Sam shakes his head. "No. She didn't die. Electrocuted means dead. She got a nasty shock."

Dad rubs his forehead. "Please tell me your sisters didn't set off the alarm and cut school."

"I can't really see that happening. Sierra might daydream about it, but Soph would never go along with it and I doubt Sierra would really do anything that seriously wrong. Let me fly over there and check."

He nods at me. Sam runs off to his bedroom. As Dad starts to call the electrician, I hurry out the back door and jump into the air. While my logical side is pretty sure imps are to blame for my sisters' disappearance, I'm consumed by worry... enough to where I don't realize I forgot my shoes until I'm already cruising over the middle school. A fire engine sits by the main entrance, lights still flashing, and a large maintenance crew is working to clean up the mess caused by the sprinkler system going off.

Wet, frigid grass at my toes startles an *eep* out of me when I land on the lawn. A worker in a grey jumpsuit turns at the noise, almost yells in shock at seeing me come out of nowhere, and gives me a 'what are you doing here?' look. He radiates more confusion than hostility, so I walk up to him.

"Hey, what happened here?"

"Ehh, someone set the fire alarm off a little after one this afternoon. Figure some kid pulled it as a prank... but that normally wouldn't have triggered the sprinkler system. Only heat does... so the FD's been back and forth through the school for hours searching for the hot spot. Finally declared it a false alarm only like an hour ago."

"Oh. That's good."

"Yeah. Sprinklers did almost as much damage as a fire though. Fried computers, televisions, ruined books. The school's gonna be shut down probably until next Wednesday if not longer. If they catch the little bastard who set off the alarm, they're gonna regret it big time."

"Yeah, no kidding. False alarms are not cool. Thanks." I wave at him and start walking toward the entrance, but he lightly grasps my arm.

"Sorry, kid. Can't let you in there. Closed, and you're neither a teacher nor a student. You shouldn't be on the property."

I face him. "My two little sisters go here, and neither one of them came home today."

"That's an issue for the cops. Call the police. I can't let you go roaming around."

"I'm not roaming around." I force my thoughts into his mind. "I'm looking for my sisters. And that's totally okay."

He blinks. "Oh, yeah. Sure, no problem. Just be careful."

"Thanks."

Workers in jumpsuits and firemen swarm the front entrance. I can't mind-zap all of them, and I'm sure they'll try to keep me from going inside. Life isn't a video game… I don't fool one 'guard' and have the entire faction go neutral at once. So, I duck around the side of the building, heading for the back doors. It's been a while, but this is the same school I went to as a kid. The cafeteria has doors straight to the parking lot behind the school. Technically, it's a small atrium between the cafeteria on the left and the gym on the right, but still, it's a way in.

I hurry across soaked grass to the parking lot and jog through icy puddles on the blacktop to the row of six double doors. Empty picnic tables stand to the left, a cluster of big dumpsters on the right. Ignoring both, I grab the first set of doors and pull.

Of course, they're locked.

One by one, I try each set, hoping to find a pair that's unlocked, but no luck. Ahh well. I grab one door and pull until the mechanism snaps with a loud *clank*.

"Help!" shouts a tiny voice.

I freeze, listening.

"Hey! Help me!" calls a tiny voice from the direction of the dumpsters. "Is someone there? I heard you."

It sounds just like Ashley when she'd been in the kennel... supernaturally muted. Oh, son of a bitch. I rush over to the four dumpsters.

"Which one are you in?" I ask.

"Sarah!" shouts Sophia.

The faintest of thumps emanates from the second dumpster, one of the two brown ones intended for trash—as opposed to recyclables.

I grab the lid and shove, but it's stuck. So, I try again with both hands, pushing with my entire body—until the dumpster lifts off the ground, tilting backward. Oh, holy shit that lid is on there good.

"Aaah!" shouts Sophia. "Eww! Don't tilt it."

"Sorry. The lid's stuck."

"I know! Please get me out of here! It stinks so bad!"

Hmm. The lid might be stuck shut, but it's still made out of plastic. I extend my claws and float up so I can reach the top. It takes a bit of doing, but these new razor-sharp nail extensions I've got slice this thick plastic like marshmallow. I make a square hole that I think is big enough for Sophia to fit through, and peel the flap up. Heck, she's so skinny she could probably stuff herself into a Pringles can.

And oof. The smell *is* bad. Egads. I didn't realize cafeteria food fermented.

Trash rustles inside. A bag rolls to the right, exposing Sophia's face with a banana peel draped over her head. She fights her way out of the garbage, struggling to stand on top of the ever-shifting mountain of awfulness. Once she has her footing, she shoves her pink backpack toward me. I grab it, set it on the lid, and reach back into the hole to grasp her arms.

She closes her eyes, hanging limp like a caught fish as I haul her up and out of the dumpster, setting her standing beside it on the ground. I keep holding her wrists so she doesn't clamp onto me while covered in horror. Her pink dress looks like a Jackson Pollack rendered in mustard, ketchup, chocolate milk, soy sauce, and... I don't even want to know what that dark blotch is.

My sister makes a face like she's gonna throw up and squirms to get away from my grip, so I let go. She takes two steps to the side, drops to her knees, and dry heaves a few times, but stops short of vomiting.

"How'd you wind up in there?"

Sophia coughs, reaches up to wipe her face, but stops—not wanting her hand anywhere near her mouth. "Stupid imp stole my backpack during lunch. I chased it all over, and when it threw my bag in the trash, I climbed up like an idiot to get it. It pushed me in and the lid slammed. I couldn't get out. Oh, and my phone's dead."

"Yeah. They did the same thing to Ashley. Killed her phone, I mean."

"Ugh, this is so disgusting." She sits back on her heels, looking herself over. "I think they're angry with me now because I told them to go home."

"Do you know where Sierra is?"

"Umm, no. I haven't seen her all day since we got here. She has gym right before lunch, and she wasn't at lunch."

"Maybe they stole her clothes while she was in the shower and she's hiding."

"Nah." Sophia shakes her head. "Sierra would be too angry to care and just go home naked... like you did."

I laugh.

Sophia stands. "If I take a shower and wrap myself in a towel, will you carry me home? I'm gonna throw up if I don't get out of this filthy dress like right now. It's sticky *everywhere*."

"Yeah sure."

"Cool." She runs inside, spaghetti and tomato sauce flying out of her hair.

Ugh.

I follow her across the gym and into the girls' locker area. She sets her backpack on a bench, then strips out of her fetid clothes, nearly throwing up again at noticing some of the stains soaked through to her skin. Gagging, she dashes into the shower. A moment later, the hiss of running water starts up.

While I want to go look for Sierra, it doesn't feel right leaving Sophia here alone and defenseless. After about fifteen minutes, she emerges from the shower area covered from armpit to shins in a white towel emblazoned with the school logo. Her skin's gone a little red from the heat, but she looks *much* happier. Such a heavy 'soap' fragrance surrounds her that it waters my eyes. Still, beats what she smelled like before—utterly rancid. Considering she's willing to go outside wearing only a towel, she probably feels the same way about the stink.

She walks past the pile of stained clothes and stands in front of me. "Okay. Let's go."

"What about your stuff?"

"They're soaked in ick. Burn them."

"Aww, it's nothing a cycle in the wash won't fix."

She stares at me.

"Okay, a *few* cycles in the wash."

Sophia makes this little diva wave. "If *you* wanna touch them, go right ahead."

"Wait here a sec."

She sighs.

I run across the cafeteria to the kitchen and grab a plastic trash bag. Sophia stops pacing around when I return, standing there fidgeting while I stuff her clothes in the bag. The pink backpack is pretty nasty, too, but it's made out of waterproof plastic so I send her back into the shower to give it a quick rinse.

"Where are your shoes?" asks Sophia, upon emerging with the dripping pack.

"Home. Dad mentioned you guys went missing and I ran out the door so fast I forgot them. Worried about you."

She hugs me. "Gonna be smelling that dumpster for the rest of my whole life. I really don't like imps."

"I'm starting to agree with you."

"Really, we didn't mean to summon them. Just open a doorway. I thought it was like something *we* could use. Like to teleport around. I'm really sorry for summoning demons."

"C'mon. Let's find your sister. Do you think she's still here at the school?"

"Probably."

She holds my hand with her left, keeping her towel tight to her chest with her other hand. "If anyone I know sees me walking around with just a towel on, you will make them forget."

"I promise."

"Why is there water on the floor?"

"Sprinklers went off."

She cringes. "I'm in so much trouble…"

"You didn't set off the sprinklers."

"No, but the imps did, and they're here because I messed up."

I stop near the doors out of the cafeteria and smirk at her. "If you confess to your teachers that you summoned minor demons and they set off the fire alarm, you won't get detention, you'll get an appointment with a psychiatrist. Don't feel guilty about lying. People can't handle this truth."

She bites her lip. "Okay. That makes sense."

We creep around puddles into the hall outside the cafeteria. Voices murmur in the distance from the work crew cleaning up after the sprinkler deluge. Sophia starts trembling.

"What?" I whisper.

"People are here. I just know the imps are gonna steal my towel." She goes scarlet in the face at the mere thought of it.

"You're a little too big to carry, but if it makes you feel better, I'll hold on to you."

She appears to be considering it for a moment, then shakes her head. "Nah. It's okay. Just keep them off me."

I gaze down a hallway full of lockers at various classrooms.

Shadows move in the atrium at the far end where two guys squeegee the floor with giant versions of those things people use on windshields at gas stations, shoving the water toward the door. Soft bumping comes from somewhere up ahead on the right.

"Sierra?" I ask, not quite loud enough that the workers will hear me.

The bumping picks up speed. It's damn quiet, but I imagine Sierra trapped inside a locker, banging and fighting the door with all her strength.

"Ooh. Locker!" says Sophia. "My gym uniform is in there!"

She runs off ahead of me. I chase her about three-quarters of the way down the hall until she stops at a locker on the left, opens the padlock, then rummages out a pair of gym shorts and a white T-shirt with the school logo on it. She steps into the shorts and pulls them up under the towel before dropping it and hurrying into the shirt. Dressed, she sighs in relief before putting her socks and sneakers on.

"Sierra?" I ask.

Banging continues from further down. The school assigns lockers based on grade level, which puts Sierra's in the next section, two classrooms' distance farther down the hall. It doesn't take me long to home in on the sound of enough swear words to get my sister grounded until she's my age. I grab the combination lock and peer through the little vent slats at Sierra's hazel eyes. She looks furious, but also like she's been crying. Pretty sure I know why—more than simply being trapped in a locker.

"People weren't ignoring you. They can't hear you. There's magic making you quiet."

"Please get me the hell out of here!" shouts Sierra. "I can't hold it anymore!"

"What's the combo?"

"14-11-20."

I dial the combo in, pop the lock, and pull at the latch. It takes way more strength than I would've had as a normal girl to open it, but not enough to bend the metal. A bright yellow flash bursts away from the door as it swings open.

Sierra shoves the door aside, stumbles over a pile of collapsing books into the hallway, and runs off, disappearing into a bathroom about thirty feet away. I repack her stuff in the locker, but don't secure the padlock yet. Not sure if she needs anything in there for homework.

A few minutes later, Sierra trudges out of the bathroom, walks up to me, and grabs on. "You ever get so angry you cried?"

"No... can't say I have." I rub her back and give her shoulder squeeze. "You okay?"

"Yeah. Just angry. I kept screaming for help whenever someone went by, but they all ignored me."

"I didn't hear you at all, even standing right here." Sophia flails her arms. "The school's like super quiet now. I *still* couldn't hear you."

I pull out my phone and poke the contact entry for Dad. "You guys know how sensitive my ears are, and even I barely found you."

"Sarah," says Dad. "What's going on?"

"Found them stuck at school. Imps. They're both okay, but a little upset. We need to get out of here before someone catches us and we get in trouble, so I'll give you all the details when we're home."

He exhales hard. In the background, Mom starts machine-gunning him with questions about the girls.

"You want me to fly them home, or would you rather come pick them up?"

"I'll be there as soon as it takes me to drive," says Dad. "Going out the door right now."

Sierra grabs a few books and notebooks from her locker, stuffing them in her backpack.

"We'll be outside waiting. The girls are okay."

"No, we're really not," says Sierra. "Those things are going to keep coming after us."

I hang up. "C'mon. Let's get outside before the workers see us."

Sophia tries to look determined and comes off totally adorable. "We can get rid of them. It's just gonna take a while. I tried to end the spell in math this morning 'cause Rachel fell down the stairs."

"I spent—" Sierra looks at me. "What time is it?"

"6:12 according to my phone."

She points at Sophia. "I spent six hours stuffed in my locker because you tried to break the spell alone?"

"It locked me in the dumpster for six hours. My clothes got soaked in disgusting crap! That's why I'm wearing my gym uniform." Sophia flaps her arms. "At least you stayed clean."

"Eww," says Sierra.

"Yeah. Sorry for trying to break the spell alone but I was scared. I didn't want it to hurt Rachel. She almost broke her arm and her face was all bloody from a nosebleed. She smacked it on the floor at the bottom."

"Oh, gah... did she break her nose?" I ask.

Sophia shrugs. "They sent her back to class in like twenty minutes, so I don't think so."

"Don't do that again." Sierra grabs her. "If you wanna break the spell, tell me and we do it together."

Sophia nods. "Okay."

"What the hell is wrong with us?" Sierra sighs. "I'm talking about spells like they're real."

"Did you or did you not wind up stuck in a locker all day?" I ask.

"Anyone could've pushed me from behind, slammed the door, and locked me in." She folds her arms.

"How many of your classmates are capable of casting a silencing spell on the locker after doing so?"

"You and your logic." Sierra sticks her tongue out at me.

I take my sisters' hands and walk them down the hall, across the cafeteria, and out the back door to avoid being seen by the work crew. The fire truck is gone by the time we reach the front, and no one pays us much attention standing around at the far end of the wide sidewalk where parents usually pick kids up after class.

A few minutes later, Dad pulls up in the Yukon. I toss the trash bag of putrid clothing as well as Sophia's backpack in the cargo area, then climb in up front. Both girls show Dad their dead iPhones, drained entirely of battery power as proof they hadn't ignored him and Mom trying to call them. He seems to take the explanation of supernatural activity in stride, clearly not happy that the girls wound up trapped all day, but there's little point to becoming upset about it at this point. He's also relieved that nothing *bad* (like an abduction) happened to them.

Pretty sure that making us all angry at each other is exactly what the imps are hoping for... to mess with us.

I examine my fingernails.

Until those mystics come up with a way to close that gate, it looks like I'll need to go hunting.

At least the kids' school will be closed for a few days. That will at least let the littles stay close to home and make it easier to watch over them.

I hope.

LUCKY

I arrive at Computer Science class really late, only twenty minutes left in a one-hour class.

Fortunately, the professor, Olive Garcia, accepts my excuse of missing tween-aged sisters without my needing to use mental powers on her. Once the official class period ends, I have a one-hour gap before my second intro calculus class for the week, so I use that time to sit with Professor Garcia as she gives me a quick, condensed version of the material I missed.

She asks about my sisters, so I relay a slightly watered down version that a bully threw them into a dumpster at the school during a fire sprinkler incident and they couldn't get out on their own. I claim my parents both freaked out thinking they might've been kidnapped and ran around in a panic until the girls turned up safe.

Anyway, Professor Garcia is rather laid back and decides not to ding me for an absence. School policy states that being more than ten minutes late counts as an entirely missed class, but the period today had been fairly light. I manage to catch up the work with time to spare before calculus.

Dr. Mercer, my math professor, is a slow talker. Without fail, her classes always run twenty minutes or more over time. It's beyond tempting to give her a mental prod to increase her verbal speed, but I think people would legit think she'd been kidnapped and replaced with an alien if I did that.

I'm one of the few people in the room who doesn't sit through calculus with the 'I'm only here because it's required' glower, and because of that, she seems to like me. The woman's on a roll tonight. We only go overtime by fourteen minutes.

When she finally says goodnight, I sling my backpack over one shoulder and join the stampede of students rushing for the doors. Once outside, I hurry to the cover of darkness by the parking deck. A gurgle in my stomach changes my plans from going straight home to diverting for a snack.

To be on the safe side, I've gotten into the habit of not feeding near school. In fact, I try to vary location around the city as much as I can. Not that I'm going to run out of people to feed from in a place like Seattle, nor am I leaving mangled bodies in my wake, but better safe than on YouTube again. A naked run out of the morgue is all the blurry, unrecognizable celebrity I'll ever want. I am *so* thankful those security cameras have crappy resolution and my face wasn't recognizable on that video.

I land in an alley off Union Street, a few blocks from the Seattle Art Museum, and wander out into the sidewalk looking for someone I can borrow for a few minutes. It's not long before a thirty-something guy in business attire comes power-walking in my direction with a look of mission in his eye. He's alone and no one seems to be paying attention to the guy. Hopefully, whatever he's in a hurry to get to won't mind a five minute delay.

He stops short when I step in front of him. For an instant, he appears ready to scream at me, but instead blinks, like he's not entirely sure what to make of me.

"Hi," I say, dive into his head... and almost throw up.

Normally, when I'm about to feed, I insert a mental command that blanks the person out so they stand there loopy and docile. This process doesn't involve any sort of mind reading as it's normally a one-way transmission. But if someone's got a really strong thought rattling around in their forebrain, I can't help but see it clear as day. Picture someone stuck at a boring job all day long, dying to get home so they can play video games. All day, they're thinking of video games and just *can't wait*.

That's how this guy is… only he's not desperate to get home for gaming.

His head is full of sick thoughts about what he wants to do to his stepdaughter. I mentally cringe away as fast as I can react to the images there, but it's enough to tell me the girl's younger than Sophia. Apparently, his wife is going somewhere tonight, so he's going to be home alone with the girl and intends to take full advantage.

I grab the guy by his suit jacket and drag him into the alley, swing him around, and ram him into the building, glaring into his eyes. The brain stun I hit him with has a muting effect on the slideshow of depravity playing out in his forebrain. It's difficult for me to tell memory apart from fantasies, but still. He's definitely abused that kid to some degree. Oh, that poor girl. Sierra was right… it *is* possible to get so angry I cry. Though, I'm heartbroken for that kid, too.

My tears are not purely liquid anger.

Doing my best to ignore the worst of the memories, I bore into his consciousness. His stepdaughter is only eight. He married her mother mostly so he could gain access to the girl, and tonight, he's planning to take things farther than he's gone before, thinking she's ready for more than 'simple touching' and posing for pictures.

Ugh. I let go of his jacket. I don't want to touch this piece of shit, much less drink his blood. The mere thought of feeding from this creep makes me sick to my stomach. I sprout claws, inches from slashing his throat out, but stop myself.

No… I'm not… I can't. Despite what he's going to do to that child, I can't just kill him. That's not who I am. Murdering this scumbag will haunt me for the rest of my life. Maybe I'd feel like I did a good deed for the first thirty seconds, but killing is still killing. Scott doesn't count. He was already dead when I lit his ass on fire. Burning that Jeep was no different from an undertaker cremating a corpse.

This guy…

I dive into his head again, implanting a command that he really wants to go to the nearest police station and show them the illegal photos he's got on his phone of the girl, plus tell them what he did to her... and what he wants to do to her tonight. And, whenever the cops get around to letting him use a phone, he's going to call his wife and confess to her.

Oh, shit. I think he suspects the wife is onto him... and she's either ignoring it or really hasn't noticed. Dammit. I grab his wallet and copy the address from his driver's license into a note file on my phone. They're in Federal Way...

It takes an amazing amount of self-control for me not to punch this guy or break a bone. I do, however, compel him to record a video right here in the alley where he confesses to molesting his stepdaughter and intending to 'go all the way' tonight. Yeah. I gotta. I make him upload the video to his Facebook wall, then send him off to the police.

Too sick to think about blood, I jump into the air and fly toward Federal Way.

Tears stream out of my eyes, blasted by the wind over the sides of my face. I can't help but think about what Mom said when she worried that Sophia acting weird might have been due to someone touching her. I'm sure Mom will be relieved to learn she'd only summoned a plague of minor demons.

The more I try not to think about those sick memories in that guy's head, the more they haunt me... especially the 'please stop' look on that poor girl's face. I flash between fury and sorrow, close to turning around and changing my mind about killing the guy. Someone told me once that like five out of six girls are sexually abused before adulthood. I feel so damn lucky that I made it to eighteen without having anything worse than the occasional random butt pat happen to me in public. Sure, I'd been stared at, whistled at, and so on. Hell, I had a grown man at the mall say 'nice ass' to me when I was thirteen.

How messed up is that? I was murdered at eighteen and I feel lucky.

No one ever did anything to me like what that man did to his stepdaughter. I can't stop thinking about that pitiful look on her face, and burst into tears.

Again, I come close to turning around in a moment of anger.

What the hell is wrong with people?

No... no... I can't murder him. Even a piece of shit like that. Glim would, but if I told him about it and he did, then I'd still feel guilty for causing the death. Maybe forcing him to confess would be the same thing if some other convict breaks this dude's neck in prison. Though, it's possible he might've been caught eventually anyway without my interfering... but who knows how much damage he'd have done to that girl by that point?

My conversation with Professor Heath regarding ethics comes back to me. That makes me start wondering if what I just did to that guy crossed some line. If I randomly stumble into someone's head and find out that they've committed—or are about to commit—a serious crime, is it unethical to act on that knowledge? Is it less ethical *not* to? I shudder at the thought of what would've happened tonight had I not randomly decided to land at that particular spot of city. That poor kid is already facing some issues, but tonight would've definitely killed her inside if he'd done everything he'd been thinking about.

I turn around... and zoom for about twenty seconds before I stop myself.

Wait, no... can't kill the guy. That's not me.

Doesn't mean I can't daydream about it though.

With a sigh, I resume flying toward Federal Way.

Yeah, I gotta do something. A piece of shit like that? Definitely. Maybe if someone was merely intending to embezzle money from their job, I could say 'not my problem' and walk away, but a killer, rapist, or kid-toucher? Hell no am I capable of walking away. I don't even care if it's unethical. Screw his rights to private thoughts. What about that girl's right to not having her childhood stolen?

I'm not gonna kill him. If—dammit why am I even thinking this—but if anyone did that to Sophia or Sierra... or Sam, damn straight I'd rip their head right off. And, how many people have I fed from since my Transference? How many of them had been molesters, or killers, or thieves? Could this guy possibly be the first one I ran into? Derp-slapping them so I can feed doesn't go deep into their heads. This guy was super obsessed with that girl, probably had been thinking about her all damn day, the notion of what he wanted to do practically leaked out of his eyeballs. I couldn't help but get blasted by it the instant I established contact with his thoughts.

Other people I've fed from probably had dark secrets, but they'd been buried. Should I start deep-scanning everyone I feed from? If I let a murderer walk away without realizing it, and they kill someone, is that on me?

Ugh. I can't play vampire thought police. I'd never have time to do anything else, and I'd probably want to throw myself into the sun after a few months of seeing everyone's darkness.

I'm half-tempted to find Aurélie and ask her to make *me* forget seeing that girl in this guy's mind. How in the hell do the cops who investigate this crap cope with it? I caught fleeting glimpses here and there and I just want to go home and curl up in a ball and cry for that poor kid. Imagine having to look at horrible shit like that day in and day out as your job.

I shudder, and gain new respect for cops.

My GPS app leads me to the home in Federal Way. I drop out of the air on their lawn and jog to the front porch. A moment after I ring the doorbell, a dark-haired woman in her later thirties answers. Since she doesn't appear upset, I assume she hasn't seen his Facebook post yet.

"Hi." I say. Since it's impossible to explain this situation in any way that makes sense to someone who doesn't believe vampires and mind-reading exist, I simply plunge into the woman's head without further ado.

Her eyes flutter rapidly in response to her brain stalling.

The daughter, Avery, tried to confide that her new daddy made her undress and pose for pictures, then touched her, made her touch him back... but the woman rationalized it off as the girl 'acting out' in response to them marrying after only six months of dating. She thinks

Avery always disliked the guy, and is probably making it up to get rid of him. I don't doubt that the girl always disliked him. Kids have a sense about people. Sadly, this woman doesn't want to lose a man she thinks genuinely loves her.

Ugh.

I about scream in frustration. Dammit! Listen to your kid!

At least she's not actively cruel to the girl, just desperate for love and lying to herself. I erase that doubt, implant the knowledge that the man is a dire threat to her daughter, and make her believe what the child tried to tell her. I also drop in a strong urge to go apologize to Avery for dismissing her claims.

A cell phone inside the house erupts in a flurry of messenger notifications. Aha. Mutual friends probably saw the video and are freaking out in chat.

Good.

"Go inside. Your daughter needs you." I start to walk off, but turn back to her. "Oh, and get a divorce."

She stands there dumbfounded, lost to the mental fog.

I walk off in a huff, still not quite sure of my decision *not* to kill the guy. A moment after I'm in the air, the woman backs into her home and shuts the door. For a while, I just hang there in space, too emotionally wrecked to commit to doing anything else. It doesn't help my emotional state when a child starts crying inside. However, overhearing the woman promise Avery she won't let that man near her again makes me feel better.

My stomach has gone quiet, no longer demanding food. That's certainly a product of my mood. I really ought to go find someone to eat, even if my appetite is long gone. Dammit. When did I turn into a superhero?

With a sigh, I swing around to face downtown again, and force myself to go look for a meal.

DEADLY GAMES

The next man I ambushed had no icky skeletons in his closet. His blood tasted like buffalo bites. Guess I wanted some after all. At least eating chased away my nausea. And a mental impression of flavor that's not real won't incinerate my nether regions later.

I'm cruising in over my neighborhood when a brilliant blue flash erupts in the distance up ahead with a cannon-like *boom*. Looked like Leota or nearby. The brilliant aurora fades, shrinking down to a fire at the top of a utility pole. A large area around the burning pole has gone dark.

Ugh.

I zoom toward the burning transformer, certain there'll be a charred imp stuck to it. Surprisingly, upon gliding up to the flaming metal canister, I can't find any sign of one, burnt to a cinder or otherwise. I search the area, finding plenty of cars with slashed tires, but no imps.

Dammit. This is getting out of hand. Apparently, the imps have not only become aggressive toward my sisters, they've slipped any sense of control and are causing random chaos regardless of how Sophia or Sierra feel about someone.

"Crap. This isn't good."

I rush home.

The instant my sneakers touch the deck behind our house, Coralie appears out of thin air next to me, still wearing her 1800s black dress.

"Eep!" I shout, jumping back.

"Forgive me for startling you, dear. I have to warn you."

My annoyance evaporates to a shiver of dread. "Umm. Warn me?"

"Something deadly is going to happen to Hunter tonight."

"What?" I jump at her, trying to grab her arms, but stumble right through her, then spin around. "Where? What's going to happen?"

Coralie shakes her head. "I'm sorry, Sarah. I don't know that much detail. It's going to be tonight…" She gets a far-off look in her eyes. "Wait… there is fire. I see a small boy with blonde hair lying on the side of the road. He's covered in blood."

"Ronan?" I ask. "No! Hunter's little brother is only nine… What do I have to do to stop this?"

"I haven't seen enough of the situation to understand how it will come to pass… only that it will happen."

I pull my phone out and try to call Hunter. Of course, it goes right to voicemail. "Argh!"

It's 10:17 p.m. He'd be at Mi Tierra until ten, assuming nothing kept him late. He's going to be driving home from work. *Shit!* "Wait. Why would Ronan be with him at work?"

"I'm unable to answer that."

"Thanks, Alexa."

Coralie tilts her head at me. "Are you feeling well?"

"No, not really. But that was a joke. I gotta go. Thank you!"

She nods.

I chuck my backpack onto the deck and jump into the air again.

THE SPEED WITH WHICH I FLY TO THAT MEXICAN RESTAURANT IS enough to tear a dress right off me.

Luckily, I'm wearing a T-shirt and jeans. The place is in

Woodinvile, which isn't far from where I live in Cottage Lake. Hunter's beige Buick land boat is still in the parking lot. Seeing it there is so much of a relief that I almost fall out of the air.

Hunter and his little brother emerge from the restaurant's back door and head for the car.

I dive toward them, landing close behind them in a sprint. "Hunter! Wait!"

He spins. Ronan whirls to look at me as well.

"Oh, hey." Hunter catches me when I run up to him. "Great to see you. What's up?"

"There's something wrong with the car. Don't drive it."

"Uhh." He scratches his head. "How am I supposed to get home? Are you sure?"

I smile at Ronan, trying to reassure him. "Yeah, call it a hunch."

Hunter raises an eyebrow.

Coralie told me you were going to get into a crash tonight and die... Ronan, too. I choke up at the thought and cling to him. "Please just check."

"Okay, but… we can't just stand here all night." Hunter pats me on the arm, releases the hug, and walks over to the car. "This totally fits with the night I've had."

"What happened?" I ask.

"Hey, Sarah. What's going on?" asks Ronan. "Is the car broken?"

Hunter stops beside the car, peering over the roof at me. "Got a bad case of clumsy tonight. Food kept trying to fall off the tray. Dumped like six entrees. Had to pay for them or I'd have been let go. Couple of other servers had the same issue. Only reason I didn't get fired. Manager thinks someone might have been doing it to us on purpose."

"Damn imps," I mutter.

"I didn't do it." Ronan gives me an adorable wide-eyed innocent face.

"Heh." I ruffle his hair. "You're not an imp. You're way too cute."

He blushes, but grins.

I stand there talking about comic books with him while Hunter crawls all over his car, checking it out. He opens the hood, looks around, closes it, goes inside, then crawls under it.

"Oh, son of a…" grumbles Hunter.

"You found something?" I ask, walking over with Ronan trailing behind me.

"Yeah. Brake line is… chewed on. Fluid is everywhere."

Ronan gasps. "We would'a crashed."

Hunter shimmies out from under the car and stands. "I'm guessing this isn't the work of a homicidal raccoon?"

"No. Imps… minor demons. Probably also why you had the dropsies today."

"Oh, crap," whispers Ronan.

He eyes the car. "So, what did I do to wind up as a featured guest on Imp My Ride?"

I stare at him. "That's not funny! You could've been killed."

Hunter walks around the front end, pulling me into a hug as soon as he's close enough. "But I wasn't. What's the point of being upset over something that didn't happen?"

"Umm…" I let my head loll forward, resting against his shoulder. "I'm having a weird night."

"Something you want to talk about?"

I glance at Ronan, then back to Hunter. *Nothing I want to say in front of him. Went to feed from this guy and as soon as I looked into his head I saw he was on his way home to… do stuff to his little stepdaughter.*

Hunter squeezes me. "What's wrong with people…?"

"That's what I said."

"Right, so the car… shit." Hunter runs a hand up through his hair, his expression pained.

"Are you gonna call the cops?" asks Ronan.

Hunter shakes his head. "And tell them an animal chewed on the brake lines?"

"Oh, right." Ronan kicks at the ground.

"It's okay. I can help you with the tow."

He gawks. "You're strong enough to pull a car?"

"Probably, but... that's not what I mean." I fish my wallet out. "Covering the tow."

"It's fine. You don't have to—"

I cut him off with a kiss, then lean back, shaking my head. *$150 or whatever this is going to cost isn't as painful to me as it would be for you. Please don't make a big deal about it. I insist.*

He emits a resigned sigh.

Hey. Don't feel ashamed. Our financial situations have nothing to do with either one of us, just our parents. There's nothing for you to feel bad about. Technically, my parents are covering the tow since I'm an unemployed slacker.

Hunter laughs. "Okay... okay."

I lean against him while searching via my phone for a twenty-four-hour tow place. Hopefully, Dad won't yell at me *too* much. But better a little yelling than Hunter and Ronan dead. I'd fall to bits and start crying if not for being furious with the imps. What they did to Ashley and Michelle is on the high end of annoying, but *this*?

They've just pissed me off.

BATTLE STATIONS

The tow truck shows up about twenty minutes after I call.

While we waited, Hunter and I talked about school, work, and life in general. He's clearly in a mood over not being able to afford the tow, but at least he's not reacting like I think of him as a charity case. I don't. It's merely a matter of being practical. Besides, he already has to buy replacement brake lines, new fluid, and take the time to put it on the car. At least tomorrow is Saturday and he'll have plenty of time since he doesn't have to be back at work until four in the afternoon.

While the guy is winching the Buick onto the flatbed, my phone goes off with Mom's ringtone.

I swipe to answer. "Hey, Mom."

Kids scream in the background. Someone's banging pots and pans around. Dad is shouting like he's roleplaying a pirate captain going into battle, directing everyone to war.

Mom screams, "Sarah! I need you home right now!"

"Holy shit, Mom. What's all that noise?"

"They're *everywhere!*" She lets out a shriek like someone dumped ice water over her head.

"Okay, I'll"—a heavy slam happens in the background—"be home as fast as I can."

"Hurry!" yells Mom. "Go away you little bastard! Not you, Sarah. I meant the... whatever that thing is."

"Imps. I'll be home soon."

"Dad, look out!" yells Sierra.

My father emits a grunt like he's jumping out of the way of something, then the crash of an entire drawer full of silverware falling to the floor comes over the line.

"Aha! Foul beast. You think I am slow? I shall—"

A hollow *bonk* makes me cringe.

The line drops.

"That doesn't look good, judging from the face you're making," says Hunter.

"It's not. There's a bit of a situation at home. Sounds like World War III going on."

He nods. "If you need to go, it's okay."

"I gotta pay the dude first."

A few minutes later, we all pile into the tow truck and drive to Hunter's house. I deal with the payment once we're there—which the guy wanted before he lowered the car off the truck. That done, I hug Hunter, not wanting to let go. I really need some boyfriend time. If not for these damn imps, I'd have stayed here all night until he went to bed. Alas, the family needs me. So, I slip off into the dark and fly home.

The sounds of battle reach my ears before I land. Not a good sign. Nor is every light in the house being on. I land on the deck and rush inside. Mom's standing on the dining room table swinging a frying pan at an imp flying circles around her. Buzzing like a forty-pound bumblebee comes from the living room.

Dad runs into view chasing another imp with a weed-whacker in his hands and a red necktie around his head like a Rambo headband. The sight of his goofiness kicks me square in the feels, reminding me how lucky I am to have him for a father and not some piece of shit like that guy I ran into earlier.

I just start laugh-crying, unable to hold it in.

The imp he's chasing flies up through the ceiling like a ghost, vanishing in a puff of smoke. Dad sighs, then notices me standing there giggle-sobbing. "Uh oh. I think Sarah's finally cracked."

Clank.

An imp sails past me headfirst, hits the wall with a thump, and bounces away, laughing at Mom.

"Allie, I don't think blunt weapons work on them," says Dad while walking up to me. "Are you okay, hon?"

I grab him and squeeze. "Dad, thank you for being awesome."

He pats me on the back. "While I don't necessarily refute your assessment, I am curious as to what brought it up."

Thuds and rapid footsteps go back and forth upstairs along with Sierra shouting war cries and Sophia screaming. Mom climbs down off the dining room table, spinning in a slow circle while holding her frying pan ready for another strike.

"I ran into this guy while feeding, and"—the living room curtains burst into flames—"Shit!"

"The guy shit?" asks Dad.

"Jonathan!" yells Mom. "The curtains!"

He spins. "Dammit!" Dad tosses me the weed whacker and runs to the hall closet for a fire extinguisher. An imp ducks out from behind the curtains, cackling with glee. I toss the weed eater to Mom and run after it. The little bastard goes down the hall and darts between Dad's legs. I jump up and fly over him, diving at the imp with both arms outstretched, claws extended.

The imp spins with a huge grin, probably expecting to laugh at me crashing into Dad. It emits a panicked squeal at the sight of me pulling a Supergirl heading right for it, then zips to the left. I turn to follow, but not quite fast enough to avoid crashing into the kitchen cabinets sideways. It goes under the table and back down the hall to the dining room, cackling with glee, making a finger-snap at Dad, which sets off the fire extinguisher in his hands, blasting him square in the face. He falls over backward, sputtering. I spring off the cabinets, flying as fast as I can manage inside the house. Again, the imp screams at the sight of me catching up to it with ease. It jumps into flight, racing toward Dad as he picks himself up and starts to hose down the living room curtains with the extinguisher despite having so much white crap on him he looks like the marshmallow guy from *Ghostbusters*.

"Dad, look out!" I yell.

He spins, yelps, and wallops the imp with the extinguisher. The tank hits the creature in the head with a dull *thump*, redirecting its flight path into a crash course with the front door. I'm on it before it can peel itself away, grabbing it by two hands around the neck.

The imp sneezes at me, and my pants drop around my ankles.

Okay, I blush a little, but I keep squeezing its throat.

The imp sneezes again… and my panties drop.

"Gah!" As fast as I can move, I grab my pants and pull them up.

After raspberrying me, the imp darts up over my head and zooms at Mom. She swings the giant frying pan over her head in a two-handed grip like something straight out of *Conan,* walloping the annoying thing square in the face before it can reach her. The *clank* of the pan hitting it and the *thump* of the imp smacking into the floor are near simultaneous.

I secure the button on my jeans. "Oh, I really hate these damn things."

"Ow!" yells Sophia upstairs.

"I got it!" calls Sierra.

"*Ow!*" screams Sophia, louder.

The imp Mom whacked appears stunned, taking its sweet time trying to get up again. She wallops it again, but it looks about as productive as trying to beat a giant gummi bear to death. I hurl myself at it in a flying-devil-cat-from-hell pounce. The imp springs forward at the last second, leaving me with two handfuls of carpet shreds.

"Jonathan, your daughter is tearing up the carpet," says Mom.

"Anxiety? Do you think we should've gotten her a scratching post?"

"Guys," I sigh.

Mom looks up and starts to scream.

I twist sideways to see what scared her—and spot Sophia falling headfirst off the top of the stairs. She's near-cocooned in a jump rope, arms pinned at her sides, about to land on her head. I leap up and catch her before she breaks her neck, then hand her to Mom.

"Be right back."

The imp cackles at us from under the dining room table. Another one at the top of the stairs calls me a 'silly bitch,' then runs out of sight. I dive at the one under the table, chasing it in circles around and around the dining room, gradually inching closer. After three laps, it seems to notice I'm gaining on it and breaks off, heading for the kitchen.

I nearly catch it at the top of the stairs, but crash into the wall when it dodges down to the basement. Dislocated shoulder is a small price to pay… easy enough to ignore. The imp isn't laughing anymore, evidently aware that I can outrun it. It also appears to believe I can kill it—unlike my parents—as it looks scared.

And not the extreme terror the one at the vet place faked either, this is subtle enough to feel genuine. I fly down the stairs, my claws mere inches from its back, pursuing it across the main basement room to the throw rug my sisters used to hide the summoning circle.

Like something out of a Wile E. Coyote cartoon, the imp jumps into the air, hands together, and dives into the floor—vanishing in a flash of blue light. I slam on the proverbial brakes before going face first into the wall, and pull the rug aside. The circle still looks like childish vandalism, but a faint blue light lingers a few seconds in the middle before fading back to ordinary carpet.

"Okay, so they can jump through it whenever they want…"

Sierra screams in pain.

"Damn."

I race up from the basement to the second floor using a mixture of flying and running, following the sound of my sister's whimpering. I find her on the floor in her bedroom, curled up in a ball. A huge kitchen knife lays beside her, and she's bleeding profusely from the left forearm. My heart about stops until I notice she's not cut, but bitten.

Sierra looks up at me, face angry red but also wet with tears. "Kill that fu—"

I put a hand over her mouth. "Mom will still ground you for saying that."

She grabs my hand and pulls it away from her face. "I'm bleeding!"

"Gimme a sec." I take her arm like a corn cob, extend my fangs, and bite the same spot the imp bit. As soon as I want the wound to close, it does. I try extremely hard not to think that my little sister's blood tastes like black cherry syrup. "There."

"Wow, that's cool." She gazes at the healed skin.

"What's going on up there?" yells Mom. "Shit! Jonathan! Kitchen curtains!"

"On it!" yells Dad.

"I got a piece of the bastard." Sierra points under her bed.

I crawl over and pull the spread up. An imp lays on its back, dark black liquid seeping from a stab wound in its chest. The thing is still breathing, but otherwise, appears dead. I grab it around the neck and spike my claws into its chest.

Its eyes snap open as it emits a polyphonic death wail that lasts for six seconds before the creature falls limp.

"That's for biting my sister."

The *fwoosh* of a fire extinguisher goes off downstairs.

Sierra sits up. "They like declared war on us. Shit's gotten real."

"Yeah..."

"Guess I didn't kill it." She frowns.

"Close enough. It probably would've been stunned for a long time. If you get another one, carry it downstairs and throw it into the circle."

She nods. "Is that gonna work?"

"Just saw one jump through to get away from me. Gonna test it out with this dead one."

"Ooh. I wanna see."

I rush to the basement, Sierra right behind me. When I get to the circle, I fling the dead imp at the rug. The instant it hits the circle, a tunnel of blue light opens, swallowing the creature, then the area promptly goes back to being a normal rug. I poke a finger at it, but jab solid carpet on top of concrete.

"That's really messed up."

Sierra nods. "Yeah. Did those mystics figure it out yet?"

"No. At least, they haven't called me."

Her eyebrows form a flat line. "Maybe you should call them before this gets out of control?"

"It's already out of control."

"True dat," says Sierra.

I trudge upstairs. A haze of smoke and fire extinguisher fumes hangs in the air. The house smells like burnt hair. Sophia, free from the jump rope, clings to Mom, who's taken up a defensive position in the corner of the living room, still holding a frying pan.

"Sierra!" shouts Mom. "What happened? Why is her nightgown covered in blood?"

"Imp bit her," I say. "She's okay now. Dad's right. Blunt weapons don't work. Use a knife."

"Aha!" yells Dad. "See? Twenty years of D&D comes in handy."

"So it's finally good for something," mutters Mom.

"Hey now..." Dad walks in, hands on his hips. "Basic math. Creative thinking. Conflict resolution. Strategy. Imagination..."

Mom gives him side eye. "I've spent the past hour and a half playing wak-a-rat with..."

Dad, the girls, and I all say "Imps," at the same time.

"Whatever." Mom sighs. "Are they gone?"

I hold up a 'wait' finger, and listen. Only the sound of video games from Sam's room breaks the stillness. Amazing. The boy sat through that mess without even noticing. Maybe he heard it but didn't realize the sounds weren't coming from a movie.

"I think so, but it's premature to relax." I pull my phone from my pocket and head for the deck out back. "Need a minute."

Once outside, I call Darren.

It rings ten times and goes to voicemail.

"Hey, it's me, Sarah. Have you guys found anything yet? It's getting super crazy."

An incoming call beeps in my ear. I swipe over… to Darren.

"Hello? Sarah?"

"Yeah. Have you guys had any luck yet? I think the imps are angry. They've been coming after us."

"We're still working on comparing the photo you sent us of the ritual circle to our information. So far, we can't agree on the tradition involved. It seems like whatever the summoner did is using bits and pieces of several different traditions that shouldn't be combined. I'm hesitant to think that's actually the case since the ritual obviously worked. Do you have any more information? What about the text the summoner used for reference?"

I grumble. "No, I couldn't find it. Let me go ask them about it."

"If you don't mind me asking, who did this?"

"My sisters."

"Oh. Seriously? The little ones?"

I rub my sinuses. *So* glad vampires can't get stress headaches. "Yeah. When you guys borrowed her body, it kinda did something to her. Unlocked a buried talent in her head."

"Hmm. All right. If you find the book they used as a reference, please send photos as soon as possible. There's no way a little kid made this stuff up. She had to get it from somewhere."

"Okay. I'll call you back in a few minutes."

"Sorry it took me so long to answer. Phone was in another room. I'll keep it close now."

"Thanks."

I end the call and head back inside. Mom and Dad are cleaning up the mess in the kitchen, no siblings in sight. The aftereffects of the fire extinguisher blast to the face make my father look like he tried to snort all the cocaine in California at once.

"Where are the girls?" I ask.

"Upstairs," says Mom. "Sophia said they wanted to look up ways to deal with imps."

I nod, then run upstairs. Both girls are in Sophia's room, sitting back to back on the floor in their nightgowns, surrounded by a ring of salt, each staring into their tablets.

"Does that salt thing really work?" I ask.

They look up at me.

"Considering we're not trapped somewhere, bleeding, or under attack, it could be working," says Sierra.

"Any luck?" I ask.

"Not yet," mutters Sophia.

"Hey, where did you guys find the info on that gate?"

"Online," says Sophia.

"Can you send me the link or screenshots? The mystics want to look at it."

The girls nod.

"Sure." Sierra swipes at her tablet screen. "I got it."

A deep growl comes from across the hall.

Both girls gasp, squeezing together in their salt circle.

"That came from Sam's room." I frown, and walk over there.

Sam's sprawled on his floor, playing *Soul Caliber*... with an imp. The little demon's sitting beside him, legs crossed, controller in hand. When I peer in at them, it waves at me and resumes playing. What the...?

"Hey, Sare," says Sam.

"Why is there an imp in your room?" I ask.

"He wanted to play."

The imp nods.

I'm almost afraid to ask why it's not pranking him or causing general chaos. I hope video games are just that addictive and he doesn't consider my brother a kindred spirit. Seeing this thing sitting there like some other kid—albeit a tiny one—hanging out is just too much, and I stand there bewildered until the match ends. (The imp won).

I point. "Please go back to the portal."

It makes an 'aww, Mom' pouty face at me.

"Sare, it's only the second of three. Please let it stay to finish the round? He doesn't have a PlayStation where he lives."

I sigh. "Fine. Whatever."

The imp grins.

They play to a draw, somehow managing to 'kill' each other simultaneously. The game goes for a fourth round. I fold my arms, watching. That time, Sam wins by a hair.

The imp emits a disappointed noise, but fist bumps my brother.

"Okay, you really need to go home. It's late and Sam has to sleep."

The imp is almost cute as it stands, hangs its head, and walks out of the room, grumbling. I follow it downstairs, across the ground floor, and down to the basement. It heads right to the gate and jumps in, vanishing in a blue flash.

Well, that's weird. I'm almost surprised it listened.

My parents walk up behind me.

"Ack!" yells Mom. "What happened to the rug?"

"It's washable marker. It'll come out once it's disenchanted."

She stares at me.

"What were you about to say before?" asks Dad. "This guy you were going to bite?"

I shudder, then hug him. "Ugh. I've never been so sick to my stomach and heartbroken in my entire life…"

By the time I'm done telling them about it, *both* of my parents are close to tears.

"That poor child," whispers Mom.

Dad squeezes my shoulder. "Hon, if anyone ever so much as thinks about doing something like that to you or your siblings, you have my full permission to delete them from the gene pool."

I sniffle-chuckle. "I'm not sure I could kill someone, but if anyone did that to the guys, I probably could. Good to know you won't be upset at me for it."

"So…" Dad glances at the stairs. "Wanna watch *Critters*?"

"Jonathan, it's almost one in the morning." Mom blinks at him.

"Are *you* going to sleep any time soon?" asks Dad, wagging his eyebrows.

"No, but… do you think it's a good idea to watch a movie about little monsters after what just happened?" Mom yawns. "And where's that sword you used to have?"

"They're in the attic. They've been in the attic since Sierra started walking and climbing. Are you asking me to get a sword for you?"

"I think I am," says Mom, staring into space. "Does that mean I'm losing my grip?"

"If you're going to be swinging a sword, you better not lose your grip." Dad kisses her.

I turn away. "Guys. Get a room."

They laugh—and keep on kissing.

A SLIGHT MISCALCULATION

Not wanting to watch my parents get cute, I hurry upstairs.

Sophia's room is empty. I check Sam's on the other side. He's in bed, but probably not asleep. At least, his breathing doesn't sound right for being asleep. Doesn't seem like he's faking it, since he *just* went to bed. It used to take me a while to actually pass out after crawling in bed, too.

I check Sierra's room and find her sitting up in bed, staring at her tablet.

"Hey. It's past one. You should be asleep."

"It's Saturday."

"It's Friday night."

She looks over the tablet at me. "It's past midnight, so it's Saturday. I'm not staying up too late, I woke up too early."

"C'mon. Go to sleep."

Sierra sighs, rolls her eyes at me, but shuts off the tablet and scoots down under the covers.

I walk over.

"If you kiss me on the head, I will punch you."

"Heh."

Her glower softens. "It's okay if you want to."

I kiss her on the forehead. "Night, kiddo."

"Night. Sare? Did we eff up?"

"Maybe a little, but it's not like you played with something dangerous knowing it could blow up. Neither one of you expected magic to work."

She smirks. "We should have. I mean, you're a vampire now and Sophia got knocked out of her body. We should've been more careful."

"Maybe. Bit late to worry about that, but don't freak out. We'll fix it. Try to get some sleep."

"Okay."

I walk out of my old room and go one door over to the one my sisters used to share, now Sophia's room. She's still not there. I check the bathroom, find nothing, and go back to casa de pink. "Soph?"

"In here."

The voice came from the closet. I pull the door open to find an empty closet—and Sophia standing on the wrong side of the mirror. Like *inside* the mirror. Behind her is a creepy version of the bedroom in black and white. All her unicorn figures and pictures are reflected as grotesque creatures. The curtains, masses of long, black tendrils, writhe about.

"Crap!" I yell, jumping back.

Sophia slaps at the glass. "I'm stuck."

"What did you do?"

"I thought I found a way to close the gate, but it didn't work. Umm... I think I did it wrong." She looks back over her shoulder. "It's really scary in here, like our house but *so* messed up. Nothing looks *too* bad though... at least I haven't seen anything moving."

Sierra's laugh comes from behind me. "Oh, great. You've gone to the upside down."

"No!" Sophia starts crying. "Why did you say that? Now I'm scared there's gonna be monsters in here."

"Don't be scared." Sierra grins. "If monsters were in there, they would've got you already."

Sophia screams.

"Hey, don't make it worse." I pat Sierra on the head, then look at the mirror, poking at it. "I'll figure something out. Might take a while though."

"I don't wanna be in here," whines Sophia.

The parents walk in, no doubt having heard her scream.

"Why are you girls still awake at this hour?" asks Dad.

"Umm…" I raise my hand. "I claim undeath."

"Not you, I meant the small girls."

"I'm traumatized," deadpans Sierra. "And Soph is stuck in an alternate dimension."

The parents finally notice that Sophia's standing *inside* the mirror rather than in front of it.

Mom screams.

"Whoa," says Dad.

"What is going on!" shouts Mom. "Sierra what did you do?"

Sierra huffs. "Why is it always my fault?"

"No, Mom!" Sophia shakes her head, tossing her long blonde hair back and forth. "Umm, I thought I found a way to undo the gate we opened, but it kinda backfired on me."

"Interesting." Dad rubs his chin.

Thud.

Sophia shivers at the noise. "Something moved down the hall. I'm really getting scared now."

Mom looks back and forth between my sisters. "Good grief. What are you two *doing* summoning demons? I should ground you both for the rest of the year."

"What is it with tween girls and messing around with magic?" asks Dad.

"I never did anything like that." Mom frowns. "Most of my friends did, though."

Sierra holds up a finger. "Experimentation with occultism and magic, often involving the symbolism of a powerful female goddess, gives some girls a sense of empowerment and control over their lives in a patriarchal society that systematically denies them any true sense of autonomy."

Mom, Dad, and I all stare at her, speechless.

"Wow," says Sophia.

"You know what?" Mom throws her hands up. "Never mind. You're not grounded. I have nothing to come back at that with."

"I was only trying to help and undo what we did, but it blew up in my face." Sophia bounces on her toes. "Please get me out of here."

"Gonna make a few calls and see if anyone has any ideas." I pull my phone out of my pocket.

Mom presses a hand to the mirror. Sophia puts her hand on the other side.

"The next time this family is due for more strange crap," says Dad. "Can we maybe have another vampire war or do the undead boyfriend drama thing again? Imps and mirror walking is too damn dangerous."

I glance sideways at him. "Sure, Dad. I'll get right on that."

16

UNRAVELING

I wander into the hall, but hover close to the doorway while tapping the contact entry in my phone for Aurélie.

"Oh, *Allo* there *mon cheri!* It is so good to hear from you."

"Hi. I need some advice."

"But of course."

I explain the situation with the imps, the gate, and Sophia stuck somehow inside the mirror. "Can you think of anything I can do to get her out of there?"

"Hmm. I 'ave 'eard some rumors of such things, though unfortunately, I am not well versed in *magique*. Too dangerous, *cheri*."

Ugh. I hang my head. "I understand."

The obligatory conversation with her about random nothingness follows. Everyone seems to have that one friend who's simply incapable of a thirty-second conversation. Like 'how long do I need to boil an egg' turns into a two-hour phone marathon. My life is now blessed with two of those friends. Used to think Ashley was bad for talking, but she's got nothing on an almost four-century-old vampire noblewoman.

I do my damndest not to sound like I'm in a hurry to get off the phone.

"Oh, one moment... *La Petit Papillion* says... Mm-hmm. *Oui.* Yes. I will tell her."

I blink. The little butterfly? That has to be one of her dolls. One of her *possessed* dolls. As if imps didn't creep me out enough. Somehow, those dolls freak me out more, despite they're not being malicious.

"She says if you are not well versed in *magique,* there is no way for a person to escape."

"Umm... That's not exactly good news. Are you saying she's lost for good?"

Mom and Dad gasp behind me.

"No, of course not," says Aurélie in a bright tone that makes me picture her big smile. "*You* are not a person. At least not an ordinary one. You would need to go where she is, and then you would be able to tear the veil from the other side."

"So you're saying if I can somehow go into the mirror with her, I can rip open a hole that we can both come back through?"

"Indeed."

The 'rents sigh with relief.

"Do you have any idea how I can get in there?" I scrunch my nose up at the mirror.

"Alas. I do not."

"All right. Thank you. And thank *Papillion* for me."

"*Bien sûr.* Oh, you must need to attend to your sister. The poor dear must be terrified. I shall not keep you longer."

"Thank you. Good night."

"*Au revoir.*"

Next, I call Darren... and might as well put him on speakerphone.

"Hey," he says upon answering. "I got the email. We've been looking it over. You're going to need to conduct a counter-ritual to close the gate."

"But... they don't know how they did it."

"Hmm. That could be a problem."

"Is there anything you can do to help?" I ask.

"Where did they get this ritual from?"

"The internet," says Sierra.

Darren mutters something inaudible, though contempt is clear. Guess looking up magic from the internet is the mystic equivalent of putting ketchup on filet mignon.

Sierra runs to her room and comes back with her tablet, showing me a page full of weird markings and scribbles among typed text. "Here."

I skim some of the writing, almost breaking out into laughter. It's way overwrought. Like, this is the kind of stuff a twelve-year-old boy would write if they made the dialogue for an evil wizard from a D&D campaign. "In the eleventh hour of the night under the watchful eyes of Imbrelor, begin the preparations... the dried eye powders of a raven? Seriously? Where did you get 'eye powder' whatever the hell that is?"

"It would be the dried-out eyeballs of a raven, ground into dust," says Darren.

"Eww." Sierra cringes. "We didn't do any of that."

"What the heck is an Imbrelor?" asks Dad.

"That would be the name of a lesser devil affiliated with cruelty and mischief," says Callum over the phone. "Any ritual invoking or associated with him is almost assuredly going to result in demonic activity."

"Oops," say Sierra and Sophia at the same time.

"We had no idea!" whispers Sophia.

I gesture at the tablet. "This is the same information we sent Darren. It looks like nonsense. Like who would ever take this seriously?"

Sierra shrugs. "The imps, apparently."

"Okay... but honestly..." I sigh. "Does all magic look like this? If I read this without seeing actual imps running around, I'd have laughed."

"I *did* laugh at it." Sierra shrugs. "Soph thought it was cool."

"In her defense." Dad leans closer to me, reading the spell. "It did work."

"Jonathan!" Mom rubs her sinuses. "You're not helping."

"Please get me out of here!" yells Sophia while banging on the glass.

I look down at the phone in my hand. "Darren, Sophia's trapped on the inside of a mirror. Do you have any idea how we can get her out? Will breaking the glass help?"

"No, don't do that!" says Callum, voice raised. "That will destroy her entry point and permanently trap her."

Mom and Dad exchange worried glances.

"Not entirely permanent," adds Landon. "Though it would involve multithreading dimensions to reconstitute a symbiotic portal in a proximal reality. No one alive in the order these days has that kind of skill."

"So for all intents and purposes, she would be trapped there permanently. That's what I said." Callum sighs.

"Yes, but permanence isn't literally true, just functionally accurate," says Landon.

"Pedant," mutters Callum.

"Umm. Fascinating." Darren hums in thought. "Allowing your sister back into the mortal plane is an entirely different question than closing an accidental summoning portal. I'll need to check other books. Can I call you back in about half an hour?"

"Does she have that long?" asks Sierra.

Sophia squeals in fear.

"If she hasn't seen anything dangerous yet, she should be fine. Just tell her to stay where she is and not go exploring. It's easy to get lost in alternate dimensions. I'll call you back as soon as I have something. I should be quick as it sounds like the gate is unraveling and will be a threat to your sisters before long. Imps will grow more and more bold with each passing hour."

"Okay. Please hurry," I say.

"We are working as fast as humanly possible."

"Thanks." I hang up.

"The imps are probably going to do something super horrible," says Sierra. "Like make your dance outfit vanish in the middle of class."

Sophia gasps. "They wouldn't dare!"

I shake my head. "I don't think the imps would swipe your clothes."

Both girls exhale with relief.

"They're going to steal your souls."

Sophia starts crying. "I don't want my soul taken *again*."

Sierra just stares at me.

"Sarah, why would you say something like that?" Mom glowers. "You're scaring your sisters."

"Sorry." I pace around. "This is a bit much for me to deal with, too."

"So… we just sit here and wait for that guy to call back?" asks Dad.

"Unless you know how to open a doorway into wherever the heck Sophia is, yeah." I gesture at the mirror.

Sophia jumps and gasps, spinning to put her back against the glass. "Something's coming. I hear it walking."

17

THE TROUBLE WITH NEIGHBORS

Sophia looks like she's about to run off into the otherworld at any second to hide from whatever she hears.

"Hey, what exactly did you do to get over there?" I ask.

"Umm." She peers back over her shoulder at me, still pressing herself into the mirror. "I found a spell to close doorways and I was making the circle for it, and I just wound up here. The magic must've blown up and shoved me backwards. Stopped sliding in here."

I look around her room. A large art pad sits on the floor near her bed with occult looking scrawl marks around a circle. An incomplete symbol has a line that trails straight off the paper toward the bed, continuing on the rug, too. I crouch and look under the bed. A blue marker sits uncapped among a veritable army of Barbie stuff that's plowed aside. Just because that sort of thing bugs me, I pick it up and cap it before it can dry out.

"That's weird. Whatever she did blasted her straight away from the pad. She made it halfway under the bed before she slipped across the dimensional wall." I feel around the rug, but don't get that odd prickly feeling the gate in the basement caused.

"Wow." Dad raises both eyebrows. "I'm not sure what disturbs me more… hearing you say that like it's a thing, or that Sophia apparently *did* switch dimensions."

Mom swipes the tablet from Sierra, looks it over, and shakes her head. "Young lady, I don't want you messing around with any more black magic."

"Aww, Mom!" says Sierra.

"Well, at least not until your sister is no longer stuck in a parallel dimension. And you should stick to white or grey magic."

Sierra flails her arms. "But, Mom! What if messing around with this stuff is how we get her out of there?"

Mom looks around for a few seconds like she isn't sure what to do with the tablet, then hands it to me. "You do it."

"Why her? She has no clue." Sierra gestures at me.

"Thanks," I mutter.

Mom massages the bridge of her nose. "She's older."

I glance down at the tablet, a page of weird markings that looks more like Joey Rivera's high school notebook doodles than anything legitimately magical. "Older? I have no idea what I'm doing with this stuff. Boobs don't come with occult powers."

"Depends on the boobs." Dad wags his eyebrows at Mom.

She and I both blush. Her, because of the way he's looking at her. Me, because the comment and the looks on their faces has once again made me think of my parents being romantic with each other. Gah.

Sierra grabs the tablet and tries to pull it away from me. I don't resist too much, but I also don't let go of it, giving Mom the eye.

"I don't want you getting stuck in there, too. Didn't you hear Aurélie? Sarah can get out." Mom turns away, grabbing Dad and trying to hide that she's about to start crying from worry over Sophia.

I let go of the tablet. Sierra almost falls over backward, but keeps her balance.

Wham!

The whole house shakes.

"Oh, please tell me that isn't Zuul," mutters Dad.

"What are you talking about?" Mom blinks at him.

Car alarms go off outside.

We all run across the hallway into Sam's room, on the front of the house, and cram together at the window to look outside. A silver BMW has embedded itself in Mr. Neidermayer's porch. Deep, muddy tire trenches gouge the lawn in an arc to the cul-de-sac.

An imp standing by the end of Neidermayer's driveway doubles over with laughter at the guy behind the wheel who appears to have been knocked out by the crash. I almost chuckle at the thought that our mean neighbor is going to keep the BMW for straying onto his lawn the way he does with Frisbees and balls.

Lights come on in Neidermayer's house upstairs.

"Be right back." I hand my phone to Dad. "Might wanna call 911."

"Where are you going?" Mom blinks at me.

I open the window. "There's an imp behind the car. It caused the crash."

"There is?" asks Dad.

"Haven't you been paying attention?" Sierra looks up at the parents. "They're invisible to mere mortals."

"But we—" Mom makes a walloping gesture.

"They can allow people to see them if they want," I say, then dive out the window.

Impressive. Neither of my parents scream in alarm. It's probably a bad sign that watching me jump out a second-story window *doesn't* bother them.

"What the Sam Hill is going on?" yells Mr. Neidermayer from behind his front door—which he can't open due to the car pressed into it.

I swoop down on the imp like an eagle after a field mouse. My moonlight shadow gives me away and the little bastard runs off screaming. At least I don't eat grass this time. I pull up to avoid a collision, swerving to the right and following the imp down the cul-de-sac to the street. With no obstructions out here, I gain on it easily.

For having such small legs, the imp is surprisingly fast on foot, but it's not 120 MPH fast. Seconds before I get a hand on it, the thing darts to the right and goes under a car. I pull up to go over the car—no way am I stopping in time—and swing back to land beside it. As soon as I crouch down to look for the imp, it gives me a double middle finger.

This is the demonic equivalent of three-year-old Sam running into the men's room at the mall to get away from Mom after an argument... and it works about as well. Mom went right in there after him.

Me? I push the car aside. Hey, not that impressive. It's only a Honda Civic.

The imp yelps and runs. For some stupid reason, I chase it on foot for a moment—we're about the same speed—before leaping into the air and flying again. The imp jumps onto its wings, straining to outrun me but having little chance. Though, it is quite a bit faster while flying than running.

I edge closer to it as we sail back and forth over the neighborhood some 500 feet in the air.

A flash of pale white catches my eye from a yard down below. A woman about Mom's age is stranded naked in—I'm assuming—her backyard. As soon as I look down at her, the imp I'm chasing cackles. No doubt, her situation is also his handiwork. Or its. Still haven't figured out if these things have a sex. I can't quite remember that woman's name since we haven't met despite living a half-mile from each other, though I do remember her showing up once or twice in an effort to talk my parents into joining her church.

She can wait. I can't let this thing get away.

It leads me on a roundabout chase past several small fires, yards with knocked-over statues, and two small boys trapped on a first-floor roof extension jutting out from beneath a window on the second story of their house. What in the hell? Grr. They look terrified but not in immediate danger as long as they stay away from the edge. If I break off from chasing this imp, I'm going to lose it.

Worrying about the maybe six-year-olds pushes me to fly faster. At the approach of distant sirens, the imp swerves left, evidently drawn toward an intersection where a sedan sitting at a red light is in perfect position to get t-boned by an approaching police car if it should suffer a sudden mechanical failure and accelerate.

The temptation for such calamity evidently proves irresistible to the imp.

It dives left toward the car. I drop straight down for about thirty feet, pulling up into a curve that puts me on a collision course with the distracted imp. It barely has time to scream before I grab its tiny chest in both hands and squeeze my claws in as hard as I can, gritting my teeth to tolerate the painful heat of its insides. My fingers piercing its body hurts like I've tried to grab just-out-of-the-oven lasagna with my bare hands. Leathery wings slap me in the face when the imp lapses into death convulsions.

The instant it stops twitching, I pull my fingers out of it and whimper at the burns. Ow. Fortunately, they heal in seconds. After a brief detour home long enough to drop the dead thing in the back yard, I rush to the house where the two boys sit huddled on the small side roof.

They look up at me with pure awe when I land behind them. Sorry kids, you can't remember seeing me fly. You live like a ten-minute walk away. Thankfully, five- and six-year-old brains are super easy to reprogram. I erase their memory of seeing me as well as seeing the imp that tricked them into going out the window. Another window— with no roof under it—two rooms down the side of the house is open enough for them to fit through, so I ferry them one at a time over there.

With the kids back in their house, I head over to the reluctant nudist moonbather.

She's muttering under her breath about some little demon attacking her in the tub, stealing her towel, and running outside. The poor woman's too mortified to leave her yard and ask neighbors for help and has been standing there for over two hours trying to summon the courage to do more than hide.

I can sympathize. Without the freakiness of waking up in a morgue, I probably would have done the same thing a few months ago when I found myself stranded outside nude. Hmm. Careful not to let her see me, I orbit her house twice in search of a way in before noticing an open window on the second story. Perfect. I slip inside, but stop short with a gasp at the scene.

It looks like an army of imps trashed the place. Curtains are shredded, books tossed all over, furniture ripped up, wall hangings thrown around, plates smashed. Ugh. What did this woman do to deserve this?

Taking care not to touch anything, I fly down the hall to the stairs. The rest of the house is equally trashed. Smashed dinnerware litters the dining room. Crisscross scratches mark every painting in sight. The kitchen is a mess of thrown food and broken dishes. A large bath towel lies on the floor by the back door, still damp and smelling of bath bomb.

Wow…

I grab a paper towel and use it to unlock the deadbolt, then turn the knob. Guaranteed this woman is going to call the police over the destruction inside the house. The last thing I need would be for them to find my fingerprints here. Not that I couldn't fix things eventually with mind control… but that's a massive pain in the ass I'd rather not deal with.

The woman runs inside and stops short, staring at the mess. After a second, she turns her head to the left and stares at me. Before she can scream, I dive into her head, erase myself, and slip out the door.

I really hate imps. They're more annoying than telemarketers.

In fact, it wouldn't surprise me if companies didn't *hire* telemarketers as much as summon and bind them to servitude.

On my way home, I spot another imp on a telephone pole about to touch a transformer in a bad place. The moon's in front of me this time, so no shadow gives me away when I dive at the thing. By some miracle, I manage to nab the little monster without eating a few thousand volts, carrying the limp body back home with me.

My cul-de-sac is awash with flashing lights from numerous police cars and an ambulance dealing with the crash. Plenty of distraction on the ground makes sure no one notices me glide overhead and land in my backyard. After retrieving the dead imp, I go inside to the basement and throw them both at the gate, which frustratingly remains solid to me.

That done, I head upstairs. Mom and Dad are in Sophia's room by the closet door mirror, doing their best to comfort her. My sister's curled up, sitting on the floor with her back to the glass, shivering in fear while repeatedly apologizing for 'doing magic.'

I take my phone from the nightstand. "Gonna call these guys again."

The parents nod at me, so I slip out and head down to the living room. Actually, I go to the basement. If Darren doesn't have good news for me, this phone call will most assuredly involve some screaming, and I don't want to freak Sophia out.

18

NONSENSE

So, yeah, Darren's still 'researching.'

I pace around my room, frustrated to the point I can't make a choice between screaming and kicking stuff around or merely collapsing into a heap and sobbing. The parents haven't gone nuts yet, so I take that to mean Sophia's still okay. It's tempting to call the mystics every ten minutes, but that will only piss them off. They don't *have* to help. So, as much as it infuriates me being unable to do anything, there's little choice but to wait.

I sit by the computer and open Google, but I can't even think of what to search for. Mirror world? Magical portals? Demon summoning or banishment? Yeah, that's going to give me a mountain of useless bullcrap to sort through… probably plenty of movies Dad would want to watch though.

"Argh!" I collapse over my desk, banging my head repeatedly into my folded arms.

The rapid soft thumps of someone small running down the basement steps snaps me out of my frustration tantrum.

Sierra appears at my door looking freaked out. "Sare! There's something growling in my room."

"An imp?" I ask.

She runs over and grabs me, trembling. "I dunno. It sounded huge."

It's bizarre to see her so scared. She's usually the one who rolls her eyes at horror movies that even make Dad hide behind a pillow. Though, there's a distinct difference between watching a horror movie and being in one. Those imps are not special effects.

"Okay. I'll go check."

No, I don't think it's weird that she ran to me instead of Dad. It's going to take more than a weed whacker to destroy whatever's crawled into her bedroom. I head upstairs, Sierra right behind me as if afraid to be alone anywhere in the house. She hovers at the doorjamb as I walk into her room. It's weird to think of this space as hers instead of mine. Sure, the entire layout is different, but its position in the house, walking down the hall to *that* door, the window overlooking the backyard I spent so many hours staring out... it all still feels like I'm going back to my personal sanctuary. This had been my room from like age two until only months ago.

Nothing's growling presently, so I check the closet, then peek under the bed, under the computer desk, and check the closet again just to be sure.

Sierra creeps in, looking around like she's trying to sneak across a minefield. "Is it gone?"

"Seems to be. I can't find it."

"Will you stay here for a bit?" asks Sierra in an out-of-character shaky voice.

"Yeah sure."

She pads over to the bed and starts to climb in, but a black hand comes out of nowhere, grabbing her by the right ankle and dragging her, screaming, under the bed. She rolls onto her chest, clawing at the rug in a futile effort to stop herself.

I dive at her, but she vanishes into a cloud of eerie blue light before I can get close, leaving me grasping empty rug. Stunned, I lay there on my stomach staring at the emptiness under the bed.

"Dammit!" I shout. "No!"

Mom and Dad run in.

"What are you screaming about?" asks Mom.

As guilty as if I'd done something, I have to fight tears while pointing. "Sierra's gone."

"What?" blurts Dad.

"Something pulled her under and she just disappeared. I wasn't fast enough."

Mom runs over and crawls headfirst under the bed, reaching around and patting at the floor. Dad tries to comfort me, saying it's not my fault. It kinda is in a way. Maybe not for being too slow to grab Sierra, but if I'd behaved myself as a vampire and gone off into the night instead of trying to stay with my mortal family, my sisters wouldn't be in danger now.

No. I can't think like that. I can't. Every time something supernatural happens to or near my family, I'm going to beat myself up over not staying away—and that's bullshit. If they thought I died, they'd be emotional wrecks. Even Sierra, as cool as she acts, likes me a lot for some reason even if she's nowhere near as obviously clingy and adoring as Sophia. Really, I have no idea why they're like that with me. I haven't done anything exceptional for them other than simply being older. And, admittedly, I *was* kinda rude to them for the last year or so before I died. Nothing extreme, just the usual 'I'm too mature to hang out with little kids' crap.

Okay, Sarah, focus. Now is not the time to think sad thoughts.

My parents' voices cease being meaningless sound blurs.

"... are we going to do about this?" asks Mom.

"I have no idea. Maybe I should start studying the occult?" Dad's trying to keep up a sense of humor, but the worry is clear in his eyes.

"Give me a sec." I pull my phone from my pocket and call Darren.

"Sarah, we—"

"Sorry to bug you. Really. Something new happened." I explain Sierra being dragged under the bed. "Oh, shit." I stare at my parents, run out into the hall, and take the closest door left into Soph's room. "Sophia didn't do *more* magic to wind up on the other side... she got grabbed, too." I point at the marker line trailing off the pad onto the rug.

Mom and Dad look at it.

I flop on the ground as I imagine Sophia would have been, propped up on her elbows while drawing, her feet right by the bed. "It just grabbed her by the leg and pulled her straight under the bed."

Using flight, I mimic being dragged backward, trailing the (still capped) marker off the pad.

"So she *didn't* do that?" asks Darren and Dad at the same time.

"They made the gate, but no, Soph didn't send herself across. She didn't even finish whatever spell she'd been trying to do here."

"I'm still trying to make sense of how your sisters were able to get anything from that website to work. We haven't been able to identify the specific tradition because it's using symbolism from various unrelated schools. There's Thelema, Wicca, Satanism, Druidry, a few esoteric Christian markings, too. Those haven't been used since the Middle Ages. In my professional opinion, this is Hollywood style nonsense, not real magic."

"What?" I blurt, staring at the phone. "But there *is* a gate. You saw the imp."

"I know," says Darren. "I'm unable to explain how anything from this website could have possibly worked, but I'm not giving up yet."

"You're saying it's nonsense?" asks Dad, leaning closer to the phone.

"Put it this way." Darren pauses. "It's like the girls decided to invent a bunch of random marks, wrote a few lines of poetry to go with them, called it a system of magic, and then managed to successfully summon demons with it."

I stare down, sorrow welling up inside me like I'm never going to see my sisters again. "Oh…"

"Hey," says Dad. "What if it's not the spells on paper that did this? Could Sophia be a sorcerer?"

"Pardon?" asks Darren.

"You know, like wizards have to study ancient rituals and specific phrases, follow certain rules. Sorcerers just point and want stuff to happen and it does." Dad gestures like a wizard tossing a fireball.

"Are you talking about magic or D&D?" I ask. "Dad, be serious."

"I am." He gestures at the phone. "This guy is saying that there's no way what the girls did should've had any real effect… but here we are up to our collective tits in imps."

Something explodes in the distance.

"Oh, that didn't sound good," mutters Mom.

"The ground didn't shake. It can't be *too* bad." Dad smiles. "But random explosions are usually not good."

"Amazing. You might actually have something there, Mr. Wright," says Darren. "Landon is telling me he's heard of certain people who were able to command paranormal forces but not through any known system of mysticism. I realize your idea is based on the lore of a fictional game, but… it bears consideration. This material is functionally worthless to an actual mystic, but your daughter—or daughters—may only need a mechanism that allows them to focus their thoughts. Since they don't know they can 'just do' things, their belief that something is going to happen when using this bogus occultism made the difference."

"Sierra didn't expect anything to happen at all," I say. "But… Sophia might have, since she'd already seen magic work once."

"Sorry!" yells Sophia from the mirror. "I swear I won't play with dark magic again. Didn't think 'doorway' would be evil."

"The dark overtones of this ritual, ridiculous as it is," says Darren, "likely influenced your subconscious and tainted the effect. Perhaps, if it is true that you possess some manner of intrinsic power, you *do* have the ability to open a doorway from that side."

"Are you suggesting she try to do magic again?" Mom blinks. "What if that makes it worse?"

"I'm scared," whispers Sophia.

"Is Sierra in there with you?" asks Dad.

Sophia looks away from the mirror, listening for a moment. "I dunno. I thought I heard her scream a little bit ago, but it's quiet. Something heavy is walking around."

"We have a direction now at least," says Darren from the speakerphone. "Instead of attempting to undo a specific spell, we will work on creating a new one that may shut the gateway down, hopefully drawing all the imps back where they belong in the process."

"Great." Dad nods.

"Okay. How long will that take?" I ask.

"Maybe an hour or two."

I nod. "Sounds good. Please work."

"We are…"

"I was talking to the universe."

Darren chuckles. "All right then. Call you soon."

19

OFF THE RAILS

The instant I hang up the phone, it rings again.

'Mrs. Carter' shows up on the caller ID.

I answer. "Hey, Mrs. C."

"Sarah! What's going on? There's *something* in the house. Dishes are flying around, doors are opening and closing, I almost fell down the stairs. My curtains keep trying to light themselves on fire."

"Umm." I stare at the gap under Sophia's bed. "Something's here, too. It grabbed both my sisters."

Ashley's scream comes over the phone.

"Hey!" yells Sierra from the desk.

We all turn.

My middle sister's face appears in a small, round cosmetics mirror. She knocks on the glass. "I can see you guys."

Mom rushes over and picks it up. Kinda looks like she's Face-Timing on a round phone. "Honey, where are you?"

"You're asking me?" She blinks. "Something grabbed me and dragged me down this long, weird hallway. I kicked it in the face and got away. I heard you guys talking and found this little hole in the wall, but I can't fit through it."

"Umm," says Dad. "You've appeared in Sophia's cosmetics mirror."

"Sarah!" yells Mrs. Carter. "Ashley says you can do something about this... *thing.* Please! It's trying to kill us."

Sierra gasps. "Oh, shit. Something's in here with me."

I run over to Mom and pull the mirror over so I can look at her. "How do I get in there?"

"I dunno!" whines Sierra.

"Sit tight," I say. "I'll find a way to get you out of there."

Ashley's shriek is loud enough—off speakerphone—for everyone to hear.

"Go," says Dad. "Ash is in trouble now, and there's nothing we can do here until your mystic friends call back."

"Not sure I'd call them *friends*, but... well, I guess. They are trying to help the girls." I scowl. "Half of this is their fault for enchanting Sophia in the first place."

Mom and Dad exchange pained grimaces.

"Okay, Mrs. Carter. I'm on the way."

"Thank you!" she yells, then shrieks. Glass breaks in the background.

I run downstairs and go out the door, not bothering to waste the time necessary to put shoes on. Ash only lives four houses up the street from my cul-de-sac, and it's not like cold ground bothers me anymore.

Ashley and her mother screaming inside their house reaches my ears before I'm even halfway across the cul-de-sac to the street. The instant I grab the doorknob, I notice watery splashing in the distance. Something about it strikes me as significant... so I jump into the air and fly over the house toward the noise. In the yard of the house right behind Ashley's, a dark stain covers most of a large in-ground swimming pool, with an irregular edge exposing water all the way around it. It takes me only a second to realize it's not an oil slick, but a pool cover that's become detached. It is, after all, November. Someone appears to have fallen into the pool and gotten tangled up in the plastic.

Oh, shit... what a horrible way to drown.

I dive toward the struggling man, at least I'm assuming man based on the gasps and gurgles coming from the tangle of plastic sheeting. He's become cocooned in it, already sunken a few inches beneath the surface. Hovering over the pool, I grab two handfuls of the material and drag him to the side. There, I land on my feet and haul him up onto solid ground.

Rapid pattering from behind gives away an imp charging at me, likely intending to shove me into the water, too. I spin and grab the bastard out of the air with a fist around its spindly neck before it can crash into my back. Its scream of surprise grows to a multi-voiced death wail when I ram my claws into its chest.

The man continues fighting the plastic, hopelessly disoriented and tangled up in it. I'm sure he'd prefer having to buy a new pool cover to suffocating, so I slash it open with my claws like I'm freeing a butterfly from its cocoon.

A late-thirties guy coughs up water and gags a few times before looking up at me. "Holy shit… thank you!"

I grab his hand and help him out of the plastic, hiding the dead imp behind my back. He's shirtless, wearing pajama pants, and shaking from adrenaline, fear, and November-cold water. Poor guy. That's going to leave a mark. Ashley's distant scream reminds me I've got places to be and things to do.

"Sorry, I gotta run. Friend's in trouble." I dash across the yard to the tall wooden fence, which I 'climb' by flying, and head to Ashley's place.

The back door is open, fire glows from the kitchen window, and there's no sign of anyone.

I run inside, tossing the dead imp in the sink for the time being, then rip the burning curtains down, also throwing them in the sink, before hosing them with the sprayer attachment on the faucet.

"Open goddammit!" shouts Mrs. Carter from behind the basement door at the back corner of the kitchen.

"Hang on," I yell, then run over and grab the knob, giving it a sharp yank that breaks the lock plate.

The door pops open amid a flash of yellow light. Mrs. Carter stumbles out into the kitchen wearing a bathrobe covered in dirty smudges, a length of black cord around her neck. I catch her before she falls on the floor.

"Gah! Mrs. C, are you okay?"

She coughs. "What's going on? This wire came to life and tried to strangle me." She removes the power cord from around her neck and tosses it aside. The poor woman looks exhausted.

"I don't really have time to explain everything in detail. Imps are loose."

"Imps?" She blinks. "Is this more vampire stuff?"

"No. Minor demons. There's a dead one in your sink. Don't worry about it for now. I'll take it with me when I leave. Where's Ash?"

"Upstairs as far as I know." Mrs. Carter wanders over to the sink, peers in, and screams.

"It's dead. It can't hurt anyone." I run across the house to the stairs.

The upstairs hallway is marked here and there with soot stains, like small fires started all over the place but didn't burn long. I'm about to call out for Ashley, but upon hearing the raspy giggle of an imp up to no good, decide stealth is a better option.

Clicking and squeaking, like a cat desperate to get out of a slippery tub, leads me to the bathroom at the end of the hall. Ashley's left foot sticks up from inside the tub, oriented like she's face-down. An imp hovers by the faucet, turning the water on. I pad up as quiet as I can be, springing forward at the last second and grabbing the tiny horror from behind.

It shrieks, then wails as I crush my claws into its chest, killing it.

Ashley, in her nightgown, lays unconscious in about an inch of water, a bedsheet coiled around her body like a python, trapping her arms. A smear of blood on the wall matches the blood on the right side of her head. The imp had only just turned on the water, so it hadn't yet covered her face. I pull her upright, propping her in a sitting position before shutting off the faucet and opening the drain.

"Ash?" I pat her on the cheek. "Ash!"

She moans. "Ow."

A moment later, her eyes flutter open. She squirms, struggling at the sheet tying her arms to her sides. "Stupid little bastard pulled the rug out from under me. I think I hit my head."

"You did."

She squirms again. "Are you gonna untie me or are we about to do something we'll both regret."

Fortunately, I can read her mind, and know she's totally kidding. "Heh. Sorry. Just wanted to make sure you were okay." I grab the sheet, which isn't tied at all, rather held in place by inexplicable forces. A good strong pull breaks the magic and gives off a brief flash of yellow light.

The instant Ashley's arms are free, she grabs on in a fierce hug. "That damn thing was trying to kill me."

"Would it help if I told you that it probably just wanted to scare the shit out of you? They don't *try* to kill, but they think it's funny if death happens."

"That is a meaningless semantic difference." She squeezes me again. "Help me up?"

I lift her out of the tub and set her on her feet. She peels off her soaked nightgown, wraps herself in a towel, and leans against the sink, looking over her injury in the mirror.

"My head hurts and I feel way dizzy. Do you think I should go to the hospital?"

"I'm no doctor, but you whacked your head on the porcelain hard enough to bleed… yeah, better safe than sorry."

She faces me. "Did you get it?"

I point at the corpse.

Ashley spite-stomps it in the face. "Good. Was there only one?"

"Yeah." I think back to the other house where the woman had been stuck in her backyard. It would probably take more than one imp to make a mess like that in mere minutes. Given that Ash's house isn't a total disaster, I feel safe declaring it a single-imp problem. "Got him."

"Okay." She woozily staggers toward the door.

I grab her arm and help her to her room. She wants me to stay with her while she changes, in case she passes out and falls over, so I do. It's not weird for us to change in front of each other even if she is into girls as much as she is boys. We're as close as sisters. Nothing romantic could ever possibly happen between us, as it would be far too icky.

Once she's dressed, I help her downstairs. Mrs. Carter runs over, fretting at the blood.

"She fell into the tub, bonked her head pretty good. You should get her looked at."

Mrs. Carter nods. "Yes, of course. Let me get dressed."

I sit with Ashley, keeping an eye on her while her mother runs upstairs. She's not in a talking mood, so we just sit there staring at the wall. Eventually, Mrs. Carter comes down and we both help Ashley out to the car.

"I'm going to go back in and grab the two dead imps... I'll lock up."

Mrs. Carter nods and gets in the car. "What is happening?"

"I think my sisters accidentally opened some kind of interdimensional gateway that let these things out. They're out of control and spreading."

Ashley blinks. "Your sisters did this?"

"Not intentionally."

"Can I lock them in a kennel at work for a few hours?" mutters Ashley.

I laugh. "Sierra would just sit there giving you the finger the whole time and Sophia would cry."

Ashley sighs. "Yeah, you're right. I'll settle for an apology."

"Michelle's going to kill them." I bite my lip.

"What did they do to her?"

I shoo them off. "Go get checked out. You sound loopy."

Mrs. Carter nods and starts the car.

"You're not coming?" asks Ashley.

"I want to, but can't. The girls are trapped on the wrong side of mirrors. Those mystics I told you about are working on a way to get them out of there, and I need to be here in case they call with a spell that can open a doorway."

Both Ashley and her mother stare at me.

I pat the roof of their car twice. "Yeah. It's a weird night."

Mrs. Carter backs out of the driveway. I run into the house, grab the two dead imps, and leave after locking the doors. Halfway down the street to home, I pause to sigh at the stars. I'm standing in the middle of the road at like one in the morning with a dead minor demon in each hand, my sisters trapped in an alternate dimension, and I'm *not* totally freaking out.

Wow has my life gone off the rails.

20

ONE BY ONE

U pon returning home, I head to the basement and toss the dead imps at the marker circle on the rug.

Both creatures vanish in a blue flash, disappearing into a narrow, spiraling wormhole like sending turds down the drain. Shaking my head, I hurry back upstairs. Speaking of turds, a flush comes from the bathroom at the end of the hall. Sam, eyes not quite open, walks out into the hall and trudges for his room. A sudden sense of worry makes me rush after him. The instant he raises one knee to climb into bed, an ink-black hand closes around his other ankle.

I leap into a dive, grabbing him from behind and falling flat on my back with him on top of me, my arms secure around his chest, feet braced on the bed frame. Sam screams, but it's the kind of noise any normal kid would let out on a rollercoaster ride.

The force trying to steal him is *way* stronger than those little imps could possibly be. I strain to keep it from dragging my little brother away. An imp-like voice in his closet chatters angrily… almost like it's yelling at the one grabbing him. Weird light and foggy mist fill the space under the bed, so I can't see what the hell has him. Careful to control my strength so as not to hurt him, I shove with my legs, lifting the bed up on one side, while pulling at him.

Little by little, the battle goes in my favor.

"Ow!" yells Sam. "It's got my leg."

It's so tempting to pull with all I have, but I would never forgive myself for breaking his spine. Rather than rely on a surge of brute strength, I gradually push harder with my legs, easing him out from under the bed. Mom and Dad run in at the commotion. It takes them a second to process what they're seeing, then they grab his arms to help pull. Inch by inch, we extract Sam from the force attempting to pull him across dimensions. When his feet come into view out of the mist, I trust my parents' hold to keep him steady and let go, reaching down to swipe my claws at the hand clamped around his ankle. Steam hisses out of the slashes where my claws slice leathery, black skin.

A high-pitched demonic shriek fills the air. The hand lets go of Sam, who flies back into my parents with enough force that all three of them land in a pile, legs in the air. I roll over onto all fours and start to crawl toward them—but hands close around both my ankles.

I'm about to sink my claws into the rug to hold on but... no.

I let it take me. This is my ticket inside.

The force yanks me under the bed. Sam's bedroom blurs away, shrinking to a squarish point of light amid endless blackness. Despite seeing nothing but darkness, it still feels like I'm being dragged backward. A moment later, I'm abruptly in a corridor with grey stone walls and a dusty floor. I stop sliding and find myself sprawled out with my arms stretched over my head. The sense of hands gripping my ankles is gone.

I flip over into a seated position, but there's nothing behind me. The hallway stretches off into infinity with dozens of arched passages on both sides, not a single trace of whatever grabbed me anywhere in sight. This place has no ceiling, merely an opening with a view into endless void. It sorta reminds me of a rat maze without a lid, like I've been tossed into the Minotaur's labyrinth.

There are no apparent sources of any light, but the area appears illuminated. This, of course, doesn't surprise me as I'm a vampire. Even in the total darkness of a sealed room, I can still see fine. It's a little annoying not being able to tell if it's dark or not, but I have bigger issues to deal with at the moment than quibbling over night vision.

Rings of purple slime mark my jeans where the creature grabbed me. The substance has no smell and the consistency of cherry pie filling, as warm as if it had just come out of the oven. I decide to ignore it.

Hmm. According to Aurélie, I have the ability to somehow cut the veil and go back across to the normal world. That makes me wonder why the creature decided to pull me in here. Either slicing it off Sam made it angry enough to stop thinking and lash out at me, or she's wrong about me being able to escape. Or, maybe it simply doesn't realize I have the ability to get out of here. Are creepy demonic forces that abduct children by dragging them under their beds omniscient? And where the heck does it keep the fog machine?

While I'm definitely flying blind here, I at least feel better that I'm with my sisters. At least, I hope I wound up in the same place.

"Guys?" I shout. "Soph? Sierra?"

My voice echoes in two directions. Distant growls and gurgles reply, but nothing that sounds like a tween girl. More like a frat house at eight in the morning the day after a big party. I spend a little while turning side to side, trying to decide which way to go. Eventually, out of sheer randomness, I walk in the direction I'd been facing. At each archway, I peer in at chambers that look like macabre recreations of houses or offices. The proportions of the furniture are slightly off, everything angled and skewed into surrealism, and no bright colors. Objects that ought to be colorful and cheery are black and morbid. There don't seem to be any people or other creatures alive in any of them.

Some archways look in on *weird* scenes that aren't the insides of buildings. In one chamber that resembles a pine forest, a stream flows uphill to a waterfall that disappears into a purple sky. In another, I spend a moment gawking at the ruins of a castle that absolutely ignores the laws of physics. A stretch of stone that starts off as a support column becomes a bridge supported by an archway near the top. On the left, what starts off by the ground as four columns holding up a section of wall becomes three at the top.

Ugh, this is like one of those perspective illusions made physical. My brain hurts.

I wander for what feels like hours until my right foot explodes in pain like I stepped in a deep fryer.

With a shriek, I jump back, gawking down at long shards of obsidian glass sticking up from the top of my foot. The floor ahead of me is awash in an inches-thick layer of deadly shards. Whimpering, I hop backward two steps and sink to sit on the clear floor, stunned at the sight of thirty or more jagged slivers of black glass impaling my foot.

Honestly, sneakers probably wouldn't have helped. These damn things would've cut most shoes to ribbons and still totally pierced me. The smaller shards, the ones that didn't go completely through my foot, start working their way out as my body heals. The big ones aren't going anywhere without help. Gritting my teeth, I grab the shards by the wider ends, wiggling them back and forth, screaming as each bladed slice of glass slides out of my foot—especially whenever one scrapes bone.

I'd say I managed not to cry, but that would be a total lie.

Once the last bit of glass is out, I curl up in a ball and cry until the pain stops. My foot is bloody, but intact. Right. Lesson learned. Watch where I'm going. And that hallway of shards? Yeah, it can go eff itself.

I stand, flip the middle finger at the hundreds-of-yards-long stretch of pain, and turn away.

Not three steps later, the sound of Sophia sobbing comes from behind me. Of *course* she's on the other side of that ridiculous mess.

"Oh, screw you." I hang my head, then yell, "Soph? Is that really you?"

"Sarah?" replies a distant yell. "Yeah, it's me. Where are you?"

"What's the name of your cat?"

Silence.

Hah. Thought so. I keep walking away from the shards.

"I don't have a cat," yells Sophia... and her tone shifts to excitement. "Wait, did you get me a cat?"

Dammit. That's really her. I stop. "No, just testing to make sure it's really you."

"Butt!"

Speaking of testing, I attempt to fly—and it works. Okay, that's oddly surprising. I tuck my feet up behind me and glide forward, cringing at the sea of razors passing below.

"Where are you?" yells Sophia.

"No idea. Just keep talking so I can find you."

Every ten or twenty seconds, Sophia yells things like "I'm here!" or "where are you?" or "I'm scared."

The pile of deadly shards ends before Sophia sounds any closer. I land on clean, grey floor that could be stone or hard-packed silt. A few minutes later, I pause at a four-way intersection where the impossibly long hallway I've been traveling down crosses another impossibly long hallway going perpendicular to it.

"Sophia?"

"Here!" she yells, from the left.

Considering how far I've walked since hearing her, I shouldn't have been able to hear her at all. Sound must work differently in this place. Then again, waterfalls don't usually go into the sky. Fair bet, nothing in this place is going to work the way it should. Seven archways down on the left, I find the one that her voice is coming from. While the unending corridors don't have a ceiling, the chamber she's in does—and she's standing on it.

I step past the arch, staring up at her. "Well, that's not something you see every day."

The room is massive, basically a ten-story building made completely hollow. All four walls are covered in doorways linked by a confusing network of interwoven stairways that look like an MC Escher drawing. One starts off right side up and ends upside down on a different wall. Whoa. I could totally stare at this room for hours.

Sophia, roughly at the middle of the ceiling a hundred feet above me, jumps up and down, waving. Gravity appears to be working in reverse for her. Neither her hair nor nightgown are draping down like they should be. From my point of view, *I'm* the one on the ceiling looking down at her. Considering I can fly, this is a fairly familiar feeling.

"Sarah!" yells Sophia. "You got in! Did you do magic?"

"Nope. Something grabbed me… just like you."

"What?"

"Sec!"

I jump into the air, flying straight up toward her.

21

NOWHERE

Twenty feet from the ceiling, gravity abruptly inverts.

I go from flying to 'power falling' and plow face first into the stone ceil—floor.

Something cracks, and I'm pretty sure it's a bone, not the ground.

"Ow." I flop over to one side, limp.

"Eww!" yells Sophia, cringing away from me while hyperventilating and crying.

"Relax, Soph. I'm fine."

"No, you're not fine! Your neck is broken!"

"Oh, is that what that snap was…?"

She screams. "Stop!'

"I'll be fine in a minute. Damn, that was stupid. I should've expected up and down to flip."

Sophia gags.

"It's not that bad. Did I pop open or is my head just at a weird angle?"

"Stop!" shouts Sophia. "I'm not looking."

She stands there with her back to me for a few minutes. Eventually, my neck knits with a soft *crunch*, at which point, I sit up. "Okay, all back to normal."

Sophia risks a hesitant peek, then relaxes and flings herself into a hug. "Make me forget seeing that. Please!"

"Are you sure?"

"Yes! That was *so* disgusting. The bone was like sticking a lump in your throat." She shivers.

"Okay." I peer into her eyes and force her brain to remember me simply gliding in to land like a non-idiot.

While she floats in the momentary mental fog of vampiric mind alteration, I pull her to sit in my lap.

"You made me forget something, didn't you?" She glances at me. "I feel funny."

"You asked me to."

"I did?" Sophia blinks. "What did I ask you to make me forget? You promised you wouldn't."

"If I tell you, then you'll remember. I hurt myself and it looked scary."

"Oh. Okay. It's fine. Yeah, I wouldn't want to remember that." She gazes up and around at the bizarre room, then randomly giggles, though it's tinged with fear. "So, how'd you hurt yourself?"

"I crashed. Gravity's not supposed to flip over without warning."

"People aren't supposed to end up on the wrong side of mirrors either, but here we are."

"Any idea where 'here' is?" I also look around at the impossible stairways. "If I had to guess, I'd say we're at the intersection of WTF and hell no."

Sophia shrugs. "We're nowhere. This place doesn't really exist." She holds up her arm, showing off some cat scratches. "The imps tried to grab me, but Sierra started fighting them. They all piled on her and dragged her off. I ran after them, but fell into a hole and went down this long slide."

"C'mon. Let's find her. I'm going to have to carry you over the glass."

"What glass?"

I stand. "You didn't see that whole hallway full of broken glass?"

"No."

"Damn."

She tilts her head. "Why would you be unhappy that I *didn't* find a hallway full of dangerous broken glass? I don't have any shoes on and you don't—aaah! Your foot's bloody!"

"It's healed." I pat her on the head. "The problem is that if you didn't see that glass, it means this place doesn't have a consistent layout. We took two totally different paths to get to the same place."

"Sure, there are stairs on the wall to upside-down doorways. This place *doesn't* make any sense."

"Yeah. I mean, trying to go back the way I came in from doesn't necessarily guarantee we'll find the way out."

Sophia shakes her head. "We don't need to find *the* way out. Just any way out. I think this place is connected to the real world by mirrors. They glow from this side, like windows at night with lights on inside. If you look through them, the other side is normal."

"Like you were in your door watching us."

"Yeah. But I got lost. I can't find my room again. I've been looking." She sniffles. "Then I heard Sierra shouting bad words. I found her, but the imps came after us. She grabbed the one off me, threw it, and kept punching more that tried to get us. They jumped on her and dragged her away. I tried to stop them, but I got scratched."

"No idea where they took her?"

Tears roll down her cheeks. "No. She could be dead."

I shudder, then yell, "Sierra!" as loud as I can.

A tiny F-bomb detonates in the distance.

Sophia brightens in an instant. "She's alive!"

"C'mon!" I grab Sophia's hand and run across the floor-ceiling to the nearest door that lines up with the direction of Sierra's swearing diatribe.

When I open it, a great vacuum wind sucks us through into free fall. I shift from falling to flying, and zip over to grab Sophia, who's screaming shrill enough to shatter glass. Forces beyond my strength keep pulling her downward, but my attempt to stop her acts like a parachute. We land atop a massive heap of human bones filling the bottom of a vertical shaft about fifty feet square that has to be over a hundred stories deep. A narrow stone stairwell leads up from the pile to a doorway at the center of one wall, maybe fifty feet higher than the top of the bone mound.

Great. We landed in hell's trash can.

Once Sophia realizes what we're standing on, she resumes screaming.

"Shh," I say. "They can't hurt you. They're already dead."

About twenty skeletal arms reach up from the pile, grabbing our legs.

Sophia faints.

Dammit.

I kick at a bony arm grabbing her leg, shattering it at the elbow, then grab the wrist of a hand clutching her hair, crushing it. Why is everyone afraid of skeletons? They're super brittle. It only takes me a moment to kick my way free of the first wave. More bony hands emerge, grabbing for us, so I scoop Sophia up into my arms and try to make a run for the stairs.

Carrying an unconscious ten-year-old while simultaneously kicking at skeletal arms and running downhill on a shifting pile of skulls requires a superhuman amount of agility. While I do possess superhuman agility, I don't have quite enough.

A skull crushes under my heel, taking me off my feet and sending us both rolling down the hill. Sophia, being lighter, stops first. I go rolling another thirty feet or so before crashing into the wall at the bottom of the pile. Dozens of bony arms erupt around both of us, trying to hold us down.

I sigh. Really? Good thing she's still unconscious. I'm not sure I could erase a terrifying memory this deep.

Arm by arm, I snap my way free, kicking and clawing at the endless assault of bony fingers. Quite done with this unstable landscape, I try to jump into the air, but that weird mega-gravity grabs me and slaps me down on my chest atop the bone pile again, triggering another mass of arms to sprout from all over, which grab everywhere and hold me down.

Beyond angry, I let off a growl deeper than any human throat should be able to produce.

Okay, this room is designed to make stuff fall. If we're not touching the floor, we get pulled. Considering my sisters opened the doorway to wherever we are, this entire place could be feeding from their nightmares, so I can't be too angry at the insane mind responsible for its existence. Hopefully, if this realm really is based on my kid sisters' darkest fears, none of it will be particularly dangerous. Then again, Sierra has seen some pretty serious stuff in her video games. Probably where this pit of happiness came from. But Sophia? She's so damn easy to scare, things she finds horrifying will probably make me laugh.

With a grunt, I do a push-up that tears me free of the bones, gasping at the two gripping my hair. More pop up and grab at me as I struggle to my feet. They're not particularly strong, but the damn things always seem to pull me at just the right angle to exploit the moving ground and make me fall again. When that doesn't work, they grab me in sensitive places that make me jump—and fall again. Cursing and shouting in anger, I eventually fly into a frenzy of smashing that gets me upright on the shifting skulls. After kicking a few more skeletal arms off my legs, I fight my way up the hill to where I dropped Sophia. By the time I reach her, she's nearly buried. Only her face and some blonde hair is still visible, the pile trying to absorb her. Frantic, I start grabbing arm after arm, snapping them like kindling branches and throwing the pieces over my shoulder. It's a really damn good thing my body doesn't get tired anymore.

Once she's free of the bones, I toss her over my shoulder like a big bag of cat food, and trudge across the mound toward the giant stairway, spitting a curse every so often when my bare feet find a tooth or sharp piece of bone. Arms keep trying to grab at us, but I simply trudge through them, breaking them by refusing to stop.

When I reach the stairs and get a few steps up from the hill, the arms sink out of sight.

"Wow. This is really messed up. Is this the kind of stuff you have nightmares about?"

Sophia, still unconscious, doesn't reply.

I head up the rest of the giant staircase to a door at the top, which I punt open, revealing another corridor with no ceiling. Sierra's voice emanates from straight ahead, so there's hope. I stand there with Sophia draped across my arms, holding her until she wakes up a few minutes later in a flailing, kicking frenzy.

"Hey!" I yell.

She freezes, staring at me with saucer-sized eyes, again hyperventilating. Once she figures out the skeletal arms are gone, she breaks down crying.

I hold her, patting her back. "Relax. Just a bad dream, right?"

"It's not," she whispers. "We're really here."

"Mother f… son of a… bastard… coc—"

"Sierra!" I shout. "Where are you?"

"Is she gonna get grounded for cursing?" whispers Sophia.

"What happens in creepy alternate nightmare dimensions stays in creepy alternate nightmare dimensions." I wink.

Sophia nods. "Okay. I won't tell on her if you won't."

"Hang on, you've got bones in your hair."

Sophia freezes. "Eww."

I pluck a few fragments out of her hair and toss them aside, then set her on her feet, take her hand, and run toward the stream of cursing. It feels like we run for twenty minutes, but somehow only travel about a hundred yards. I skid to a stop at an archway looking in on another plain room. This one is only two stories tall, the walls and ceiling covered with tiny doorways just big enough for imps.

Sierra's sitting on an imp's chest, punching it over and over in the head, accenting each hit with a curse word. Three other imps lay around her, one apparently unconscious, two dragging themselves away from her, evidently unable to stand up. Her nightgown's taken some damage, claw slices and shreds in spots, but it's still intact enough not to fall off. Blood trickles down her arms from numerous cuts, and she's also bleeding from bite marks on her legs and back. Fortunately, none appear serious, more like she got into a fight with a pack of housecats. Another imp stands behind her with a two-handed grip on her long mouse-brown hair, trying to pull her off its friend. She either ignores or hasn't noticed him, too focused on beating the one she's perched on to death.

Finally, she notices us standing in the doorway and looks over. "Sare?"

The imp pulling her hair drags her over backward, wraps her hair around her neck, and proceeds to strangle her. The one she'd been punching simply lays there out cold. Sierra grabs the hair at her throat with both hands, struggling. I run over and jump on the imp, seizing it by the chest.

It hisses at me—so I extend my fangs and hiss right back.

"Eeeee!" shrieks the imp, scrambling to free itself from my grip.

As soon as it lets go of her, Sierra sits up, pulls her hair off her throat, and gasps for air.

I stab the imp in the chest with my thumb claws, killing it, and chuck the rubbery body aside.

Sierra twists, gives the corpse the finger, then stares at me. "What are you doing here? You're supposed to be getting us *out*, not end up trapped, too."

"Sort of a last minute idea. Aurélie thinks I can tear open a doorway from this side. It tried to grab Sam, but I got there in time to catch him and it dragged me under the bed."

"Wow." Sierra blinks. "So *can* you get us out of here?"

I shrug. "No idea, but I'm gonna try everything I can think of."

Sierra pushes herself up to stand, cringing at all the scratches. "Ow. Death by a million paper cuts. Hey, you might wanna kill the other ones."

It's surprising that Sierra *was* able to beat them into unconsciousness. Then again, if we are in Sophia's nightmare, that makes sense. She thinks of her sister as a total badass. And, hell, I'm probably a goddess in here. Unless, of course, this is some other demonic realm that's merely taking inspiration from what scares her.

I walk over and ram my claws into the chest of the one Sierra had been sitting on. It wakes up, emitting the polyphonic death wail I'm becoming entirely sick of hearing. It's like sticking needles in my ears.

Speaking of needles in the ears, Sophia shrieks.

I spin.

My youngest sister is flat on her back, under attack by four imps, grabbing her arms and legs like they're trying to play wishbone with her. Sierra's wrestling with another one that's sitting on top of her chest, trying to bite her in the face. She's got a hold of it by the ears, barely managing to keep its teeth away from her, but doesn't look like her strength is going to last much longer.

"Get off!" Shouts Sophia, struggling to kick at the ones on her legs. "Let go!"

I sprint into a field goal kick at the one on Sierra. My foot hits it with a meaty *splat* like slapping a pair of raw ribeye steaks together. The imp blurs across the room and hits the wall, exploding in a shower of black goop.

"Thanks," rasps Sierra.

I nod, then pounce at the others.

Sierra grabs the imp trying to bite Soph on the left leg. I step on the one clinging to her right shin, grab the one holding her right arm, and drop kick it. It bursts upon impact with the ceiling, showering us with hot, black slime. Sierra lets off a battle cry like she's in taekwondo class, and kicks the imp clinging to Sophia's left arm. Though the critter doesn't fly off with enough force to pop like a water balloon, it bounces across the floor and stops a good distance away, laughing at her the way they laughed at Mom for walloping them with a frying pan.

Snarling, Sierra runs after it and jumps on it, once again going off with a stream of swears as she punches it in the head repeatedly. The imp she pulled off Sophia's leg jumps on her back, about to bite her on the neck.

I zoom over there, grabbing its oversized head like a bowling ball —only I make new holes with my claws.

Sophia gurgles in disgust at the black goop leaking out of the dead imp's nostrils and mouth. Shuddering, she turns away. With a sharp twist of my wrist, I break the neck, then chuck the creature's rubbery corpse aside. Sierra keeps pummeling her imp until it loses consciousness, then gives me this 'okay, your turn' look, and climbs off it.

A quick claw stab finishes the thing.

"I *really* don't like this place," rasps Sierra, out of breath.

"Yeah. I'm not fond of it either."

She looks at the splat mark on the wall. "Wow… you'd be awesome at soccer."

"Nah," I mutter. "The balls would explode."

"Or she'd kill the goalie," says Sophia.

Sierra shakes her head. "Naw. She'd just put the ball *and* the goalie into the net. Huh… would that count as a point? Like if the goalie stops it, but goes flying into the net with the ball, is that still scoring or would they call that a save?"

"Guys!" shouts Sophia. "Can we like not debate sports rules until we're no longer stuck inside a mirrorverse?"

Another imp leaps out of nowhere at Sophia's throat. Time seems to drag to a near standstill from my vampiric reflexes kicking in. I hurl myself at it as fast as I can move, sinking my claws into its body, stalling its flight a mere inch away from tiny fangs tearing open Sophia's neck. The imp is dead before either girl realizes I moved.

Both of them shriek.

Sophia spins, about to yell at me for scaring her until she sees the dead imp in my hand, its mouth still gaping open and way too close to her. At that, she just stares mutely at me, shivering.

"Can we go home now?" asks Sierra.

I sling imp goop off my fingers, take my sisters both by the hand, and hurry back to the corridor. "Yeah. That's the plan."

22

SPELLCASTING 101

We walk down the endless corridor for a while in silence until Sophia randomly bursts into tears.

"I'm sorry!" she yells. "This is all my fault because I'm different now."

I keep pulling them along. "It's fine. And you're not different."

"I am! I have magic or something. Like, I could see Coralie." She sniffles. "I'm sorry for summoning those goblins."

"They're demons, dumbass," mutters Sierra.

Sophia gives her a hurt look.

"Imps are more like mini-demons. They're not *that* dangerous, and don't call your sister dumb."

"Saying dumbass doesn't mean she *is* dumb. It means she said something dumb. Gawd, stop being so sensitive."

Sophia sniffles.

I squish them together in a hug. "Don't start fighting here. They might be minor demons, but they're still trying to claim you."

Sierra stares at me with a 'say what' expression.

"Claim?" Sophia wipes tears off her face. "What does that mean?"

"I'm not totally sure, or even if that's true. The mystics had a book about these things. Apparently, if whoever summoned them acts against their own spell, it like breaks whatever implied deal exists. That makes them angry and they want to 'claim' you. I think when you changed your mind and tried to shut the gate in your math class, that made them mad."

Sophia wails, "I'm really sorry! It was just messing around. I didn't think it would really work?"

"Umm, am I included in that claiming thing or is it just Soph since she's the one with magic?" asks Sierra.

I blink at her, too stunned at her to say a word.

She wipes at the blood on her arms. "I'm not gonna let them take her. Just want to know if I have to watch my ass, too, or I can concentrate on protecting hers."

"Oh." I slouch with relief that she didn't mean it the way it sounded. "No idea. Depends on if the imps consider you part of the spell or a spectator."

"Where are we going?" asks Sophia in a teary voice, eyeing a passing archway.

"Good question. At the moment, I think I'm just going straight."

Sierra twists back and forth, looking around. "How do we even know where to go? This place keeps changing."

"The location might not matter as much as just finding the inside of a mirror big enough for us to fit through." I stop and peek into an archway on the right.

Twelve nine-foot-tall mice, all perched on their hind legs holding tea cups, turn their heads to stare at us. The room around them looks like an old English study, with giant cat heads the size of SUVs stuffed and mounted on the walls around the fireplace.

"Oh, how nice of you to send for snacks," says the lone white mouse, before licking at its whiskers.

"Umm, that's a big fat nope," says Sierra, pulling at my hand.

"I agree." I pull the girls onward at a fast walk in case the giant mice try chasing us.

Fortunately, they don't.

We peer into each archway we pass, all of which contain bizarre surrealist landscapes without a mirror in sight. The one with trees floating in the sky is particularly mesmerizing, and we wind up standing there in awe for a few minutes until a neon green centipede the size of a school bus comes into view, crawling along the ground.

Amazingly, Sophia doesn't scream.

Sierra looks up at me. "I don't think we should go in there."

"Agreed." I pull the girls away from that arch and keep going. "So… what made you decide to start off in your magical experimentation with summoning portals instead of doing something less… dangerous? I mean, gateways aren't exactly basic magic."

"She's got a point," says Sierra. "Why not like try making light first?"

Sophia leans around me, pointing at her. "You're the one who found the spell and said 'hey, it's Halloween, we should do witchy stuff'. It's not all my fault."

"You could've said no way."

"You could've *not* suggested we try doing magic the night before Halloween."

"Girls, girls! Stop!" I yell. "Arguing now won't fix anything. And Darren said the stuff you found isn't even real magic. He has no idea *what* it is. Said it's totally made up nonsense."

"See?" asks Sierra. "I told you it wouldn't work."

Sophia looks down. "It said 'gate' and we thought it might be like teleporting."

"Opening a wormhole," adds Sierra.

"Sorry. Are we in trouble?" whispers Sophia.

"Well… I think Mom was *going* to ground you, but she'll probably be so thrilled that you're safe she might forget. Besides, who would ever believe magic is real? It's not like Mom thinks you guys *wanted* to set those imps loose."

Sierra exhales in relief.

A little while later, we run into another patch of black glass shards on the floor. Or maybe it's the same one from last time.

"Speaking of nope," says Sophia, curling her toes in imagined pain.

"Do we have to go that way?" Sierra points back the direction we came from. "There's an intersection we didn't try. Two totally different hallways *not* full of ouch."

"What do you mean 'have to'?" Sophia flails the arm she's not using to hold my hand. "We *can't* go this way. It'll cut our feet off. Straight ahead isn't even an option."

"Technically, I could carry you both while flying."

"Does flying work in here?" Sophia looks up at me. "It's been weird before."

I float up off my feet. "Yeah, feels fine."

Sophia lets go of my hand and turns in place a few times before shooting an 'I hate you' stare at the glass. "I think we should go that way."

"Seriously?" Sierra scrunches her toes up. "That's painful just looking at."

"Yeah. I feel something."

Sierra frowns. "We're gonna feel something all right. A lot of pain."

"Might as well. So, how do you want me to carry you? Like firewood? Over my shoulders? Hanging on my back?"

"Whatever will result in the lowest chance of us landing in broken glass," says Sierra.

"Okay, then not relying on you two to hold on to me then." I position the girls to hug each other, then scoop them up horizontally in my arms with Sophia on top.

Slow and steady, I lift off and tuck my feet up, then glide out over the shards.

"Wow, this looks like it would be almost as painful to step on barefoot as a Lego brick," says Sophia.

"What is it?" asks Sierra.

"Sky." Sophia points up. "The void breaks sometimes and the pieces collect here."

I blink. "Are you just being randomly creepy or do you somehow know that?"

She shrugs. "Guessing. Sky's black. That glass is black. And there's no windows or anything."

"Right." I shake my head.

A few minutes later, we reach bare floor. I land, set the girls down, and walk with them until we reach a six-way intersection. The walls tower over us, easily five stories tall. It occurs to me that this place must have actual light since my sisters can see. That makes it all the eerier as there's no apparent source of illumination anywhere. Then again, being freaked out by inexplicable daylight is probably stupid after having a ten-foot-tall mouse refer to us as self-delivering snacks.

"Which way?" asks Sierra.

"Umm." Sophia looks around, shivering. "I'm scared. They all look dangerous."

"Well," says Sierra, "we could pick a hallway or just stand here until we starve."

Sophia glances sideways at her. "Why did you say that?"

"Because I don't want to stand here and starve."

"If you're gonna put it like that…" Sophia rubs her stomach while studying the hallways. Eventually, she points at the one branching off diagonally ahead to the right. "Umm. That one."

"Okay," I walk out in front, taking the lead. "Let's go."

23

THE NIGHTMARE SPIRAL

Chattering in the distance makes the hairs on the back of my neck stand on end.

We've been walking for at least an hour. Or at least it feels like it. It's certainly been a long time as both girls are dragging their feet and complaining about being tired. By some miracle, they press on. The ephemeral whispering becomes steadily louder.

"What's that?" asks Sierra, hearing it for the first time a few minutes after I noticed the sound.

"Imps." Sophia shivers. "Maybe this is the wrong way."

"Or maybe it isn't." I raise an eyebrow.

Both girls emit uneasy whines out their noses… but we keep going.

The rasps lead us to a smaller archway than the others we'd passed, this one only the size of an ordinary door—as opposed to being wide enough for a car. I creep closer and peer into a large courtyard. It's big enough to hold four of our house, surrounded by giant castle walls but no ceiling, only more of the black void that's been over our heads for-seeming-ever. The space is swarming with imps, mostly clustered around a glowing blue hole at the center of the room. Every so often, one of them jumps down. One even pinches its nose like it's cannonballing into a swimming pool.

"This is the other side of the gate!" whispers Sierra. "We should close it!"

"We gotta go through it first!" Sophia bounces on her toes. "But there are so many imps…"

"You guys wait here," I say, and sprout claws.

The girls nod.

I rush past the archway, charging headlong into the sea of knee-high mini-demons. They scatter in all directions, hissing, growling, and shrieking at me. A few I catch unaware, or those dumb enough to stand their ground, drop dead to single claw swipes. Others jump on me from behind, biting me in the shoulders or back. Their teeth don't cause too much damage, but it's like being stabbed with hot soldering irons.

My world becomes a blur of tiny bodies, flapping leathery wings, and minuscule jabs of pain everywhere. At least until one bites me on the tit. I roar more in anger than pain, grabbing that one's head, and crush it between my hands. Oh, lookie. These things *do* have brains. About a third of the imps break and run away screaming at that.

Sophia's shriek comes from directly above me.

A cluster of imps have her by the arms, flying her into the room. She's at least thirty feet off the ground, kicking her legs and screaming. Sierra tumbles in the door, partially being dragged, partially fighting the group attacking her. Sophia's scream-crying is a pretty good indication that they're biting her.

I punt one off my leg and fly straight up, intercepting Sophia before they can drop her onto the stone floor. Imp by imp, I grab them off her and throw them aside. Finally, Sophia clamps onto me, shaking, no longer under attack.

"Little help here!" yells Sierra.

A crowd of imps have pinned her to the floor, at least six apiece on each limb, holding her arms and legs out in an X. Another much bigger imp—almost three full feet tall—stands on top of her nightgown between her knees, looking down at her with an unimpressed frown. That one's got a wicked obsidian sword balanced across its shoulder, which I'm sure it's about to stab her in the heart with.

"Like, now!" shouts Sierra, struggling but unable to get up.

I swoop low by the portal, drop Sophia on her feet, and fly straight into the giant imp right as it raises the blade to take Sierra's life.

It emits a squawk like a kicked goose when I hit it, hauling it off its feet by sinking my claws into its back. The giant imp flails and shrieks as I zoom with it into a crash against the wall. Furious that this thing was about to murder my little sister, I pin it in place with a foot at the middle of its back, reposition my claws near its shoulders, and shred down its back, flaying it alive. It emits a horrible wail of agony.

Twenty tiny imp voices behind me all cry out in alarm.

The critter's scream makes me feel just a little bit guilty for torturing it, so I ram my right hand like a claw-tipped spearhead into where its heart should be, forearm deep into its body. The big—relatively—imp sags, dead. Its onyx sword, a massive two-handed thing to it, but a little smaller than an ordinary broadsword to me, clatters to the ground.

"Ooh. Thanks. This will make things faster." I remove my hand with a slurp, pick up the sword, and charge the imps holding Sierra down.

After I cut two clear in half, they panic and run in all directions, letting go of her. Sierra rolls to her feet and tackles one, punching it in the back of the head over and over again as she spews curses like a *Call of Duty* player who's died for the fortieth time in the same round.

"It's not working!" shouts Sophia, while clapping.

Say what?

I twist around to look at her. She's not actually clapping—that's her foot hitting the floor in the middle of the 'gaping hole.' It's as solid as the basement floor was, despite appearing to have an opening.

"Better close the damned thing," snarls Sierra. "This is probably where they're going through from."

The imp she's pummeling twists around and bites her on the left ear.

"Ow! You shitbag!" she yells, rolling to the side, grabbing at it.

I lunge and stab that one in the head, then flick it away from her with the sword.

She whines. "Did it bite my ear off?"

"No… just a red mark."

"Sare! The portal!" yells Sophia.

Sierra springs to her feet and engages three imps, trading punches and kicks for little claw swipes. The sight of her in a nightgown fighting tiny demons like some bizarre kung fu princess anime would be hilarious if not for the chance we could seriously die in here.

I rush over to the portal. It looks more or less exactly like the marker scrawling on our rug in the basement, only instead of ink, these lines are carved into the floor and glowing. All the symbols around the outside emit cobalt light, and the hole continuously peers down into a twisting vortex of luminous energy. The one back home only showed the wormhole for a few seconds when I flushed an imp.

Sophia screams and ducks an imp flying at her head. I lean back, bringing the obsidian broadsword around with a hasty upswing—but still manage to hit it. Half an imp goes left, the other hits her and bounces off.

"Eww, gross!" she yells, gagging while swiping at imp blood on her shoulder. "Hurry up and like scratch the markings or something."

I jab the sword at a random squiggle. It bounces away amid a wash of sparks, not damaging the carving. Okay, need more force. The second swing gets beyond-human strength… and the sword ricochets up from the ground with at least double the power I put into it, throwing me into the air. I land on my back and slide for a few feet.

"It didn't break!" yells Sophia.

A cluster of imps charge at her. She shrieks and runs around in circles.

Two jump on my chest, trying to bite me in the face. I grab the one on the left and bite the other imp before he can get me.

Oh, that's a mistake.

Gagging on a flavor like two-year-old rotten eggs, I hurl the imp I grabbed, grasp the one in my mouth, and rip it apart with my claws—then start retching.

A huge pile of imps drags Sierra to the ground. Still fighting the urge to puke, I hurry over to the sword, recover it, and rush at her since Sophia appears to be able to outrun her group for the moment. I snag the nearest imp, hold it up, and slice its head off like I'm cutting the greens off a carrot. This obsidian sword is either wicked sharp or it's got magical properties that work super well on imps. The second time I pluck one and kill it, the others abandon their hold on her and explode in random directions doing a spot on impression of roaches when the lights come on.

"I hate these things!" Sierra huffs. "I feel like a damned dart board!"

She's covered with tiny wounds, but none look serious.

"Help!" yells Sophia.

Sierra grabs the collar of my T-shirt and pulls me down nose-to-nose. "I don't think you can scratch the runes. Soph's gotta close it with magic. She couldn't do it outside, but it's gotta be able to work from here. I'll distract them. You tell her to close the damn portal."

"Umm, what do you mean you'll distract them?"

"Just do it." She lets go and jumps to her feet.

"You're eleven. I'm not letting you do something dangerous."

Sierra points at Sophia running from a pack of imps. "We're already doing something dangerous. And these things are irritating, not deadly. Go."

"Fine."

I sigh, then jump into the air, flying in a strafing pass with the sword at the dense pack of mini-demons chasing Sophia. One swing kills like five of them and wounds two. They also scatter in random directions, abandoning their chase. Sophia stumbles to a halt and stoops forward, hands on her knees, out of breath. I turn and come back toward her. One imp realizes he's running straight at me, and skids to a stop screaming... but doesn't have the time to move before I chop his head off.

Sophia grabs on to me when I land next to her.

"Hey. I can't close that thing. You have to do it."

"I don't know how," she whines.

"The same way you opened it. Dad thinks you have magic and you don't really need written spells to make it work. Just want something to happen. The spell you guys found is total made-up nonsense."

She peers up at me, no longer crying. "What?"

"It's a mess of different things. Some of the symbols are one thing, some another, some made up entirely. Darren said it's nonsense. That spell didn't make the magic work. *You* did. Just focus at it and want it to close."

Sierra stands by the gate, arms out, and starts babbling made up words like she's trying to fake her way through Latin class. Evidently, imps aren't geniuses. They all charge at her, desperate to keep their highway to mischief wide open.

My eleven-year-old sister vanishes under an avalanche of tiny bodies that drags her across the room, only her feet sticking out.

"Now!" I yell.

Sophia raises her shaking hands toward the gate. Her initially terrified expression melts to neutral, then almost confident. She appears to be reacting to something I can't see or detect. Curious, I peer into her thoughts. Whoa, she can feel the power flowing in and out of the hole like a brisk wind. Her desire to stop imps from invading the normal world and close the gate causes a shift in the flow. A sense of tightness manifests. Sophia grunts, struggling like she's trying to twist the lid off a stubborn jar of grape jelly.

A few imps sense the change in the magic and jump away from Sierra to come running at us. I play goalie, running in circles around Sophia while slicing down any imp that gets close. The seventh time one runs at her, I line up a perfect slash to cut it in half—but it stops short, my swing passing an inch shy of its nose. Rather than laugh at me, it looks bewildered for an instant, then slides backward toward the hole, its three-toed feet clawing long scrapes in the rock.

The mass of imps on top of Sierra flies into the air, swirling around and around, carried by an invisible cyclone before plunging into the glowing blue opening. In the span of six seconds, every imp in sight flies screaming into the hole.

"What the?" whispers Sierra.

Seconds later, a small group of imps comes sailing in from *way* far off, falling into the hole—which promptly slams shut.

Sophia faints.

Sierra, bleeding from hundreds of tiny cuts, sits up. "…and we're still stuck."

"Maybe we'll be able to go out a mirror now," says Sophia without moving.

Guess she's not unconscious after all.

"Soph? You okay?"

"I'm tired."

I walk over to Sierra. Her nightgown is smeared with blood, but after checking her over, I'm confident she's not in any real trouble. And dammit, she still smells like black cherry syrup. "You okay?"

She holds her arms up, looking herself over. "You remember that time I crashed my bike and went flying into a thorn bush?"

"Ow. Yeah."

"This is about the same, only there aren't little stickers all over me." She cringes. "Hey, at least the imps are gone."

"True. I sure hope we didn't flush them into the house."

Sierra gasps. "Don't even joke about that."

"No, they're gone," says Sophia, making no effort at all to move. "Maybe with the gate closed, we can escape out a mirror now… if we can find one. But can we rest a bit?"

Sierra grumbles and forces herself up to stand. "I wanna go home. We can rest when we get home."

"Ugh. I'm not on speaking terms with walking right now," says Sophia.

"C'mon, kiddo. Don't you want to get out of this place?"

"Yes, but in a minute."

Sierra folds her arms. "What if time passes differently here and waiting even five minutes means we go home fifty years from when we left?"

"I hate you," mutters Sophia, but she sits up. "Doing magic is exhausting."

THE NIGHTMARE SPIRAL | 209

"But you did it!" Sierra grabs her in a hug. "You closed it!"

Sophia frowns. "I'm the idiot who opened it. Don't be proud of me for undoing what I broke."

"I'm not. I'm proud of you for having fu—umm actual magic." Sierra flashes a cheesy smile at me.

"C'mon." I head out the door back into the hallway

The girls follow close.

"So much walking... This is like Disney World," mutters Sierra. "With murder."

Sophia groans. "They had the giant mouse at least."

A distant rumbling noise starts up behind us. I peer back over my shoulder and have a momentary brain lock at the sight of a wall racing down the corridor in our direction, like the hallway is erasing itself. It's rushing closer at a speed much faster than highway traffic. No damn way can we outrun that... even if I flew as fast as I could without carrying two kids.

"Crap! Move!" I grab the girls and dash for the nearest archway.

Mere seconds after we leap through, the 400-mile-per-hour wall rockets by with a deafening roar and an air blast that throws us all to the ground on our chests. When the dust settles, I push myself up and look back at solid wall. The entire archway vanished as if it had never been.

"I guess we go this way." I cough on dust.

"Why is this grass black?" asks Sophia.

"Everything in this place is black." Sierra stands.

The room, or chamber, in front of us stretches way off into the distance, packed with strange jungle-like trees, vines, flowers, grass... most of it black. Some of the leaves are purple. The girls gasp and grab each other, pointing around.

"There's people watching us," whispers Sierra.

Sophia points to the right. "There's tons of them. They're trying to sneak up on us."

"I don't think they're people." Sierra shivers. "Just wraiths. Nothing but shadows."

There's nothing there as far as I can see, even right where the girls point at 'a big monster' staring at them. "Guys. It's only a trick of darkness. I don't see anything."

They peer up at me, confused.

"Night vision. I can't even see shadows." In their heads, I peek at what they're seeing—a forest much different. It's quite dark, and stuff *is* moving around, but I'm sure it's an illusion. "Trust me. It's not real. This room isn't dark to me."

They both grab my arms.

"Okay," says Sophia. "I believe you."

I lead them deeper into the 'dark garden,' trying my best to go straight. After a few minutes, the foliage is too thick for me to tell which way we came in from and it also conceals any walls—so I have nothing to navigate by. There's no sign of any animal life, imps, or other monsters here, just creepy shadows that I'm lucky enough not to see. My sisters jump and scream every so often when one gets too close, and cling to me the same way they did at the haunted house two years ago. Well, to be fair, Sierra hadn't been half this scared at that place. We'd made it about a third of the way in before Sophia had a meltdown and scream-begged not to be forced to keep going. After the actor dressed as a zombie clown grabbed her arm, the poor kid legit had a panic attack, I think. Mom took her back out while Dad, Sierra, and I continued.

"There!" Sierra points at an archway on the left where the jet-black ivy parts, revealing a stone wall like from a medieval castle. "A way out."

"Do we trust it?" I ask.

The girls do rock, paper, scissors. Sophia wins. They stare at each other.

"Umm, does that mean we go that way or not?" asks Sophia.

Sierra shrugs.

"Feels right to me," I say.

They both nod.

I take point, walking up to the opening and pulling the black ivy out of our way. The next chamber looks like a dungeon out of a medieval fantasy movie. Skeletons hang in manacles around the edges, propped up against the walls. A few more skeletons and random chains with empty shackles litter the floor. It's as big as the gym at my old high school, with another doorway at the far end leading to a corridor.

"Eww," says Sophia. "Like, dead people."

"I hope they stay dead." Sierra leans in to look around.

I heft the onyx sword. "They better hope they stay dead."

We advance into the room, carefully stepping around bones and chains.

Roughly a quarter of the way across, a metallic *clink* comes from behind me to the right.

Sophia screams.

Another *clink* happens to my left.

Sierra yells, "Sarah! Look out!"

I spin. A length of chain hovers upright behind me like a cobra, striking toward my leg within a split second of me seeing it. I jump back, my superhuman speed the only reason I evade it. The 'serpent' stops short at the end of its length, the shackle closing empty.

Sophia bursts into tears, struggling at a shackle locked around her left ankle. "Help! Sarah! It got me!"

Sierra's also trapped by one leg, but looks more annoyed than scared.

Clink.

One gets my right ankle from behind while I'm distracted at the sight of my sisters.

I look down at my leg. The manacle is uncomfortably tight due to having closed around my jeans. With a growl, I yank my foot back, breaking the shackle open.

"See?" Sierra points at me. "Sare is strong enough to break them. Don't freak out."

"We're gonna get stuck here and starve like those people!" Sophia, again starting to hyperventilate, struggles at the tether holding her to the floor.

"Do I need to give you a mental poke to calm down?"

Sophia stares up at me with a 'please no' expression.

"Then relax." I crouch, grab the chain on her leg, and snap it off. "See?"

She starts running for the door, but only gets about ten steps before another chain locks around her left ankle, tripping her. She screams after landing flat on her chest, but that sounded like total frustration.

"This is going to suck, isn't it?" asks Sierra.

Clank. I smirk at my right wrist, then snap the chain off it. "Totally."

Sierra walks for the door in no great hurry, stopping with a resigned sigh whenever another chain serpent 'bites' her.

Sophia stops struggling and stares at her. "You're not even trying to run?"

"If I ran, I'd have tripped and landed on my face. I'm gonna get grabbed again either way."

"Oh." Sophia looks down at her trapped leg. "I hate this."

After an annoying fifty yards of stopping every ten-to-fifteen feet to break someone free, we reach the hallway. A group of six animated chains hovers just out of reach like pissed off snakes. It's probably not a good sign that my sisters are starting to smell like candy stores. Both have numerous tiny cuts, though Sierra's far bloodier. I really hope it won't take us so long to get out of here that the temptation to bite—or at least lick—one of them goes past the limits of my willpower.

I really love strawberry flavored stuff, and Sophia's basically a strawberry milkshake with legs at the moment, at least as far as my nose is concerned.

"That totally stank!" yells Sophia.

"Yeah. We're lucky Sare's so strong, or we'd have been in big trouble."

"Don't even say that." Sophia shivers. "Starving is the worst way to die."

"C'mon. Enough morbid. We gotta go home." I usher them down the hall.

Plain grey walls surround us for a short distance until we reach a ninety-degree right turn. Around the corner, the hallway's décor changes, filled with huge red tapestries, life-sized oil paintings of people dressed like medieval nobles, vases, plate armor suits on stands, and small tables bearing vases.

"Wow. So do you think the armor's going to try and kill us... or maybe those big curtains will try to suffocate us," says Sierra.

Sophia whimpers.

"Let's not wait around to find out." I hurry forward at a light jog.

The girls run after me. Predictably, we don't get very far before something makes Sophia scream.

"What do you—?" Sierra screams. "Shit! Run!"

Hearing *her* shriek makes me look back.

A half-dozen glowing ghostly figures dressed in medieval garments have appeared in the hallway behind us, the large paintings having become scenes of rooms with no one in them. Another painting starts glowing, and the dour-faced man gets up from the chair and steps out into the hallway like a hologram ghost while drawing a thin rapier-style sword from his belt.

All of them brandish sharp weapons from swords to tiny bodice daggers. They're still transparent... but something about them sets off my sense that they're actual people. I can almost read thoughts out of thin air where their heads appear to be. It wouldn't surprise me if those knives *will* cut us. Something also tells me if I tried to claw those ghosts, they wouldn't be solid.

The girls haul ass, going around me on either side and up to a full sprint.

Yeah, they have the right idea.

I run after them. Every painting we pass, one every five or six feet, spawns another angry ghost. I stop counting at forty, and just run faster. My sisters scramble around a corner to the left, bumping a table and nearly knocking over a suit of decorative armor. That hallway also has a ton of giant paintings, who all start looking at us.

The girls reach the end of the hallway, crashing into a set of white double doors. They grab the knob, struggling to open it, but the doors appear to be locked. Behind me, a mass of ghosts too thick to even perceive individual people closes in. They don't appear to be in a great hurry, probably because they think we're trapped.

They're wrong.

Hopefully.

I leap off my feet into the air, flying up to as much speed as I can get in the last twenty feet of corridor before crashing into the doors. The white wood blasts open from the force of my impact, though the hit knocks me loopy . For a moment, it feels like I'm falling while tumbling head over foot until I land on something soft, bobbing faintly up and down.

Both of my sisters shrieking snaps me out of a daze.

I try to sit up, but can't, so I lift my head—my hair pulling. It appears as though I've landed in a gooey white lattice of strands, somewhat like spider silk but way goopier. Clear, sticky liquid with a consistency halfway between raw egg and tree sap coats the fibers. Sophia landed to my right, face down. Sierra's directly above my head on her back, staring up the length of a forty-foot shaft at a cluster of superimposed ghosts in a doorway. An irritated nobleman huffs at us and pulls the doors shut.

"Did I say how much I hate this place?" deadpans Sierra. "Oh, by the way, I can't move."

"Neither can I," replies Sophia in a shaky voice.

"There's going to be a giant spider, right? Oh, wait, this kinda looks like the stuff that the aliens cemented that kid with before the egg thing tried to jump on her face."

Sophia screams.

"Alien egg or giant spider?" asks Sierra, way too calm.

Sophia screams again.

"Sare, please tell me you're strong enough to get out of this."

I pull at the stickiness, peeling my arm away with the loss of only a few fine hairs. "Ow. Yeah. I'm good."

Sophia makes a wheezy noise like she's trying to scream with no air left inside her.

"Oh, that sounds really bad," says Sierra.

"Hang on. She's face down. Whatever she's seeing is under us."

Something scrapes below us.

I force my way up into a sitting position, and peer down between my legs, through the web, at the lower half of the chamber. A massive insectoid creature climbs the wall. It somewhat resembles a spider covered in a shiny, black shell, but instead of spider mandibles, it's got five serpentine necks sticking out, each with a head like a wasp's.

My heart stops. Or at least stops faking beating. "Umm. It's neither an alien nor a spider."

"What is it?" asks Sierra.

Sophia wheezes again.

"It's a mega nope-a-saurus."

"That doesn't sound fun." Sierra sighs. "Are we gonna die?"

"No."

Sophia whimpers. "It's getting closer."

Crap. Where'd the sword go? It's not on the web near me… which means it fell to the bottom. I hurl my body to the right in a twist that breaks me out of the webbing, and fly downward, fighting the glue that's sticking my arms to my sides. The giant nope monster sees me falling and rotates to follow me down. Guess it knows the girls aren't going anywhere soon, so it wants to grab the food that's getting away.

Once again, I absolutely *adore* being a vampire. The obsidian sword landed in a corner that would certainly have been pitch dark to any living eye. I dive bomb it, rolling away from the spot seconds before the two-ton nope machine slams into the ground, three of its wasp heads biting the dirt.

Part of me thinks we're all still home, sleeping, having a communal nightmare. This can't possibly be real. Giant hydra wasp-spiders don't exist. Then again, I once ran into a huge troll. As much as I want to think that had been all in my head, Garrett Alder, the vampire who wanted the potion, exists. Speaking of him, wonder if it worked or if he's still a Beast.

Shrieking wasp heads lunge at me with mandibles larger than my sword, each pair slamming shut with clacks as loud as a dude banging two-by-fours together. Crap. This thing could bite me in half. Two heads go for a simultaneous pincer strike, but the monster isn't counting on me having the ability to fly. I launch myself straight up, causing the two wasp-faces to crash into each other. A third comes at me from the left, so I turn, flying backward, and take a two-handed slash straight down at its face.

My blade strikes between its compound eyes, cracking the shell and sending a spew of yellow slime into the air. The force of my swing swats the flexible neck downward, smashing the head into the floor where it bursts open like a dropped egg. Eww.

Something splatters behind me. Probably Sophia throwing up.

All four remaining heads emit an ear-splitting screech. It's anyone's guess if this thing is in pain or pissed. Not waiting to find out, I weave to the side and chop at its left foreleg. That shell is much thinner than its skull, and the imp sword slices it with ease.

The four surviving heads all lunge at me simultaneously, emitting a painfully loud noise I'm sure is anger. For a few desperate seconds, I zip back and forth, dodging and spinning out of the way of mandibles. I'm feeling optimistic—until one shows up at a blind spot and I've got three feet of serrated bug mouthpart jammed into my stomach, it's cantaloupe-sized eyes mere inches in front of my boobs.

Such unbelievable pain grips me that I don't feel a damn thing.

Sophia screams, "Sarah!"

Growling, I raise my sword over my head, flip it upside down in a two-handed grip, and icepick it to the hilt in the wasp's brain case. I try to give it a twist, but the blade snaps off at the hilt, leaving me holding a useless handle.

The giant nope monster recoils, shrieking, swinging its body around in a circle that flings me off the mandible impaling my gut. I manage to stop myself in midair before smacking into the wall, then sink to the floor. My legs refuse to hold me up and I wind up on my knees, cradling my gut.

Stumbling around like a drunken dinosaur, the giant wasp-spider thing appears to have forgotten all about me. Good. I hope having a damn sword stuck in one of its brains hurts like hell.

Know what sucks more than having a massive serrated bug mandible speared completely through me? The itching as the wound heals. I grab the hole in my stomach and simply concentrate on not screaming. Somewhere in the distance of my awareness, Sophia keeps calling my name. I'm vaguely aware of Sierra asking what's going on.

The minor earthquake of the monster thrashing around finally stops. I lift my head and catch a glimpse of it retreating into a cave hollow leading away from the bottom of the chamber, two of its heads dragging limp along the floor. An archway frighteningly close to the cave leads into another passageway—which is luckily way too small for that thing.

"Sarah?" yells Sophia.

"Almost," I rasp.

Forget my earlier statement. The itching isn't the worst part. Feeling my intestines slide around as they slither back where they belong is *way* worse. A few minutes later, the itching and pain stops, but I'm noticeably hungry. It's not overly severe hunger, so I should be able to resist the temptation to bite my sisters.

I stand, smirk at the sword handle, and drop it. "Well, there's a reason people didn't make swords out of solid obsidian."

"She's alive!" cheers Sophia, upon seeing me stand up.

I fly upward, crashing into Sophia from below with enough force to rip her loose from the sticky. Once above the web, I roll over and dive down onto Sierra, breaking her out of the web. Neither girl has to put any effort into holding onto me, as they're glued in place. They both scream when they realize I'm flying closer to the cave where that *thing* went, but we have to in order to reach the way out.

At least, I hope it's the way out.

They keep screaming as I swerve for the corridor, not even bothering to land until we're a good forty feet down the hall, well out of reach of the monster.

I peel Sierra off Sophia's back and set her down, then unstick Sophia from my chest... and in a moment of mischief, hang her on the wall.

She peers down past her feet at the floor. "Not funny."

Sierra scrapes slime off her arm, tries to sling it aside, but it keeps on sticking to her hand. "Ugh. This is nastier than that time Billy Cortez snozzed all over my arm."

"Help," says Sophia, calm.

I pluck her off the wall and set her down.

"Eww. It's *so* sticky," whispers Sophia.

We spend a while scraping slime off ourselves and smearing it on the wall. Eventually, the stuff loses most of its stickiness, leaving us coated in clear slime similar to raw egg whites. Once no one is sticking to themselves—or each other—anymore, we resume walking down a corridor with plain grey walls and a smooth floor. It's cold underfoot, but polished. Not sure what it's made out of, but it looks like the floor in the hallways at my old school.

The passageway curves to the right in a gradual arc, eventually leading to a room that appears to be a strange black-and-white version of someone's bedroom. Rather than a floral pattern, the bedspread is decorated with skulls and thorns. Nothing is quite straight, all the furniture and walls having a noticeable slant to one side. A square of light glows from the opposite wall like a flat-panel television showing a blank screen.

"Whoa, creepy," says Sierra.

"Mirror!" yells Sophia, before running over to the bright spot.

Sierra and I rush after her.

When I get close, the blinding glow fades enough to let me see through it into the normal version of the room we're standing in. Two fifty-something adults I don't recognize are in bed, asleep.

Sophia pushes at the glass, which stretches under her hand like cellophane. "This didn't happen last time. Before, when you found me in the mirror, it felt like hard glass from this side."

I push at the mirror, gummy and squishy under my hand. Hmm. Why not.

"Here goes nothing."

"What?" ask the girls at the same time.

I extend my claws. The stretchy material warps over them, not cutting.

"Dude," says Sierra, in a fake 'popular girl' voice, "it's seriously time for a nail intervention. You need a salon big time."

Sophia giggles.

"Well, we're not getting through this." I let my arm drop. "Unless Sophia can do something."

24

THE HARBINGER OF ULTIMATE DOOM

We back away from the mirror in case the people wake up. No sense making a therapist rich.

"Wait," says Sierra, her face lighting up with an idea. "Maybe we can only get out the one we came in from? This isn't our house."

"Maybe." Sophia kicks her toe at the floor of the bizarre bedroom. "But none of us actually went through a mirror. The imps dragged us under beds."

"But what is this place?" I ask.

"It looks kinda like the bedroom on the other side of the mirror, only… nightmare version." Sierra wanders around, pulling at drawers, and peering inside them. One contains something that makes her jump with a squeal and slam it. "Don't open anything."

Sophia points at the door. "Maybe this is like some kind of shadow that the normal world casts into this dimension. Back down the hall where we saw the monsters, we'd been too far away from reality, so it goes all twisted and weird instead of looking like normal?"

"Oh, wait. Maybe this is like all the spaces between everything?" Sierra runs to the bedroom door and opens it. "I think we clipped out of the map and we're looking at the world from behind the walls. This would be a cool way to spy on people."

"That's mean!" says Sophia.

"I agree with her. Neither one of you should ever go here again. It's way too dangerous."

Sierra looks back at me with a 'no kidding' expression. "Yeah. If we ever get out of here I don't wanna go back."

"If?" Sophia whines. "What do you mean *if?* I swear I'll never try to go into a mirror again. I mean, I didn't try to go into the mirror this time, either, but... you know what I mean."

"Hallway looks safe. Let's go outside and see if we can figure out where we are." Sierra slips out of the room.

"Wait!" yells Sophia.

"Come on," calls Sierra from down the hall.

I grab Sophia's hand and run out the door into a corridor that looks like the upstairs of an average suburban house—in a nightmare. "Don't split up. I don't want to lose track of either one of you."

Sierra waits for us by the top of the stairs at the far end. When we catch up, she leads the way down and goes out the front door.

The street isn't at all familiar. Trees tilt at odd angles, every house is disjointed and... almost cartoonishly evil. Parked cars appear askew as well, with an almost face-like quality to them. Despite there being nothing else alive out here, I can't help but feel a crowd of unhappy people glaring at me... like I've asked a question in Dr. Mercer's class when we've already gone twenty minutes past the bell, and the answer to my question is going to take twenty more.

"Is this even Washington State?" Sierra eyes one of the cars. "It doesn't have plates."

"We're nowhere," says Sophia. "I don't know which way to go or if it's even real."

Sierra edges away from the car. "Umm. I think this thing just growled at me."

"It doesn't look anywhere near as bad as the hallways we've been wandering. Why don't we try going—"

Sophia screams so loud I think she ruptured my right eardrum.

I cringe, turning toward her.

A huge creature that appears to be made entirely of black fur glides toward us in the middle of the road, creeping along at a pace even a grandmother on a walker could run away from. It's about the size of a tractor-trailer cab, spherical, and has tiny wings—also black —near the top, both flapping with hummingbird speed. They're ridiculously small compared to the creature, like someone attached pigeon wings to a truck.

"What the heck is that?" I ask, chuckling. "The pom-pom from hell?"

"It's kinda cute," says Sierra. "Why are you screaming?"

Sophia backs up, her face paler than any Old Guard vampire. "T-that's F-Fuzzydoom!"

Sierra and I make the same 'you've gotta be kidding me' face at her. "What?" I ask.

"Fuzzydoom!" yells Sophia. "If he touches us, even one little hair, we're gonna die! Just turn black and disintegrate like ashes. He's my nightmare I've been having forever."

"That's *your* nightmare?" asks Sierra.

Sophia sniffles, shaking and crying like a slobbering twelve-foot-tall werewolf had cornered us. "Yeah."

"And you couldn't come up with a better name than 'Fuzzydoom?'" Sierra grins. "Like, call it the Bringer of Eternal Death? Something scary?"

Sophia's fear fades to a note of petulance. She huffs. "I was only three the first time I saw him. Once I knew him as Fuzzydoom, he was Fuzzydoom!" She clasps her hands in front of herself, looks down, and blushes. "He's *so* fuzzy. That's part of why he's so dangerous. You wanna hug him."

The giant black puffball undulates and emits a roar like a tiger.

I cover my mouth to hold in the laugh. This is adorably murderous. It is cute... cuter to think of a three-year-old Sophia coming up with that name. But, here, this thing might actually be able to kill us.

"So, all it has to do is touch us and we die?" I ask.

"Yeah!" Sophia nods rapidly. "Even one little hair touches us, we're gonna turn to ashes. We gotta run."

"We've been standing here talking for like five minutes and that thing has gotten maybe six inches closer. Why are you panicking?"

Sophia blushes. "You know how like when a monster is chasing you, no matter how fast you run, it's always right behind you? It's gonna keep getting closer really slow. Whether we stand here or run, it's not gonna matter."

Sierra dashes off about forty yards, and turns around. "Nope. It's farther away."

"That's because me and Sare are still here." She grabs my hand and pulls me into a run toward Sierra.

In seconds, Sierra's face goes from confident to 'holy crap.' She whirls and runs away as well. I peer back over my shoulder, and sure enough, Fuzzydoom is hauling ass, trucking along as fast as we are—plus a tiny bit more. Lost to inexplicable fear, I pour on speed, grabbing both my sisters' hands and dragging them up to a pace too fast for their shorter legs to tolerate. As soon as they begin stumbling, I ease back so they don't wipe out.

Fuzzydoom is still right behind us, creeping closer.

"Gah! Shit."

"Told you!" singsongs Sophia.

Sierra screams in terror, then yells, "Why the hell am I scared of a giant pom-pom with teeny wings?! It's ridiculous." She looks back with an annoyed expression, but she winds up shrieking again.

"He's really scary!" Sophia tries to run faster.

The fear gripping Sierra fades once she's no longer looking back at the creature. "This is too messed up."

"Run!" yells Sophia.

We sprint down the road for a few more seconds before I feel like a complete idiot. What the hell am I doing?

"Guys!" I yell. "Stop!"

"No!" shouts Sophia.

Grr. I scoop the girls up and fly. Once they realize we're off the ground, they cling to me, so I climb higher, well out of Fuzzydoom's reach. The damn thing doesn't have arms, after all. Or legs, or anything but fur and those tiny wings. I'm not even sure what the heck they're attached to. Is there a body inside that sphere of hair anywhere?

The black puffball flaps harder, trying to pull itself into the air, but can't get off the ground.

I hover about forty feet up, watching this thing struggle and wobble.

Sierra, hanging on my left side, seems totally unfazed and laughs at it. Sophia buries her face against my shoulder, refusing to look down. She's trembling, but I can't really blame her. If she's been having a recurring nightmare of—I snicker—a killer pom-pom, it makes sense how she'd be irrationally afraid of it. Mom used to have this six-inch ceramic owl figurine that, when I was like four, scared the crap out of me. For some stupid reason, I got it in my head that looking directly into its eyes would turn me to stone, like Medusa.

So yeah. Ceramic owl terrified me. I can't really pick on Sophia too much for the black pom-pom of annihilation.

After a few minutes, Sophia finally works up the courage to look down. She stops trembling, but doesn't let go of me to wipe her tears. "Wow… he's easy to get away from when you can fly. I never thought about that before."

"Yeah." Sierra laughs. "Its wings are smaller than the ones we get from that Chinese place Mom loves."

Fuzzydoom undulates, emitting a miffed grunt before disappearing in a puff of smoke.

"Is that thing gonna come back if we go down?" asks Sierra.

Sophia shrugs. "I dunno. I always wake up before he catches me, and I never tried flying. This is all new territory."

I rotate around, surveying the landscape below us. Unfortunately, it doesn't look like any city I've ever been in before. Also, there's no sign of ocean in sight. Granted, I'm not up *that* high. I also don't want to go higher in case one of the girls slips. We are, after all, still coated in clear snot from that web.

"Is it messed up that whenever I see chicken wings from now on,

I'm going to think of that thing?" Sierra giggles. "Why did you give it such small wings?"

"I dunno. I was three." Sophia rolls her eyes.

"We can land now." Sierra points. "It's gone."

"No!" Sophia yells. "What if it comes back?"

"You're really scared of that thing?"

"Am not."

"Are, too."

"Am not!"

Sierra looks at me. "She even argues like she's three."

Sophia raspberries her.

"Mom and Dad are probably shitting bricks," says Sierra. "We should go home."

"Yeah." I sigh at the distance. Every direction looks the same, generic town as far as I can see. "But which way *is* home?"

Both girls stare at me, worried and confused.

25

GREMLINS

Hovering in place, I continue spinning back and forth, searching the cityscape below us for anything that looks like a way out.

"Wait a sec," says Sierra. "We just saw Soph's nightmare. Are we inside her head? No wonder this place is so twisted."

Sophia raspberries her again.

I shake my head. "Nah. I really don't think we're in her head. That room with the skeletons and grabby chains? If we were in Soph's head, it would've been packed with faeries. Or unicorns attempting to force-feed us rainbow cupcakes. Or maybe dolls trying to kill us."

Both girls shudder.

"Thank you for a nightmare I'm going to have for the rest of my life," says Sierra. "Ugh. Overrun by a swarm of killer dolls."

"This place is probably created from scraps of things you both picked up from movies or nightmares or whatever." I glide down to land on the road.

Sophia peers around me at Sierra. "Do you have a nightmare monster we should watch out for?"

"No, not really. I've had bad dreams, but it's not like the same one every time."

"What about you, Sare?" asks Sophia.

As we walk down the street, I tell them about the ceramic owl. Though, I'm not sure if that counts as a nightmare since it didn't haunt my dreams. I'm more like Sierra. Nightmares happened every so often, but nothing recurring like Fuzzydoom.

Houses, shops, and cars surround us. No street looks exactly the same, but they're all so close and generic... "Civilization. This is an anytown."

"Maybe," says Sierra. "Could be why there's no street signs or license plates."

"What if we really are all stuck in my head?" asks Sophia. "And all we need to do is wake up?"

Sierra shakes her head. "Pain usually wakes people up." She indicates her bloody nightgown. "I would've snapped awake when that imp swarm covered me."

"Or the damn spiderwasp-whatever bit me." I pick at the fist-sized hole in my T-shirt. At least it's one without any sentimental significance. It won't bother me throwing it out when we get back. "That hurt so damn much."

"Sorry," says Sophia.

"Not your fault."

"Yeah it is."

I pat her on the head. "If you want to think like that, this is all Mom and Dad's fault for having us as kids. Or their parents for having them. If Grandma never met Grandpop, we wouldn't be stuck here either."

She smirks at me.

"I'm serious. That thing bit me only because I got confused trying to keep track of four heads. I wasn't gonna let it climb up and get you. So which one of you is afraid of spiders?"

Both girls raise their hands.

"Wasps?"

Again, they both raise their hands.

"Well, that probably came from all three of us then."

"Wait, all three?" Sierra looks up at me. "Is this place reading our minds in real time? Changing and twisting as we think of different crap to be scared of?"

I stop walking and put my fingertips to my forehead. "I'm morbidly terrified of ten million dollars."

The girls laugh.

"Hey, over there." Sophia points.

Brilliant white light leaks from the seams around a doorway on the side of a generic convenience store on the next corner.

"That's either the way out or goes right to the core of a nuclear reactor," says Sierra.

"Feels like I wanna go there." Sophia grabs my hand, pulling me across the intersection. "It's gotta be right."

"Okay."

We jog over to it. I grab the knob and pull the door open.

The blinding glare fades fast, revealing another plain grey corridor.

"This goes behind the walls again." Sierra walks in. "I think this city is endless, so we need to get out of it or we'll walk forever."

I shrug and go inside after her. "That makes about as much sense as anything else here."

The hallway comes to a short end at an archway that leads out onto a ledge overlooking a giant cube-shaped chamber. Stairways, doorways, and windows cover all six walls. Once again, I feel like we've walked into an MC Escher drawing. It hits me that Sophia likes his stuff. And optical illusion drawings. Like the three-pronged tuning fork. Considering the amount of pain I experienced, I don't think we're dreaming, or stuck in Sophia's mind. But, it's possible if she does have some magical abilities, that she created this dimensional reality we're exploring. As much as I don't want to believe in such craziness, no other explanation fits. But also, if this *is* a place of her design, then her idea that going into that door is the way out is promising.

"Down there." Sophia points at a doorway near the middle of the 'floor,' about seventy feet down from the ledge we're on.

I peer over at the ordinary-looking blue door. "Okay. Grab on."

"No!" Sophia shakes her head. "Remember what happened last time you tried to fly in a room like this?"

Sierra looks over. "What?"

"She went *splat!*" Sophia grabs my arm. "Your neck will un-break. Ours won't."

"Right. So how do we get from here to the floor?"

"Umm. Follow the stairs." Sophia walks on ahead, pivoting over the ledge like she just took a suicide leap off a building.

"Sophia!" I scream, and run to the end—but she's standing on a step two away from me, sticking out horizontally in defiance of gravity.

I can fly and I'm still woozy at the thought of walking over the side.

"Trippy," says Sierra.

"You're not old enough to call something 'trippy,'" I mutter.

"Come on." Sophia walks 'up' the stairs.

To me, she's walking down the stairs while standing on their front face. Yeah, Sierra's right. This *is* trippy. I hold my breath and step over the edge. My body whips up like I'm falling forward, but then gravity equalizes out and it feels like I'm standing flat again, despite the room having rotated ninety degrees backward. Sierra appears to be standing horizontally on the wall below the stairs that used to be floor to me.

"This is going to drive me nuts."

"Come on!" shouts Sophia.

She's way ahead of us, now on the left wall of the chamber.

Sierra steps over the ledge behind me. She starts screaming like she's going to fall, but stops when the gravity shift hits her. "I hate this place."

"Me too."

I follow the stairs up to an archway, then emerge on the sideways path. Sierra holds my hand, freaked out but too 'cool' to act as scared as she is. Minutes later, I'm going up a flight of stairs while Sophia—who's got a good lead on us—walks down the same set of stairs on the opposite side, passing directly under me. Three more flights of stairs plus a veranda later, I reach a flat walkway that twists at the midpoint. The visual of the room rotating to the left is super disconcerting, but it doesn't feel any different than if I'd walked on straight, level ground the whole time.

Sierra gurgles like she's about to throw up.

A curve in the path at the room's corner allows us to walk straight up what had once been a wall. Again, it feels as if the room rotates while we keep traveling on flat ground. Sophia darts along, surprisingly fearless. We've gone from nightmare to *weird*.

Eventually, I catch up to Sophia, who's waiting at the base of a stairwell leading to the blue door she spotted from where we came in. I peer up and behind me at the same ledge. I can't even fathom how we walked here from there, though we had to have gone back and forth on all six walls of this giant cube to do it.

Grinning, Sophia marches up the stairs and grabs the doorknob.

I follow, Sierra still holding my hand.

The doorway leads to a short passage with bare wood slats on either side, as though we really have gone inside the walls of a house. Sophia stops at a tall, glowing rectangle up ahead, almost as big as a door.

I walk up behind her and almost shout when I realize we're looking through a glass pane into Sophia's bedroom. This large rectangle is her full-length closet mirror. Mom and Dad are standing a few feet away, holding each other.

"We made it!" says Sierra.

The 'rents both jump and look at us, having heard her.

Mom screams a non-word. Dad sheds a few tears, but smiles as wide as I've ever seen him smile.

"We still have to get past the mirror." Sierra pushes her hand into the glass, which stretches out like gelatin.

Mom blinks.

"Whoa. That's weird." Dad grasps the protrusion that Sierra made, almost holding her hand. He tries to pull her into the room, but the mirror stops stretching after about three feet.

"Try your claws," says Sophia.

I nod, raise my right hand, and extend my claws. Cringing, I swipe at the glass, slicing it open like a sheet of plastic. A loud *bang* goes off somewhere behind us along with a stiff wind blasting into our backs. Sierra jumps through into Dad's arms. I shove Sophia after her then climb out. The wind cuts off in an instant, the mirror behind me intact.

"What time is it?" I ask.

"1:42," says Dad. "It's about six minutes after you went under Sam's bed."

My sisters exchange a glance.

"We were in there for *hours*," says Sierra.

Mom finally seems to notice all the blood and goes into full panic mode. It takes her a minute or two of examining the girls to realize they're all tiny scratches. Dad raises an eyebrow at the massive hole in my shirt.

"Giant nope monster." I say, scratching at the exposed skin. "Pretty sure I hurt it worse than it hurt me."

"Umm," says Dad.

"Oh for the love of…" Mom squeezes the girls together. "I don't want you two opening gateways to alternate dimensions again. Is that clear? *Especially* on a school night."

"But, Mom, it's not a school night. It's Saturday," says Sophia.

"Technically, it's Sunday." Sierra raises a finger. "After midnight."

Dad laughs. "You know I'm seriously going to lose it if an owl flies in the window with a letter for these two."

"Oh shit!" I gasp.

Sierra whines out her nose, going wide eyed.

Mom and Dad look at me like someone's about to die.

Sophia clamps onto my arm, staring at the mirror. "What?"

"I've got a paper due for English lit on Monday and I haven't even started it."

Mom grabs her face, muttering. Dad starts laughing.

My sibs launch a tickle-attack while yelling at me for scaring the crap out of them.

"Girls, girls," says Mom, a minute or so later, while trying to pull them off me. "You're all up past your bedtime."

Sierra looks up at her with an 'are you serious' expression. "Mom, I'm covered in alternate dimensional snot." She brushes at some of the goo. "I'm going to take a shower."

"Yeah, me too." Sophia cringes. "This is disgusting."

The girls dash out into the hallway and start arguing over who gets to use the upstairs bathroom and who has to go down to the basement. The basement one is kinda cramped and doesn't have a tub, just a flimsy plastic standing stall.

The parents both end up looking at me.

"What?" I ask, low. "The weird crap wasn't my fault this time."

Mom massages the bridge of her nose. "Are those creatures gone?"

"The imps? Yeah. Pretty sure we flushed them and jiggled the handle. The marker on the carpet downstairs ought to wash out now."

"We heard a couple odd screams in really tiny voices. Sounded like imps came flying from all over the place into the house." Dad scratches his head. "But nothing broke and we didn't see anything."

I nod. "Yeah. When the gate shut down, it inhaled all the imps back to where they came from."

"Good." Mom pulls me into a hug. "Please don't let your sisters ever do anything like that again."

"I had no idea they did... or are you asking me to subject them to continuous mind reading?"

Mom winces. "No, not that. Just... oh, I thought you knew what they were up to."

"Nope."

Dad keeps looking at me like something's wrong.

I raise an eyebrow at him. "What? Are you upset about something?"

"Nope," says Dad. "I was just wondering if you wanted to watch *Gremlins* tomorrow evening.

"Argh!" I fall into him, banging my head on his chest. "That's so wrong."

"I know." He pats me on the back. "But it's a good movie."

"Maybe if I finish that paper in time. Gonna go start on it now."

Mom swipes a dab of goo off my arm. "But you're also covered in... whatever this is."

"Both showers are in use. Gotta wait. Might as well start writing." I sigh. "How messed up is that? Save the world from imps, rescue my missing sisters, and my reward is hours of writing a boring paper. I demand recompense. Like... chocolate mousse or something."

My stomach gurgles.

The parents look at each other.

"I'll be right back. Gonna go out for a quick bite... after I change."

Mom hurries off to the upstairs bathroom to check Sierra's cuts. Dad trudges off to his bedroom. I start down the hall to go to my room, but stop at the low sound of video game coming from Sam's bedroom, too quiet for either parent to hear. Better chase him to sleep before they catch him.

I creep over to his door and peek in. His PlayStation is on, paused, but Sam's out cold in bed. A mere second's concentration on his thoughts proves he's been asleep for a while.

His closet door emits a soft *click*, as the latch closes.

I eye the TV, the fighting game paused in mid-match.

"Screw it," I mutter. "Just behave yourself."

With a sigh, I shake my head and walk out.

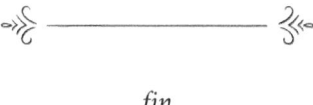

fin

ACKNOWLEDGMENTS

Thank you for reading *How Not to Summon Demons*!

I am beyond thrilled with the overwhelming reception this series has gotten from my readers. I hope you enjoy the latest bizarre twist in Sarah's unlife.

Additional thanks to Lee Sheridan for editing.
    Also, thanks to Alexandria Thompson for the wonderful cover art!

ABOUT THE AUTHOR

Originally from South Amboy NJ, Matthew has been creating science fiction and fantasy worlds for most of his reasoning life. Since 1996, he has developed the "Divergent Fates" world, in which *Division Zero, Virtual Immortality, The Awakened Series, The Harmony Paradox, and the Daughter of Mars series* take place. Along with editing for Curiosity Quills press, he has worked in IT and technical support.

Matthew is an avid gamer, a recovered WoW addict, developer of two custom RPG systems (paper & dice), and a fan of anime, British humour, and intellectual science fiction that questions the nature of reality, life, and what happens after it.

He is also fond of cats, presently living with two: Loki and Dorian.

Visit me online at:
    Facebook: https://www.facebook.com/MatthewSCoxAuthor
    Pinterest: https://www.pinterest.com/matthewcox10420/
    Goodreads: https://www.goodreads.com/author/show/7712730. Matthew_S_Cox
    Twitter: https://twitter.com/mscox_fiction
    Instagram: https://www.instagram.com/mscox.author/
    Email: mcox2112@gmail.com

OTHER BOOKS BY MATTHEW S. COX

Divergent Fates Universe Novels

Division Zero series

- Division Zero
- Lex De Mortuis
- Thrall
- Guardian
- Harbinger
- The Shadow Fixer
- Neuroshock

The Awakened series

- Prophet of the Badlands
- Archon's Queen
- Grey Ronin
- Daughter of Ash
- Zero Rogue
- Angel Descended

Daughter of Mars series

- The Hand of Raziel
- Araphel
- Ghost Black

Virtual Immortality series

- Virtual Immortality
- The Harmony Paradox

Prophet of the Badlands Series

- Prophet's Journey
- Prophet's Mercy

Divergent Fates Anthology

(Fiction Novels - Adult)

The Roadhouse Chronicles Series

- One More Run
- The Redeemed
- Dead Man's Number

Faded Skies series

- Heir Ascendant
- Ascendant Unrest
- Ascendant Revolution

Temporal Armistice Series

- Nascent Shadow
- The Shadow Collector
- The Gate to Oblivion
- The Queen of Discord
- The Burning Alchemist

Vampire Innocent series

- A Nighttime of Forever
- A Beginner's Guide to Fangs
- The Artist of Ruin

- The Last Family Road Trip
- The Phantom Oracle
- How Not to Summon Demons
- Ordinary Problems of a College Vampire
- A Vampire's Guide to Surviving Holidays
- An Introduction to Paranormal Diplomacy
- A Vampire's Guide to Adulting
- How to Stop a Vampire War in Six Easy Steps
- Ancient Vampire Death Cults and Other Annoyances
- Hunting Vampires for Fun and Profit
- A String of Seriously Unlucky Events
- The Summer of Completely Usual Strangeness
- Demonic Crisis Management for the Modern Vampire

Standalones

- Wayfarer: AV494
- Axillon99
- Chiaroscuro: The Mouse and the Candle
- The Spirits of Six Minstrel Run
- Sophie's Light
- The Far Side of Promise anthology
- Operation: Chimera (with Tony Healey)
- The Dysfunctional Conspiracy (with Christopher Veltmann)
- Of Myth and Shadow
- The Girl Who Found the Sun

Winter Solstice series (with J.R. Rain)

- Convergence
- Containment
- Catalyst
- Catacombs

Alexis Silver series (with J.R. Rain)

- Silver Light
- Deep Silver
- Silver Quarrel
- Silver Crucible
- Silver Heart

Samantha Moon Origins series (with J.R. Rain)

- New Moon Rising
- Moon Mourning
- Haunted Moon

Vampire For Hire series (with J.R. Rain)

- Moon Master
- Dead Moon
- Lost Moon
- Vampire Destiny
- Infinite Moon
- Vampire Empress
- Moon Elder
- Wicked Moon
- Moon Blade

Maddy Wimsey series (with J.R. Rain)

- The Devil's Eye
- The Drifting Gloom
- Dark Mercy
- Primal Wrath

Samantha Moon Case Files series (with J.R. Rain)

- Blood Moon

Immortal Operative (with J.R. Rain)

- Broken Ice
- Broken Wing

Four Elements series (with J.R. Rain)

- The Elementalist
- The Black Rose
- The Wakefield Curse

Witches series (with J.R. Rain)

- The Witch and the Hangman

Zeb Clemens series (with J.R. Rain)

- The Beast of Devil's Creek
- Wanted: Undead or Alive

Young Adult Novels

The Eldritch Heart Series

- The Eldritch Heart
- The Cursed Crown
- The Sapphire Soul

Evergreen Series

- Evergreen
- The World That Remains

- The Lucky Ones
- Nuclear Summer
- The Nuclear Frontier
- The World We Make
- The Threat Unseen

Progenitor Series

- Out of Sight
- Out of Mind

Diary of a Teenage Fey

(Short story series)

- Elder Horror
- The Hag of Barrow Falls
- Babysitter's Nightmare
- Lharakki
- Bauble for a Soul
- Simulacrum
- Amorphous
- Manticore

Standalones

- Caller 107
- The Summer the World Ended
- Nine Candles of Deepest Black
- The Forest Beyond the Earth

Middle Grade Novels

The Adventures of Ubergirl series

- My Dad is a Mad Scientist
- Aliens Ate My Homework
- The End of all Halloweens
- Dr. Infinity and the Soul Smasher

Tales of Widowswood series

- Emma and the Banderwigh
- Emma and the Silk Thieves
- Emma and the Silverbell Faeries
- Emma and the Elixir of Madness
- Emma and the Weeping Spirit

Standalones

- Citadel: The Concordant Sequence
- The Cursed Codex
- The Menagerie of Jenkins Bailey